"ALCOHOL WAS NOT INVOLVED"

A Shallow End Gals Trilogy

Book One

By

VICKI GRAYBOSCH
MARY HALE
LINDA MCGREGOR
TERESA DUNCAN
KIMBERLY TROUTMAN

Printed in the United States of America

LCCN: 2012910906

CreateSpace Independent Publishing Platform
North Charleston, South Carolina

ISBN-13 978-1477655085

ISBN-10 1477655085

ALCOHOL WAS NOT INVOLVED

Teresa Duncan

Mary Hale

Vicki Graybosch

Linda McGregor

Kimberly Troutman

The Shallow End Gals Trilogy

Book One

CHAPTER 1

We never made it to Hawaii. We didn't even get to the airport. Teresa and Linda were in the front seat, Teresa driving, and they screamed. Mary and I looked ahead and saw a woman standing right in our lane. Teresa swerved, and then a flash of light…then nothing.

I wasn't sure where we were. It looked like our favorite bar, the Tavern, except there were no walls or floors, and there was a cool, misty feeling to the air. Teresa, Linda, and Mary were all sitting on their regular stools, just looking at each other. It felt like coming out of a fainting spell.

There was a beautiful older woman standing on the other side of the bar smiling at us. It looked like she was wearing one of Carol's costumes, Roman Goddess. Carol is our regular bartender, who likes to dress up. The older woman spoke to us in a soft, slow, calming voice, with perfect diction, and each word we knew to be the absolute truth. She paused at the end of each sentence, which I appreciated, before she continued.

1

"You have died in a horrific car accident on the way to the Airport. Grief Angels have been assigned to your loved ones and will remain with them as long as needed."

It took me a minute to digest what she had said. I'm dead? Now I am thinking, why am I not freaking out? I looked at the other gals and I could tell they were thinking the same thing. I really should have bought that hearing aid.

"You will continue to have some mortal thoughts and skills while you are in the Transition Phase of Orientation. I will be communicating with you at a level I feel you will understand. The mortal emotion of grief is gone, and has been replaced with a very basic understanding skill. This is to assist you in moving forward in the process. I am your Orientation Guide and you may call me Granny."

Okay. This is getting bizarre. In mortal life none of my relatives looked like 'Granny.'

Granny continued, "At this time there is a scheduling issue with the previous group of Orientation Angels. So for the time being you are all stuck. Which means your mortal mind will be interfering with your spiritual mind on occasion. You knew in your mortal lives that less than ten percent of the mortal mind is used?" We all nodded slowly. "Welcome to the other ninety percent! Your mortal mind and your spiritual mind are with you for eternity," Then she smiled, "I have decided that since you died together, in order to expedite our process, you will complete orientation as a group."

Granny stopped talking and just looked at us. She was still smiling and I chuckled. This is some freakin' dream. Then she looked right at me and said, "This is not a dream." Oh shit.

She continued, "Angels are continually evolving, and as you evolve you will acquire the skills needed for your assignments. The influences of your mortal mind will mean that individually, you may notice changes that have not necessarily affected the others in the group. You are not to be alarmed by this if your mortal fear emotion is still present. I will take questions at this time."

Teresa slowly raised her hand and Granny gestured for her to speak. "Are we in Heaven?"

"Almost."

Almost?

Linda raised her hand and Granny gestured her to speak. "Can we flunk this orientation thing and go to hell? I don't test well." Linda looked pretty worried. Actually we were all interested in that answer.

"You can't flunk. The decision has been made that you all belong here."

Wow! I must have skated by that one close. Granny looked at me. Hmmmm.

Mary raised her hand, and Granny gestured for her to speak. "I'm not clear about why we are doing orientation as a group."

I couldn't believe that was her question. Really? That's her biggest issue right now?

Granny looked at me again. Uh oh, I think she reads minds.

Granny said, "I do."

She looked at Mary, "To answer your question, it was found that each of you possess very strong character traits that complement each other. You will face challenges that other classes have not had because you still retain many mortal thoughts. *Our* circumstances have created this issue of you being *stuck*, but we feel we can utilize this as a benefit. Most certainly we expect an 'interesting' transition for your group."

I really tried hard to not let my mind think, but the word 'interesting' has seldom played out well for me. I glanced quickly at Granny, and yup, she was looking at me.

I thought better of asking a question, and Granny continued, "I am handing each of you a class schedule for the Transition College. You must select, as a group, which class appeals to you the most. Once you have made your selection you will only communicate with me in cases of need. I have been assigned to you and will always assist you when called upon. However, your requests may delay your progress if deemed excessive or unnecessary. I encourage you to utilize the skills of the others in your group."

The schedules she handed us looked like menus at the bar. It struck me that a great deal was being done to make us feel comfortable. "I'm needed elsewhere for a moment. Take this time to talk, and I will return." She smiled and suddenly she was gone.

I think from the looks on our faces it was a pretty sure thing we still had our mortal emotion of shock.

"What the——," I started to say, Mary and Linda looked like they were going to jump me and kill me! Except, I guess I am already dead.

"You can't curse in Heaven!" Mary yelled.

I think Teresa had my back, but I wasn't sure.

Linda did her famous "Tst, Tst. Tst!" to shut me up.

Mary put her head in her hands on the bar, and I'm *sure* she said, "I can't believe I'm *stuck* outside of heaven with *Vicki*!"

"Hey!" I didn't see any reason to get nasty. "I think you need to work on your mortal anger issues."

At that, we all started laughing. How sick is this? Teresa decided to take control, "Okay you guys, we have to pick a class."

We all slowly opened our menus and began to read. It was really put together quite well. Each class had a description of skill development requirements, including but not limited to, estimated completion times. Some of the classes sounded like a strange version of Phys Ed. "Understanding and Controlling Your Mass." Hmmmmm. "The Art and Science of Mortal Mingling." I never did get that. "Utilizing the Spiritual Mind." Sounds hard. "Helping Mortals Do Good." Ehhhh maybe. "Defending Good." Eeeks no! That will be what Teresa wants. *Ninja* Angel. Ugh.

"Well, I know what I want," I said as I closed the menu and laid it on the bar. They all looked at me. "Let's do the diet thing."

"*What* diet thing?" Teresa asked as she looked at her menu again.

"Controlling Your Mass," I answered.

"Oh god we're doomed," Mary went down on the bar again.

Linda spoke up, "I think we could do the 'Helping Mortals Do Good'. That sounds like something angels should do, and look, it offers the most points of all of the classes!"

Teresa nodded her approval.

Mary surfaced again, her white hair all ruffled. "Yeah, that works for me."

I had to say it, "Have you noticed we all look the same? I mean, I guess I thought in heaven at least I would be skinny and young again. And we're wearing yesterday's clothes. Do we get hungry? Can we eat? Can we …poop?"

Linda started laughing so hard she took her glasses off and was wiping her eyes, "You want to ask that when she comes back? Can we poop? Oh God."

"I think we should stop saying that." This was Teresa, "The 'Oh God' thing," as she looked around.

"Hey! News flash guys, Granny can read minds!" This was me.

Mary slowly turned to look at me, "And you know this how?"

Out of the corner of my eye I could see that Granny was back. She made a throat clearing sound and said, "As I mentioned before, we expect this group to be interesting."

Granny looked at me and said, "Vicki, you would like to know if you can poop?" I didn't have a chance to answer when she said, "That is a very good question for you to ask. It shows you are forward thinking." Try not to think, try not to think. "You no longer have mortal body requirements, but you may enjoy the pleasures of aromas during your transition. If you feel hungry we have an entire aroma system designed where anything you imagine you want to eat, you will smell, and feel totally satisfied."

Wow, the capital opportunities of this little gem. Granny's eyebrow went up. Oops, I can't help myself.

"I know," Granny said looking at me. Mary looked over, and I gestured to her. "See? She read my mind."

Granny collected our menus from us and stated, "Since you have selected the class, 'Helping Mortals Do Good,' I would like to introduce you to your Education Guide." At that moment a short, older woman appeared next to Granny. Her resemblance to Betty White, the actress, was uncanny. I looked at Teresa and wondered if she thought the same thing I did. Evidently so, the three of them all had their jaws dropped and their eyes bugging out.

The short angel spoke and sounded like Betty White. "No girls, Betty White is still mortal. However, we are looking forward to her joining us some day with much anticipation. We selected her image as being comforting for your mortal minds at this time. You may call me Betty." She giggled.

I elbowed Mary.

"As you evolve, you will eventually be able to manifest your spirit into any image imaginable to serve your purpose. My assignment is to assist you through your basic educational requirements, in order for you to successfully complete your training and accomplish your first assignment." Then she tilted her head from side to side a couple of times and gave us that big Betty White smile.

With that, she made a wide gesture with her arm toward the far end of the bar and said, "Go through that door to enter the Transition College."

She was pointing to the door that in mortal life went into the ladies room. Single file we all sort of floated there. I looked at Linda who seemed to be trying to see her feet in the now foggy room. Teresa was moving her arms like she thought we were swimming. Mary was hanging on to the back of my sweater and moaning. I hope for Betty's sake that one of the 'angel' skills she has mastered is patience.

CHAPTER 2

Somehow Betty beat me to the door and pushed it open. Wow, what a beautiful campus! Lush green lawns, tall stately buildings, and…what the heck? Millions of mayflies?

Betty started to giggle, "Oh boy, you gals are going to be fun. Let's see, how do I put this? You see mayflies." She giggled again. "That is actually pretty good, yup, good one." She slapped her knee. "Ahem, okay."

About now I was thinking that I had a much different vision of Heaven when I was mortal, and it didn't include bugs!

"You see mayflies. *I* see thousands of spirit energies from the previous Orientation Class. One of the classes required in the process is, "Utilizing the Spiritual Mind." Do you remember seeing that class option?" We all nodded. "Well, one of the goals of that class is to eliminate unnecessary memories, and free that space for additional spiritual mind. Makes sense, right?"

We all nodded, even though we had no clue what she was talking about. "Your mayflies, on earth, live their whole life in one day, don't they? Your mortal mind is trying to make sense of the energy it sees here, and mayflies are your vision. The process of eliminating memories seems to trigger a type of panic unique to the mortal. They just don't want to let go! This particular class, either as a whole or because of an individual, is not ready to condense. That panic and confusion this class is experiencing, on earth would probably look like a mass of mayflies. To protect all of you from this negative energy, we have to process your group separately." She giggled again.

I had a great idea, "Can't you just explain to them that their memories are still there, just on a zip drive?"

"But that would be lying." Betty said as she looked at me.

"Yeah, but if it gets the job done?" Betty frowned. Okay. I guess you don't lie in Almost Heaven. *This is going to be very limiting for me.*

Betty continued, "The previous class will be fine, and eventually their spirit minds will sooth any feelings of panic and fear. In the meantime, we have devised an alternative process for newcomers." With that she smiled at all of us and motioned for us to follow her. "Mayflies," I heard her mumble under her breath.

Betty now sat on a bench near the little creek that appeared from nowhere and motioned for us to join her on the other benches that appeared from nowhere. "Let's take a moment to gather your thoughts." She was smiling in such a way I thought she was going to burst out laughing any minute. I liked her. She seemed real. "I bet you are all wondering why you see mayflies too, since this is Vicki's little vision?" Everyone was nodding. Mary was trying to carefully keep the mayflies from landing on her. "You are going to 'share' some traits from each other, like imagination."

Linda looked at me and said, "Uh oh."

Teresa piped up, "How can we tell if what we are seeing is real or one of our imaginations?" as she turned her head and looked at me. I am starting to get a little ticked off.

Betty laughed, "That is what is going to be so fun about this group!" She slapped her knee again. "It's all real. If you can think it, it is real. You have always had your own perceptions of everything! That doesn't mean someone else's wasn't real. The only difference now is that you share. Whoever has the strongest imagination wins!"

Ha! I seemed to be the only one happy with that answer.

"What I would like to do, since you are a group, is take you to the classroom where we help you discover the most efficient ways to travel. You will not only need to navigate your way around campus, but because you have selected 'Helping Mortals do Good', we have to teach you how to navigate between the 'planes of understanding' with mortals. Have you all seen how athletes will put a hand out and another will top that with his hand, etc., etc.?"

We all nodded. "Well, let's do that right now." We all stretched out our hands, layering them on top of each other, and Betty landed on the top. "Okay, you have now been implanted with our version of a GPS device, so you can be located in case I lose you."

Lose us? We all looked at our hands. There was a slight bluish dot that was illuminating through the skin. *Cool.*

"These devices also connect you to each other, allowing you to transfer skills among yourselves when needed. A training example of this would be maybe Linda was having some trouble navigating flying at high speed. In order for the class to progress, as a group, you could 'boost' her into keeping up, until it felt natural to her."

We all looked at Mary. We knew she would be the cautious one of the group.

Mary spoke, "Can we get hurt in this training?"

Betty chuckled and looked at her, "You are already dead, dear." Mary shrugged. That seemed to satisfy her. I wasn't completely sold yet. I had visions of having to turn left. Flying yet. In mortal life, driving, I wouldn't turn left unless there was a traffic light. It took a while to get to some places.

"Well, what do you say we get started?" We all nodded. "Stand up and think about moving to that building over there." She pointed to a large stone building about a block in front of us. "Hello? What's taking you so long?" I looked and she was standing in front of the door of that building. Wow, spry little thing isn't she? I felt myself moving forward.

Then stop. Then lurch forward. Then stop. I was stopped.

"Think about getting here!" she yelled.

Whoa! I was right next to her in a Nano-second. Mary was screaming, coming at us sideways at 90 miles per hour. Linda and Teresa were holding on to each other's arms, and it looked like they were being dragged to us with an invisible rope. Betty looked at me once we were all at the door and said "Let me have your hand." Huh? Is she taking away my GPS? "I am just adjusting your settings to decrease your influence on the others." She smiled. "Your mortal mind gave up control of travel years ago, so your Spiritual mind has no resistance. We just have to tone you down, dear." Teresa stuck her tongue out at me. Well! I think I was just insulted by an Angel.

"Okay, once we are inside, your instructors will teach you how to travel, a working knowledge of mortal connections, 'mind reading' as you would call it, and protocol requirements of your status. Once you pass through that door I won't see you again until you are ready for your first assignment. Any questions?" Betty was fluffing the ruffles on her shoulders and patting her hair.

I'm hungry.

Betty looked at me. Yup, she read my mind again. I am getting used to this. "Vicki is hungry. Just decide what you're hungry for, sniff your wrist where you used to wear perfume, and enjoy!"

We all sniffed our wrists and smiled. I burped.

"Are we ready now?" We all nodded, and Betty pointed to the door. "Go in."

There was no handle on the door. Trick. Maybe it slides. Nope. I looked at Betty, and she said, "That door is a visual obstacle only. No mass can stop you. Just walk in." And we did.

CHAPTER 3

U pon graduation from our basic training, we were told to go to the park area and wait for Betty. I think our instructors were as glad to see us go as we were to leave. I certainly never thought about having to go to college in heaven. It just never crossed my mind. I thought that angels just naturally knew how to fly. That was a rough class. Obviously, somewhere over the years I was given some bad information.

We summoned our own benches and waited. Those darn mayflies were still everywhere. I hope we don't end up like that. Getting our first assignment was exciting. We were discussing some of Mary's ideas for 'Helping Mortals Do Good' when Betty appeared. "Those all sound lovely, but we already have the first assignment for your little group." Was it my imagination, or did Betty look pretty serious?

"There is a man at the South Bend, Indiana Police Department right now," she was looking at the coolest watch on her wrist, "who needs our help. His name is Roger Dance. He is a Supervisory

Special Agent of the FBI who has been working with a joint task force to catch a serial killer." She looked at each one of us for a moment and continued, "This is a tough one. You have learned that we are actually fairly limited when it comes to mortal interventions. Sometimes, if a situation is deemed important 'higher up' (she pointed up....we all nodded our understanding), we are asked to assist if we can. We have great hopes for your group. You are the first angels to still be able to think like mortals. This is quite an advantage."

They think my mortal mind is an advantage?

Betty glanced at me, "Work with me here. When we arrive, the mortals will not be able to see or hear us. I want you all to pay close attention, and then we will assess the situation."

There was certainly a new mood, even for me. The thought that we might be able to serve a very important role was sobering. Betty instructed us to set the new watches that appeared on our wrists to the number one, check our coordinates with each other, and meet her in South Bend, Indiana. She no sooner made the statement, and we found ourselves in a brightly lit office overlooking the city. There was a middle aged, good looking man standing at the window sipping a cup of coffee.

"Over here" Betty said, and we saw she had summoned a chair and was floating near the ceiling in the far corner. We joined her.

Agent Dance had a nice head of hair, medium brown with streaks of gray. He looked to be about 6'2 and maybe 190 pounds. He had a slight stoop to his shoulders and his jacket was slung over the door handle of the office. His cheeks had faint pock marks, probably from childhood acne, but it made him look rugged in a pleasing way. There was an electric razor in a plastic bag on the credenza. It looked like he had already used it. He had a tie on, but it was hanging loosely against his light blue shirt He had puppy eyes....cocker spaniel, sad eyes. He was wearing a shoulder harness for his gun, and he looked very capable of doing some damage with it. The early morning sunlight coming through the window made him squint. We all heard him say, "I'm missing something.....what? What?" We were hearing his thoughts. In class, they told us sometimes we will hear the thoughts of mortals when we really weren't trying. This was our first exposure, and it startled us. I almost tipped off my chair.

A tall, nice looking man in a suit knocked on the open door as he walked in. He too had a coffee cup in his hand. "Roger." He sat in the chair across from Roger's desk and studied him. "Were you here all night?"

Roger slowly rolled his head and straightened his shoulders back, "No, I went for a drive. Get the cobwebs out." Roger turned and sat in his chair.

"Did it work?" the man asked as he took a sip of coffee.

Roger was shuffling a stack of index cards on his desk and just dropped them in a pile. Waving his hand over the pile he asked, "Do we have two do-ers on this? Half the victims have not even been touched. The rest are raped." Supervisory Special

Agent Paul Casey had nearly as many years with the agency as Roger. He had been through the ranks and in the Special Homicide task unit for over ten years. Roger expected that Paul would take his job as Chief Behavioral Specialist when he retired. Retire. He was supposed to have done that at the end of this year. Early retirement from law enforcement was almost a necessity. Hopefully, to start a second career that didn't totally consume your soul. Then all of this shit in South Bend.

Paul set his cup down deliberately on the desk, pushed his chin forward in thought, and leaned the chair back as he stretched. "Two do-ers has crossed my mind too. They were all strangled. Only the pretty ones raped. Why bother with the others?"

Paul sort of reminded me of a young Robert Redford. Hmmmm.

Roger leaned forward, "That's just it! You don't risk getting caught, break into someone's home, kill them, and leave. No robbery. Nothing, and yet..." He was shaking his head and twirling a pen.

"Yeah, I know, for some reason my gut says same guy too."

An attractive brunette lady, thirty- something, badge at her waist, knocked on the open door and announced, "They are ready for you in the confer-ence room." Very pretty, and projected a "strictly business" air. As she turned, you could hear her heels clicking on the polished floor and disappear around the corner.

"Wish I had some profound insight," Roger stated as he picked up the files that were on his desk and stood. He straightened his tie and headed toward the door.

Paul rose, grabbed his coffee cup and exclaimed, "I wish you did too."

The two men left the office, and Betty motioned for us to follow which we did. It was interesting to be around mortals again, but the noises were deafening and the smells…coffee, old shoes, body odor, perfume, cleaning supplies. Betty whispered for us to adjust our sensor watches. Whew, much better. Mary had her hands over her ears but saw what we were doing and fixed her watch. Linda was trying to dodge people, and she looked like the Frogger game zigzagging down the hall. I think she forgot that mass doesn't matter to us. She was probably trying to be polite. Teresa had managed to be the first in the conference room and was already floating near the ceiling.

One wall of the room was a bank of windows that reminded me of elementary school. On the other walls were large white boards filled with taped pictures and colored writing. There were calendars and maps and those awful pictures of dead people, six of them. In the center of the room were four long tables with men and women, some in uniform, all sitting, facing the front of the room. Paul took a chair and sat by the door. Roger walked to the front of the room, placed his files on the top of a small desk in the corner, turned to face the group and began to speak.

"Good morning, any thoughts since last night?" Roger looked around the room at the tired faces.

This was a good team of detectives, but the last two months had really drained their resources. Things just kept getting worse. "Our discovery of victim number six late yesterday means the pressure on this team has ratcheted up, *again*". Every person in the room looked defeated. "We're going to have to deal with this in the press. Sharon from our unit will release a statement but I am sure that each of you will be asked questions in private. I cannot stress enough how important it is to stay on text with what we release this morning. Your copy of the release is in a stack by the door." Paul half waived at everyone as they turned to look by the door.

Roger started again, "Since yesterday's four p.m. discovery of victim number six, Ginger Hall, thirty- two years old, an RN at Memorial Hospital, we have been able to confirm the following information: Single, workaholic, charitable volunteer, no children." He gave them a minute to finish writing and then continued, "Her supervisor stated that she had requested some holiday time off and in fact had been using PTO time since December 12. With today being the twenty third, that means our first priority will be finding out the last time she was seen alive. Sharon has scheduled a press release for this morning, and hopefully we will get something useful from the tip line. The FBI Crime Scene Unit should clear the scene later this morning and I will be at that site as soon as it is available. After that I should be back here. Of course you can call me for anything. We are here to help you and get this done."

I saw Linda and Teresa sniffing their wrists. I *tuned* into them…*POPCORN!* REALLY?

Roger continued, "Stan, I would like Agent Williams to accompany you on the personal interviews today."

"No problem," answered a man at the center table.

Roger directed his next comments to a woman at the far end of the room, "Sal, how are the interviews coming on number five, Valerie McDonald?"

The woman called Sal, Detective Sally Miller, stood and addressed the group as she flipped through a notebook. "We have only had the scene for a day and a half, but we have established that Ms. McDonald was a resident of Boston, and has not been seen by neighbors since before Thanksgiving. One neighbor said he thought Valerie was going to Indiana for the holiday, that maybe she had family. He wasn't sure. Also, we have subpoenaed bank records, financials, and should have preliminary forensic results from the lab later today, maybe tomorrow. Agent Dance, I would like to go to Boston and see what else may be there, visit her home."

"Good, talk to Chief Doyle about taking one of his people with you. We have a small jet here at the airport. Use that, you'll save time. Chief Doyle, you have a question?"

The Chief of Police, Edgar Doyle, had raised his hand, and when acknowledged he stood to speak. He had a kind face that showed far too many years of police work on it, a belly that suggested he spent most of his day at his desk, and a baritone voice that you didn't want to hear in anger.

"I know I can speak for the entire department that the help of the FBI in this is crucial, and appreciated. We have no experience with anything *like* this!" Many of the people in the room were nodding their heads in agreement. "But, I have to tell ya, I am *really* worried about what the press is going to do with this since we really don't have anything to tell them. This is a college town. Notre Dame! They are going to expect answers and action *yesterday*. We are in the same place we were two months ago, actually worse. And the bodies keep comin'."

The Chief sat down with a wave of his arms, and Roger spoke again, "The press release is worded in such a way as to sound as if we have more, we just can't comment. This may shake our perpetrator into making a mistake, but I doubt it. We have to address the public, we need their help. Agent Paul Casey will now update you."

Paul walked to the front of the room and lifted the pointer from the white- board tray. "We have *not* ruled out that these murders may be from two separate killers." As the people in the room moaned, he continued, "In any event, our killer, at least on the rape victims, is a middle aged man, judging from the ages of the victims, and in good health. He can drag bodies fair distances. Probably self- employed. Certainly has the ability to manipulate his time. He may be married. He is *smart*, careful and *arrogant*. No DNA, no *evidence*, from *any* of the dump sites. Each of the rape victims has been found in extremely public areas.

He is getting bolder and the space between killings is getting shorter. He is probably nearing a frenzy stage where he may start making mistakes. The victims of the rapes are not prostitutes or "throw away people" as some perpetrators call them. These are *very* attractive, working, professional women. He is able to engage these women, causing them to trust him, and get too close. They are not mutilated, simply raped and strangled. This suggests that they are useful more as playthings to him. He may have an adversity to gore. We only have the dump sites for this group. We do not know where the murders actually took place.

"In the non-raped group we know *where* the murders took place. Still no DNA or evidence, and there are no dump sites. They have been found in their homes." He shook his head as he continued and looked at the faces around the room, "We still have not found **any** connection of these victims to each other. There is a *reason* these women died. He risked getting caught to kill them." He was tapping his pointer next to the pictures of the non-raped women. "These are the types of murders that scare the community to its core. Women living alone are killed in their own homes." Paul took a sip of water and then pushed his chin out in his nervous tick as he looked at the group. He knew they were exhausted, but he had to keep them focused.

"Your Chief called for us on December 6 when the body of Darla Phillips was found south of town, here just off US31. We are calling her victim number three." He was pointing to a picture of a beautiful woman with long dark hair and perfect features. "This was after finding the bodies of number one, Nettie Wilson, on Nov. sixth, and number two, Karen Smith, on the twenty third of November." Nettie's picture on the board said she was 80, and Karen was 42, young, but homely. "Since then we have number four, Burna George, 74– and two days ago number five, Valerie McDonald– and yesterday Number six, Ginger Hall." He had been pointing to each of their pictures as he spoke.

"We have three women killed in their homes, strangled, no apparent robberies, and three women raped, strangled and dumped in a seven week period. Special Agent Dance and I feel the break we need, will come from these three." He pointed to the two old ladies and the homely one. "There *was* a **reason** they were killed. Just keep that thought as we retrace everything, *from the beginning*. Interview friends and family. *Again*. I can't tell you what you are looking for, but you will know it. It may be what is *missing* you will notice, not what is there. Oh, and Merry Christmas tomorrow."

Roger and Paul watched as the room cleared out. A couple of detectives stopped by the picture board for a look at the pictures of Ginger Hall, the new one. Roger rubbed the side of his neck as he spoke to Paul, "One of us needs to be with Sharon for the press conference which starts in, *oh shit*, ten minutes. Can you do that? I want to talk to the neighbors and friends of Nettie Wilson myself. Who knows?"

Paul said he would stay with Sharon and the Chief for a while. He also wanted to check with the lab to see if there was anything found by the CSI guys at Ginger Hall's dump site yesterday. "Why don't I check out this *Hall* scene with you later this morning?" Paul asked Roger.

"Fine, I'll call you when I'm done at Nettie's."

Paul cringed at the crowd of reporters waiting on the other side of the glass door for the press conference to start. This was his least favorite part of the job. With the technology today, the often inappropriate release of information by the press posed very real risks to open cases. He tried to disguise his resentment with a big fake smile. Paul held the door open for Sharon, and she winked at him. "Thanks handsome," she whispered as she walked through. Normally Paul enjoyed the flirting of a beautiful woman, but the ominous dread engulfing this case had him fearing anything that would disrupt his focus. He was also worried about Roger. The pressure was starting to show.

Paul forced a smile and said, "Go do your magic."

When Paul and Roger had both left the conference room, we all looked at Betty. She motioned us to circle around her, and then she asked, "What do you think?" Silence.

Okay, I'll say it, "I think Roger and Paul can arrest *me* any day! *They are hot!*" Betty shook her finger at me.

Teresa frowned at me and said to Betty, "As angels couldn't we, well probably *you,* just talk to the dead people and find out what happened?" That sounded *perfect* and easy!

Betty answered, "Talking to dead people is only in the movies gals. Remember, part of Orientation is reducing mortal memories to just pleasant ones? The dead people wouldn't be able to help. Now remember, our assignment is to help Agent Dance in any way we can. Let's continue to just observe for a while and see what comes to mind. We better move to the news conference now." And she was gone.

I told Linda to stop moving like 'Frogger' that mass didn't matter. She started to laugh, "Oh yeah, I keep forgetting that." She still made a couple of Frogger moves, but I think they were for the benefit of Mary and me. Teresa beat us again! Show off! Betty announced that she was going to Nettie Wilson's house to observe Roger and for us to meet her there after the press release. She gave us our watch coordinates and vanished. *This is so much fun!*

* * *

The sign out front said Attorney James Devon. Closer inspection of the lettering would show it had been poorly touched up with a black marker and the sign post was rotting at the ground. Who cares, he thought, as he pushed a pile of files into his bottom drawer and sprayed air freshener around his desk. Damn dog anyway...stinks.......have to have him though. Neighborhood's going to *hell!*

He saw his part time secretary pull up and park in front of the house where his office was. She was the fifth temp this year. *Bitch.* Said he was inappropriate. Right. She demanded he either let her work out of the living room on the other side of the house, or she was quitting. There may have been some implied threat of going to the Bar Association. *Whatever.*

He surveyed his small office from his desk with the beady eyes of a vulture but without really seeing much of anything. Piles of files on the floor in the corner, a thick layer of crud on most flat surfaces, a couple of dog toys under the desk. A smear on the window where someone had printed 'clean me,' and a mirror that hung crooked on the wall. *That* was on purpose. From there he could see if anyone was slipping a gun from under a coat, or sometimes look up a skirt if he was lucky. His own image in the mirror was less than appealing; sort of the human version of a pit bull. He spit on his hand, and pressed his scraggly hair down around his ears, and curled his lips up to see if any food particles remained in his teeth. He looked at his fingernails and started cleaning them with the corner of a court file.

He turned to his computer and checked his web history for the legal doc site. He needed to print out a few free business cards. Look at all the porn sites! Now that I am a *'Married Man,'* I will have to start erasing these, he noted. Married, a newlywed. Ugh, bitch, ugly bitch, stupid- ugly –worthless- *bitch.* How he made it through that ceremony was certainly worthy of an Oscar. It had been a whirlwind romance because he wanted to get it over with. If she didn't have all that money coming, he would not have married her. If he didn't marry her, he wouldn't have to kill her either. She isn't *pretty*. It's the fault of the *money* that she was going to die. Not him.

He heard his secretary knock something down in the other room. Then the intercom came on, "I'm here, so stay in your room! And you need a new TV snack table."

Cunt. Bitch. Probably a whore too, even if she is ugly.........ugly, *UGLY*. He answered her back, "I'm leaving for a couple of hours. Don't commit me to any appointments."

She came back with "Right." He knew the unspoken words were, like anyone would make an appointment with you?

Even *she* couldn't dampen his spirits today. Over the years of building his practice he had found funerals to be the best source of new clients. His practice had evolved to mostly estate planning and probate. He was cheap. Probably too cheap, but he was also smart and fast. If they wanted it done right, fast, and cheap, it was him. The price they paid for that was *him*. He *had* amassed a great deal of wealth, however, with the rich dumb ones. If they didn't have a bunch of nosey family members, he made sure they signed over their real estate to him as payment for administering their estate.

It was so damn easy, he couldn't believe it! He probably made twenty to forty thousand per month on average, just on real estate sales on properties he had never even seen. Occasionally some church or charity would call with questions, stating they had been told that so-and-so was leaving property to them. He had a standard answer, "Too bad, people lie." He savored those calls!

Today there was a funeral only about two miles away. He *loved* funerals. Went to at least two a week. Funerals were his favorite *hunting* grounds. From the obituary it sounded like a big family. *Lots* of people to watch. He didn't *know* any of these people. That's what makes it so much fun! *Especially* watching the pretty ones cry.

CHAPTER 4

B etty had decided to ride with Agent Roger
Dance in his car to the first victim's home,
Nettie Wilson. She was hoping she could gain
some insight from reading his mind on the trip. She
followed him across the parking lot toward his white
Jeep Cherokee and watched him glance at the news
trucks in the parking lot. His mind was very busy
and she decided to filter only his strongest thoughts.
They came in torrents. *What has not been done? Did I
bring the interview notes from the first detectives? Why kill
an eighty year old lady? No money.... Is he transferring?
Does she remind him of someone? Strangle her.... personal...
up close....violent.... Six. Six murders in seven weeks....he
is losing control....He'll make a mistake. He better.*

It was about a twenty minute ride. Betty found
out Roger was a good person but lonely. He had lost
a fiancé to cancer over five years ago and had not
been in a serious relationship since. He was all con-
sumed with his career, which was probably why he
was so good at it. He had thoughts that his age was
beginning to affect him, and he worried he wasn't

as sharp as he used to be. All last year he had doubled up on his fitness program and time spent at the
shooting range to compensate. He would turn fifty
in February, and this case had him stumped. Worse
than that, he was worried. This one seemed different. *Maybe the bad guys are just getting smarter*, he told
himself. He was consulting a small map and said out
loud, "Okay Roger, let's get this guy!" As he turned his
Jeep onto narrow dirt driveway to a cute little Cape
Cod style house, parked, and turned off the engine.

He leaned against the warm hood of the car,
stared at the house and surroundings, took out his
note pad, and began writing short notes. House -
fair condition/ needs new trim paint/ evidence of
past flower beds/ icicle hanging from eaves / needs
roof repair / lace curtains in windows. *House screams
old lady, not much money, lives alone,* he thought as he
moved toward the front porch. Yellow crime scene
tape hung loose on either side of the door. He tore
the tape down, wadded it up....*invitation to vandals.*
The scene had long since been released to the family.
Who was that? A niece named Joy Covington. Okay.
What did he know about her? She found the body
day after Nettie died, on the 7th, 10:30 a.m./ home-
maker/ works part time as cook at nursing home/
not much family left/ friends. Good size funeral on
Thursday Nov. 11th/ Neighbor, Mrs. Brooks, called
the niece when Nettie didn't answer phone morning
of 7th. They were supposed to go to Senior Center
for potluck.

Agent Dance used the key provided by the niece
and unlocked the front door. The temperature

outside was around forty degrees F, and it felt like the heat was on low in the house. Roger draped his wool overcoat over one of the Duncan Phyfe dining room chairs, and slowly scanned the rooms. The house smelled slightly stale, but looked very clean. He was struck at how similar all old persons' homes were. There was the recliner with a stack of newspapers and magazines crawling up the side of the end table. An assortment of glasses with straws, remote controls and little pill bottles covered the top. A small spiral notebook and pen rested next to a twenty year old cordless phone. A pile of neatly folded lap blankets, a pillow hidden underneath on the floor, and a can of wasp spray on the lower shelf of the end table, every old ladies pistol. A paper bag with the top rolled over half filled with used tissues, coupon clippings, and junk mail. A small puzzle book, giant letters, lay next to a pair of reading glasses. A pair of slippers was neatly tucked under the table. Nettie had *lived* in this chair.

He took his time looking through the rest of the house paying attention to every detail. On the walls of the hall were family pictures. One showed a handsome young couple in wedding clothes. The frame had a small gold engraved plaque that said Charles and Nettie Wilson, 1949. A walker was parked at the end of the hall, the kind that had a basket under a small seat in the middle. In the basket were a few neatly folded clothes. Behind the door at the end of the hall a stackable washer and dryer had been squeezed into an old linen closet. It looked as if the installation had been done a while ago. The ticking of the large wall clock blasted through the silence. Clocks can have a comforting sound, like a heart-beat. He didn't find it comforting today.

He walked back to where Nettie's body had been found. He ran his fingers through his hair and mas-saged his temples. Another headache was brewing. She had died only two feet from the front door on a small linoleum vestibule. Nettie was a tiny, frail woman. She had *let* someone in. They closed the door, strangled her and left. Didn't even walk onto the carpet. Why? Through the kitchen window he saw the elderly neighbor woman in her window, spastically motioning for him to come over. He had planned to. He laughed to himself that you don't keep old women waiting. He flipped through his notebook to get her name. Mrs. Brooks.

Roger locked Nettie's house and started toward the neighbor's home, Betty at his side. Then we all showed up. Betty looked at her watch and then looked at us with her eyebrows raised. "We got lost!" Teresa explained.

"But Linda figured out how to use the watch and here we are!" Mary said smiling. Linda looked pretty proud of herself. I was proud of her too. I didn't have a *clue* how to do that yet.

"This is something you'd better *learn*." Betty said to me. I got into trouble, and I didn't even *say* anything!

Somehow Betty transferred a lot of information about Roger to us automatically, or something. I don't quite know how she did that. We followed as the neighbor, Mrs. Brooks, led Roger into her home.

He was showing her his badge and explaining he was FBI when she interrupted him, "Oh, I know who *you* are Honey from the TV. You are that *good lookin'* one." She frowned and said, "Well, have you caught the **asshole** yet or not?"

Roger was a little taken back by her question but never lost a step. "I assure you Mrs. Brooks, we are doing everything we can to solve this."

"Yeah, yeah," she said as she plopped into her recliner. He noticed it looked just like Nettie's. "You sit down young man and ask me some questions. *Nobody* knew Nettie better 'en me."

We all sat around the dining table and watched. "Mrs. Brooks," Roger started, "the detective that interviewed you before probably asked you the same questions I am going to ask. We follow up like this in case you might remember more as time goes on." He continued, "Just now you clearly saw me through Nettie's kitchen window, but on November sixth, Sunday, you didn't see anyone at Nettie's house around say ten or eleven in the morning?"

"Well, like I told the other detective, who by the way isn't as cute as you." she winked.

I gagged, Betty frowned.

"Nettie didn't drive anymore, and we usually go to 8:00 a.m. mass together. I still drive."

She winked again. I did nothing.

Betty looked at me as Mrs. Brooks continued, "Then we had to stop at Andy's market for a few groceries. The senior center pot luck was Monday, the day we found her." She sniffled, "Nettie made her famous potato salad. I had to run a couple of errands after we went to Andy's, so I just dropped Nettie off and left again. I wasn't *home* to see who did this." You could tell she had been agonizing over this fact.

"That's how I knew something was wrong, you see. Nettie didn't answer the phone Monday, when I called to say I was ready to go to the pot luck. I called a *couple of times,* but she didn't answer. I couldn't see anything through the windows, so I called Joy. I have her number in case of an emergency," her voice trailed off to a near whisper, and she used the edge of her apron to dab her eyes. You could tell she really missed her friend.

Roger flipped back in his notebook, "You are speaking of Joy Covington, Nettie's niece?"

"Yes," she answered softly.

Roger pressed on, "Mrs. Brooks, I noticed that someone has straightened up Nettie's house since our crime techs were here. Everything looks clean and tidy. Was that Joy that did that?"

"Yes, that was Joy. She wasn't very happy with your people you know. Left that damn black powder on everything, moved all the furniture. Couldn't reach Nettie's cleaning gal, and had to do it herself! Took her a couple of days! I wouldn't be surprised if she doesn't have that house on the market in another *month.*"

While Mrs. Brooks had been talking, Roger had been flipping back in his notebook. "I don't think you mentioned the cleaning lady to the first detective."

"He didn't ask!" She said defensively.

36

"Do you happen to remember her name, or maybe a phone number?"

Mrs. Brooks pointed to a small spiral notebook across the room. "Hand me that book honey. I had to find this for Joy. *Twice* since you guys messed up the house again when *you* came into the picture. Let me see, here it is, you ready?" Roger nodded and had his pen ready, "Darla Phillips." BINGO, *victim number three. The first rape victim.*

CHAPTER 5

Attorney James Devon stood in the vestibule of the funeral home trying to look like he was waiting for someone. He tried to brush the dog hairs from his suit. He could see them now in the light. This was one of his favorite funeral homes. They always had coffee and cookies out in the reception area, and the chairs were crammed close to each other. A few of the people coming in he actually knew, mostly the elderly women. For the most part they all looked like smurfs to him... little blue haired dim-wits. "Oh hello Maude, good to see you out. Watch your step there..." I've got to remember to send her a bill. Tell her I had to prepare some probate form. She can afford it. He watched Maude's' caregiver help her up the four steps to the reception hall. That is one UGLY woman, he thought.

Oh yes, this is more like it....Hubba—*Hubba.* Oh my God. He held the door for a gorgeous blond in a long white cashmere coat. She wore a long gold scarf that perfectly matched her hair, and had professionally applied makeup. She was perfect! Her eyes were a little rimmed in red, and he could see that under her coat was a proper black dress. *Class act*, he thought.

He slowly followed her up the stairs and watched as she was greeted by a few of the family members. She started to walk towards the guest book, and he carefully maneuvered his way to stand just behind her. When she finished signing, he made sure she noticed him. He tried his best smile, "Hello, were you close to Janet?" He had memorized some of the info on the funeral card.

She looked a little puzzled but answered, "I haven't been as close to her as I would have liked in the past few years. My business has kept me a little out of touch. We used to be neighbors." With that she excused herself, and sat in one of the chairs provided for non-family members. He looked at her signature in the book and committed it to memory, Ashley Tait.

He made his rounds of sad smiles; there- there pats of comfort, and visited the body, twice. He checked out the floral arrangements and handed out a few business cards. He heard their whispers. "Any lawyer good enough for Janet is certainly good enough for me. Especially one that takes the time to go to her funeral! My, my, a lawyer with a heart." He was hysterical with laughter inside. This just never gets old.

He found a seat one row back, and a little to the right of Ms. Ashley Tait. He watched her out of the corner of his eye during the entire funeral. Yes! She was crying! *Oh*, this was too much to hope for! He couldn't wait to get back to his office and find out a little more about her. Thank God for Google. He inserted himself into the recession line at the begging of some old smurf and as Ashley was leaving he asked her, "What kind of business did you say were in?"

She took her time before answering and finally said, "I'm a judge."

* * *

Betty told us to get into the back seat of Roger's car. I couldn't believe it! Now she won't let us fly at all? *We have to take cars with people?* She looked at me. I was still pouting. Then she said, "We can learn from Agent Dance's thoughts on the way." Oh, yeah.

Roger was talking into his cell phone, "Paul! Darla Phillips, our number three, was Nettie Wilson's cleaning lady! We finally have our first break! Can you free yourself up to re- interview any friends or neighbors of Darla in that file?..... Great, I have Nettie's niece to talk to yet then I will be back at the station. I want that Ginger Hall dump scene before it gets contaminated. CSI should be done soon." With that he disconnected with Paul and flipped through his notebook. He dialed and waited. Finally he spoke, "Is this Joy Covington?" Roger was turning the key in the ignition. "This is Special Agent Dance with the FBI. I need to meet with you immediately." We heard him think, *Make time lady.*

He spoke into the phone again as he was pulling out of the driveway. "I appreciate that Ms. Covington. I am on my way now." He clicked the phone shut. Betty was in the front seat next to him. We were all in the back. Roger reached to the floorboard passing between Betty's legs and pulled out a big round red ball that he slapped onto the dash and turned on. Oooooh Cooooooooooool. We had sirens and flashing lights and everything!

Betty was laughing as she looked to the back seat. "You gals better calm down, or you won't be able to concentrate on Roger's thoughts." Her attempt to scold us just mildly worked. This was the most excitement we'd had since *dying*!

Betty had to filter Roger's thoughts again to get clarity. His mind was racing. All of a sudden we heard him. It was like he was talking to himself, but his lips were not moving. *Nettie was murdered on Nov. 6. Darla was found on Dec.6, a full month later. When was the last time she was seen? Nov 11. When was Nettie's funeral? Damn, I already forgot…check on that.* He started writing in his notebook. I **screamed** from the backseat, "DUDE! WATCH THE ROAD!!" I covered my eyes in horror. I think Betty changed the street lights to all green. We finally made it to a dingy looking house with a pickup truck running in the front yard, parked in the grass, and a big yellow dog tugging at a rope, and barking at *us*!

Betty advised us that most animals can see us. *Great.* Linda stayed real close to Roger, he had a gun. We all walked toward the house. Roger flipped his phone open and dialed, "Ms. Covington? I am here. Can you move your dog?" Good idea, I thought.

A minute later a woman appeared at the door and started yelling at the dog. "SHUT UP FLEA BAG!" Oh boy, she looked *worse* than Flea Bag. "He won't hurt ya....come on in...he just barks a lot." Roger suggested that she put the dog in the house, and they talk outside. She agreed. As she unhooked the rope and grabbed Flea Bag's collar, he tore away from her. He stood barking, high pitch, at the group of **us**. (Ran right past Roger.) "Crazy fool dog!" Joy said as she ran up behind him.

Flea Bag was growling, snorting, barking, yelping, and frankly just putting on quite a show at *apparently* "nothing." The four of us had floated up the big tree high enough he couldn't get to us. He was right at the trunk of the tree going NUTS! Even Roger looked up the tree with a puzzled expression on his face. He finally spoke, "Ma'am? If you could just ...."

Teresa jumped down from the tree, lunged at Flea Bag, and said "Boo!" The dog yelped, turned around, and blasted through the front door of the house nearly knocking over Joy.

"Well, I never," she said as she shut the door behind him. Betty suddenly appeared, we don't know where she went during all of this fun. She looked at Teresa. Uh oh, I'm thinking that Teresa is in *real* trouble.

"Nice call," Betty said as she turned to get closer to Roger. Huh!

Nettie's niece was in dirty sweats, her hair looked oily, and she obviously didn't own any tweezers…big uni-brow…ugh. "Look, Mr. FBI Man, I have to be at work in less than twenty minutes. I am the cook at Pleasant Rest nursing home, so I hope this won't take too long. My truck is already warmed up."

Roger was smiling, "Just a couple of questions. How long had Darla Phillips worked for your aunt?"

Joy looked surprised, "Darla Phillips? Oh, that cleaning gal. Let's see, *years* really. Pretty girl, woman, whatever. Aunt Nettie called her an angel. She took her to doctor appointments, groceries, that kind of stuff. She cleaned her house every now and then." Then Joy got an angry look on her face, "She's not claimin' to get any of aunties stuff is she? We got a lawyer and everything. *I* get that house!"

Roger was flipping through his notebook, "Miss Phillips was murdered. Her body was found on the 6th of this month. We are investigating her relationships and her connection to your aunt."

Joy Covington started jumping up and down. "Holy SHIT! She was one of them gals thrown next to the highway? Holy SHIT! I read about that in the paper. I guess I didn't catch the *name*. HOLY SHIT!" I slowly looked towards Betty. I knew I was *used* to this kind of language, but I wasn't sure how upset I was supposed to be, now that I am an 'Angel'. Mary was biting her lip and kind of rocking. Betty actually looked fine. Okay then, but I betcha *this* chick doesn't get to heaven! Oh wait, I did. Linda cleared her throat, and I glanced at her. She and Teresa were frowning at me.

Roger continued, "What day was Nettie's Funeral?"

Joy was picking at a sore on her hand. *Really? She is a cook?* "The funeral was Friday morning, and Darla was there! I remember she rode with Auntie's lawyer to the graveside services. She took cabs everywhere. Didn't have no car."

Roger asked, "Do you know Nettie's lawyer's name?"

Joy twisted her mouth in thought, "Devon, I think. I have some papers I can look for has him on 'em."

Roger pushed on, "When was it, you tried to reach Darla to clean Nettie's house the first time?"

Joy looked annoyed, "She never called me back. Let's see, it was whatever day your people called me and said I could use the house again. Couple of weeks ago anyway. Can I go now? I'm *really* gonna be late!"

Roger flipped his notebook shut, "I will have more questions later, and I will call you. Thank you for your time."

As we walked back to the car we heard that dog barking again, and Joy yelling, "Shut UP, Flea Bag!"

We were back in our regular seats, and I was trying to decide if seat belts worked for people like us. I found that I could pick up the strap, but when I snapped it, it went through me again. I think I did this about three times before Linda pointed out that if Roger looked into the back seat, he would see his seat belt moving around.

Then Teresa asked, "Afraid you might die?"

Betty spoke up and said, "You know it is fairly common to start feeling like you are mortal again when you are around them. I am surprised you can move objects so easily already Vicki. That usually takes a while longer. *Stop it!*" Okeey Dokeey.

Roger was sending his thoughts again, *Maybe Joy Covington did want Nettie's stuff and decided to move things along. Doesn't explain Darla, she was raped. Who knows Darla? Do we have a boyfriend? Should be in the office file.* He started to speed up, and reached to flip on the light and siren again. *Oh Goody!*

Betty looked to the back seat at Teresa, "Why don't you and Linda go to the nursing home and see what Ms. Covington really thought of this visit, dear? When you are done, set your watches to the number two and we will meet you at the last victim site, Ginger." Teresa gave a quick nod, and they were gone. Then Betty looked at Mary, "You and Vicki go to Valerie McDonald's house in Boston. That detective woman named Sal is on her way there now with another officer. I have a hunch that we may find something that could help."

Mary and I looked at each other. I said, "I hope *you* know how to get there." She got a determined look on her face and the next thing I knew we were standing in the middle of Fenway Park....hmmmmm.

"I think we are *close*," I said to Mary as she studied her watch. (I *have* to read that manual).

"Oh! Here we are", she said and away we went. We stopped in front of a pleasant looking brick row house. Bet this cost a penny or two. Mary double checked the address, and we walked through the front door. Literally.

It was a duplex, two units with a common vestibule. Hmmmmm. Mary decided we would do rock, paper, scissors to decide which door to go through. The door labeled "B" won! This was our first 'job' without supervision. Very exciting. We walked through the wall together and found ourselves in a living room. The TV was on, and a guy was lying on the couch sleeping. Eeek. He shifted his shoulders, stretched his arms out, and looked right at us. We were standing in front of the TV, and we couldn't tell if he was looking at us, or *it*. I couldn't think of anything to say but "Hi." He didn't say anything *or* change his expression.

Mary whispered, "I don't think he can see us." We started walking sideways to get away from the TV.

Mary started to back up when I whispered, "Stop!" I saw a pile of mail on the table next to the couch, and on the top letter was the name *Valerie McDonald*. "Look at that stack of mail. It has her name on it. He must be getting the mail for her! Remember? That Detective Sal said a neighbor had said Valerie was going to Indiana for Thanksgiving."

"I want that mail," I whispered to Mary.

Mary frowned, pursed her lips as she said, "The cops are coming here. Don't you think *they* will ask him some questions and get her mail?" She definitely did not like where this was going. I didn't like her answer.

"Maybe, maybe not. Why take the chance he may leave before they get here?" She was trying hard to think of a reason. I decided to just grab the mail and run. I got to the other side of the wall in the vestibule and noticed I didn't have the mail in my hand...dang. I went back, and Mary looked horrified. Evidently when I ran through the wall, the *"mail"* couldn't do that. From her side of the wall it looked like the stack of mail jumped up from the coffee table and threw itself against the wall.

This took our sleepy dude by surprise too. He was now staring at the mail on the floor, looking at the table, and rubbing his hair. Oops. "Now what?" Mary asked as she tapped her foot. I shrugged my shoulders. Hey, I am new to this too.

"He's a man. Give him five minutes, and he will fall back asleep." I sure hope I am right. Sure enough. He closed his eyes, crunched his pillow around his face, and started breathing deeply again. I kicked the last envelope under the door and out into the hall, started backing out of the room through the wall, and saw that he still had one eye open. I am sure he was thinking that mail doesn't usually slide under a door going *"out"* of a room. I quickly stuffed the envelopes under Apt. "A" door. I rushed through the wall just in time to hear his door open, pause for a second, and then shut. It sounded like he bolted it too.

We were in Valerie's' house on the couch cracking up. "That is something for us to remember," Mary said, *"Objects* do not pass through walls." Okay, time to get serious. I divided the mail into two piles to save time. I was sorting my half into piles of bills/ other, and I looked over. Mary was just sitting there staring at me. "I don't know how to do this." Oh. That's right.

"Well, let me teach you. *Super* focus on what you want to do. Block out everything else. I *think* that is what I do."

Mary was certainly focused, her brow was creased and BAM! An envelope leaped from the pile and slapped into her forehead! She was so startled, she jumped. I couldn't resist, "They are going to be easier to sort if you *catch* them, a little eye-hand coordination?" She stuck her tongue out at me and proceeded to the next one on her pile. Except for her tongue still sticking out, it looked like she knew what she was doing.

"Hey, look at this, a return address of Karen Smith, South Bend, Indiana. Looks like a card." Mary was almost shaking with excitement, "Karen Smith is one of the names on the FBI board!"

"Open it!"

Mary got all huffy, "I am *not* going to open it—that's against the LAW!"

I couldn't believe she said that. "We're *dead*. Hello? Are you worried I will turn you over to the cops? *Open it!*"

"No," she pouted and hung on tight.

"Okay, then *I'll* open it!"

Betty was now sitting on the couch with us. "No you won't, dear! Whew! *That was a fast trip*. Okay, we cannot *tamper* with anything that the police may need for their case. Hand *me* the letter Mary." Mary handed it to Betty and then gave me an 'I told you so' look. Huh. Betty stated "This will be very helpful

49

to the detectives because it confirms that Valerie was leaving to visit Karen Smith for Thanksgiving. I think the police will discover they were sorority sisters in college. It is signed Sis, and neither Valerie or Karen have any sisters."

I was shocked, "You can read through the envelope?" I asked Betty.

"Yes. I started to travel here when I saw you two go into the wrong apartment." She was looking at me. "Do you have anything else to tell me about your trip?"

I was shaking my head. Mary pointed at me and spouted, "She stole this mail!" Snitch.

Betty started laughing, "I saw that. It's okay. You did not interfere with the investigation really, and the neighbor is due to leave at any minute. Detective Sal would have missed him." Just then we heard the neighbor's door shut and the vestibule door open and shut. I stuck my tongue out at Mary when I didn't think Betty was looking. "Okay then, since I am here, let's look over the rest of the apartment quickly and see if there isn't something that just needs to be made a little more obvious." We searched for what seemed like hours, and then we heard a key in the door. Detective Sal and a man were entering the apartment. Betty told us to set our watches to the number two, and get back to South Bend to the last victim's dump site where we would meet up with Agent Dance and Agent Casey.

Meanwhile, Linda and Teresa had made their way to Pleasant Rest Nursing Home. They were outside the building sitting on a bench, watching people come and go, waiting for Joy Covington to arrive. "What do you think is taking her so long?" Linda asked Teresa.

"That truck of hers didn't look so good. Maybe we should call Betty?" Right then a black cat with green-blue eyes came from under the bench and started rubbing against Teresa's ankles. "Oh great," Teresa said. "First I have that crazy dog and now a cat!" She used her leg to nudge the cat away. The cat just turned around and started rubbing her leg some more. Then it stretched up and put its front paws on Teresa's knee. "Oh for pity's sake." Teresa said as she pushed it away and stood up.

Linda was laughing, "That's right! You are not exactly a cat fan are you?"

"No, I am not. They are sneaky, and they....." She couldn't finish because the cat had jumped up behind her head, and was lying across the top of her shoulders. You could see the tail wrapping around one side of Teresa's neck and the face peeking around the other side. Linda was bent over laughing. "This isn't funny!" Teresa was annoyed.

Linda worried that Teresa might hurt the cat trying to remove it. "Here, let me come around you and get it off." She pulled on the cat, but it had implanted all of its claws into Teresa's shoulders. It seemed the cat had rubber legs that could stretch to infinity. Linda pulled again. That cat wasn't going anywhere it didn't want to.

Teresa started screaming, "Yeow! Just stop it!" The cat was now craning its neck all the way around to Teresa's face. They were eyeball to eyeball. Teresa said, "BOO!" The cat jumped down. Teresa glared at it. The cat sat about two feet from her cleaning its paws. It tilted its head, kept cleaning, and watched her. "That cat is creeping me out," Teresa said as she straightened her hair.

Linda said, "Look! Isn't that Joy's truck pulling in?"

It was. Joy Covington slammed the truck door shut and started stomping across the parking lot to a side door. Linda and Teresa followed her. She went down two halls and slapped open a set of stainless steel doors into a well-lit kitchen where four startled people stood frozen at their tasks. One little meek woman started, "I made soup and the stuff for the salad bar, but I didn't know what you wanted for the entrée." She looked like she was going to cry.

Joy barked out, "How much of that damn meat-loaf is left from last night?"

The little lady rushed over to a huge walk in cooler and came out with a metal pan. "We have three logs left." She stood like a soldier waiting for orders.

Joy made a face and then said, "Start breaking that up. John, go in the pantry and get four large cans of marinara sauce and use the large pot. We're having spaghetti." Everyone started running around like they knew what to do now. Joy slammed a large pot on a gas burner and using a faucet at the stove filled the pot with water. She turned the flame on high and just stood there leaning against the counter top. Her thoughts blared across the room, but we knew that we were the only ones that could hear.

That Son of a Bitch. That drunken son of a bitch! I bet he planked that Darla. He ran over there every time she was at Nettie's. Raped, huh? Now he can get it up! He's not at the job site now either. Damn foreman thinks he's talkin' to a fool? Sure he went to get more drywall. Wait 'til he gets home. His ass is mine!

Linda was thinking that dinner at Joy's house was not going to be much fun. Joy yelled, "Who let the damn cat in here?" She grabbed a broom and started swinging at Teresa's new little friend. It looked to Linda like the cat wasn't afraid of her and was slapping back.

Teresa lunged at the cat and said "BOO" again, and it ran out a small service door that was propped open.

Linda looked at Teresa and said, "We have to find out who 'he' is." Just then the cat flew out from the service door, ran across the counter, knocked over Joy's purse, spilling everything on the floor. It circled the entire room and went back out the service door.

Joy was livid, "SHUT that damn door! If that thing comes in here again, it is goin' in the spaghetti pot."

Teresa and I were on the floor wildly trying to read any names on anything in her purse. There it is. Debit card: names Joy Covington and Jack Simpson. "Let's go." Teresa said, and they adjusted their watches to the number two.

They found themselves standing next to a busy highway. Linda saw the highway sign, US-31 South.

Betty, Vicki and Mary were not there yet. As she looked down, she saw the black cat sitting behind Teresa. "You brought the cat."

"What?" Teresa jumped, and saw the cat sitting behind her cleaning its paws.

"You brought that cat. Take it back!"

Teresa was stunned, "I didn't think we could even do that."

Linda stomped her foot, "Take it back. It's going to get hit by a car!"

Teresa rolled her eyes. "Fine," she turned around, picked up the cat and vanished. A minute later she reappeared.

Linda was giggling. "You think this is funny?" Teresa was not amused. The cat was perched on the back of Teresa's neck looking at Linda over Teresa's head. "You know we are graded as a 'group' in this little job. I wouldn't be laughing too hard."

Right then Betty, Vicki and Mary showed up. Mary looked at Teresa and said, "I bet there is a story." The cat jumped off Teresa and stood up on its hind legs. Teresa braced for it to jump on her again, but it started dancing. Really good dancing.

Betty giggled, "Girls, I requested some extra help here!" Suddenly Ellen DeGeneres was dancing next to Teresa! We knew it wasn't the real Ellen, but wow!

"Oh my Gosh!" We were all jumping and clapping. I always wanted to meet Ellen, maybe get on the show. Fall through that hole in the floor.

Ellen stopped dancing and said, "You guys know I am not Ellen, right?" We were all nodding. She soooo looked like her and sounded like her that it seemed real. She looked at Teresa and said, "I was just messin' with ya." Yup, that's what Ellen would do.

Betty spoke up, "This assignment is going to get increasingly difficult from here on. Ellen volunteered to help us until the end, give me a little break, but I'll be back." She made the motion of wiping her brow, still smiling, "I think there is a hammock in the park with my name on it. Catch you gals later." With that she was gone.

CHAPTER 6

Jack Simpson had decided since it was December and there still wasn't any snow cover it was a sign from God to take an extra-long lunch. Maybe he'd have a few beers, see what the guys were up to and check out any gals that might wander in. Of course he knew that if there had been a blizzard, or even a few flakes, he would have taken that as a sign from God to do the same thing. Pretty much any event was a sign from God if you looked at it right, he thought.

He entered his favorite bar, the Pub. Once his eyes adjusted to the dark, he saw his favorite bartender Larry wiping down the counters. "Hey Man! Since when do you do days?" Jack plopped onto the corner bar stool and waited for his beer.

Larry looked at him and asked, "Don't you ever work?"

Jack grabbed the remote and changed the channel on the TV. Too early in the day for a game, so he stopped on the news and turned it up. Larry and some old guy at the end of the bar were the only ones there. Of course it was only 11:00 a.m. and the Pub had just opened.

Larry brought a beer over and placed it in front of Jack. "You mean the day people start with you, and I have to end with you? How the hell do you pay your bills?"

Jack sat up straight, "I'm not here every morning!" Jack declared, "I had to get supplies for the job. Foreman's going to be gone all afternoon. When the cat's away...." He downed half a mug in one gulp, finished it off with the second. "Why don't you hit me again, and this time don't give me a mug with a hole in the bottom." Jack thought he was pretty funny, sat smiling at his wit, as his attention was diverted to the TV.

The news anchor was standing next to some highway and talking about the FBI. Jack yelled down toward Larry, "Hey Dude, what do you think about these broads poppin' up dead all over town? Cops say we got ourselves a g-e-n-u-i-n-e serial *killer*...rapes too!" Jack laughed, "Not easy gettin' a piece of ass anymore."

Larry set the second mug down in front of Jack, "You know, I told my wife she better be careful. She is so good lookin'. This guy is going' for some gorgeous chicks!"

"Well," Jack sat up straight, "That is precisely why I didn't even bother to mention it to Joy. She has nothin' to worry about!"

Larry shook his head, "Cold man, real cold."

Around four o'clock Jack decided he should take the supplies to the job site and spread some dry wall mud on a wall before tomorrow. They wouldn't let him throw darts anymore anyway, and the only thing on TV was all the damn murders.

At six o'clock he pulled into the driveway and saw Joy's truck was home. Good, she would have his dinner ready. Flea Bag was barking by the front door. Kind of nice to have a buddy greet you when you get home. He fell, sat down on the ground, and played with Flea Bag a couple of minutes. He managed to pull himself up to go on in. He decided after dinner he'd better take a nap before going back to the Pub.

He had one arm almost out of his jacket when the first frying pan flew past him and hit the wall. "Whoa there!" He ducked too slowly, and the second one hit him on the side of the head. "What the Hell? What's your problem?" He managed to slink behind the kitchen island and was bobbing along the floor trying to get to the living room.

Joy looked like she was possessed. "The FBI was here! You know that hot piece of shit Darla you're always droolin' over? They said she is one of them dead women. I know damn well you killed 'em both! My poor ol' auntie and Darla just cuz she wouldn't give ya some!" Jack was peeking from the living room around the wall. Joy continued, "And if I can figure this out, it's only a matter of time 'fore them FBI guys are back here!"

Now she was holding another pan at her side, crying. "Tell me I'm wrong you son of a bitch." Still crying, she saw Jack stand up and start walking slowly toward her. He had a strange expression on his face, and he whispered as he leaned across the island.

"You- best- not- piss- me- off. Now shut up, and get my supper." Then he turned his back to her and walked into the living room. He turned the news on, and laughed as loud as he could as the family members of victims told the news reporter how devastated they were.

Jack wasn't about to take any shit from her. He smiled. Darla. Pretty, pretty Darla. FBI. Huh. The longer he sat in front of the TV, the heavier his eye lids got. As soon as he was passed out, Joy slipped out of the house and tore out of the driveway in her truck.

* * *

Ellen was getting information from Mary and Vicki about their visit to Boston when Agents Dance and Casey arrived. They parked on the shoulder of the highway, left their flashing lights on so traffic would slow, and were walking toward them. "Okay, here come our guys. Let's see what's new," Ellen proclaimed as she produced a director's chair to sit in. (Said Ellen on it.) We all joined her and watched as both Roger and Paul slowly walked around the taped off area, looking at the ground, feeling the grass and dirt, looking up and down the highway.

Finally Roger said, "This goes beyond arrogance."

Paul was nodding, "No shit."

Roger watched the traffic, "How do you dump a body along the side of a highway, busy highway, in the middle of the day and not be seen? Have you had any good updates from the tip line?"

"Not so far," Paul said as he crouched down at the side of the road and looked back toward the pavement. "Wouldn't there be some drag marks?"

Roger walked to view from the opposite direction. "There may have been. Remember there was a car accident along here, and I'm sure there was clean up by the county boys. Initially, our girl Ginger was presumed to have been part of the auto accident, until the Coroner notified us she had ligature marks, signs of rape and dehydration. Also, family members of the wreck victims said they didn't know her."

Paul and Roger both saw it at the same time. A small piece of duct tape stuck to a branch of a small bush. When the sun was just right, it reflected like a mirror. They walked over, and Roger pulled a small bag out of his pocket while Paul put rubber gloves on and got a pair of tweezers out of his pocket. Paul carefully snapped the small branch, put the whole thing in the bag, and sealed the top. Roger scanned the area and said, "How did that get all the way over here? We are at least thirty feet from the highway now. This probably isn't part of our scene."

Paul answered, "Crime tech told me they had a lot of debris they collected. Let's have them run trace on it anyway."

They were slowly walking in circles around the place where Ginger's body had been found when

Paul said, "So tell me about the connection between Darla Phillips and Nettie Wilson."

Roger cleared his throat, "Visited Nettie's house. I don't think our guy even went past the foyer. Goal was just to kill Nettie, for whatever reason. Neighbor lady said Darla was like a caregiver to Nettie. She would take her to the doctor's office, grocery store, clean her house. Now here is something too. Neighbor said Darla didn't have a car and would take a cab to Nettie's, use Nettie's car for errands they did together, and then take a cab home. According to Darla's neighbors she hasn't been seen since the day of Nettie's funeral. Nettie's lawyer gave Darla a ride to the cemetery service, and that's the last time she saw her."

Paul made a quick push motion with his chin, "Do we know where Darla went after the cemetery? We need to talk to that attorney and see where he dropped her off."

Just then Roger's phone rang, "Agent Dance." He listened for a couple of minutes and then said, "Good work Sal. Finish up there, and get back as soon as possible." He snapped his phone shut and looked at Paul. "That was Sal Jones. She and Ed are at the home of Valerie McDonald in Boston, our Number five. Found a greeting card there from Karen Smith, our Number two. Thinks they were sorority sisters. Card is postmarked the day before Karen Smith died and has a note saying, 'I hope you found a way to have Thanksgiving with me,' signed Sis."

Paul couldn't contain his excitement, "This is it....we are linking!" Roger started walking back toward their cars with Paul at his heals.

We could hear Roger say, "Let's get this son of a bitch."

Ellen told us to go to the conference room at the station and compare our thoughts on what we had seen so far. She would meet us later.

CHAPTER 7

Linda, Teresa, and Mary were sniffing their wrists. "What are you having?" I asked them.

Mary answered, "I'm doing breakfast. Orange juice, French toast, bacon....ummmmm"

Linda said, "I went for a cheeseburger."

Teresa said, "I think donuts! We're at a police station." She smiled as she sniffed. I wasn't hungry yet. Maybe Betty was right. Half the time I ate as a mortal I probably wasn't hungry. Why didn't I figure this out as a mortal? We decided to go ahead and sit at the conference table since no mortals were in there.

Teresa shook her head and said, "You wouldn't believe what Ellen did to me at that nursing home."

Linda started laughing, "If you could have seen Teresa's face."

Then Mary piped up, "Vicki *stole* this guy's mail!" Snitch.

It was my turn, "*Mary* learned how to move objects."

Linda and Teresa both said at the same time, "Teach Me!"

I looked at Mary, and she said, "I'll teach you. After all, I am the teacher of the group."

"Second grade," I whispered.

Mary frowned at me, "You are just lucky I wasn't your teacher. I can do this!"

She saw a coffee cup on the desk in the far corner and started frowning at it. All of a sudden it raced from where it had been to the air space right in front of her and stopped. Then it dropped on the table and the handle broke off. "Wow!" Teresa said, "How did you do that?"

Mary answered, "I have to remember to catch things, but you just focus on what you want it to do." Teresa and Linda both looked at the remaining cups on the desk and started frowning at them with their hands out like baseball catchers. I was laughing until both cups flew at us and crashed onto the table top. Two more broken handles. This is dangerous!

Linda looked at me, "Okay what are we doing wrong?" I didn't know, so I shrugged. I looked at the stack of remaining cups, lifted the top one from the pile, had it gently float to me and land safely in my hand. Then I sent it back and put it gently on top again.

I looked at the rest of the girls and said, "What I was concentrating on was the whole thing. Each step, in my head I was saying, 'Carefully lift the cup. Come to my hand slowly,' I don't know, try that." They were all moving cups back and forth like pros in about ten minutes.

Linda said, "This is so cool. Boy, the power of the mind."

What we didn't know was that across the grassy area, outside the bank of windows, were the holding cells for nonviolent offenders (usually drunks). Simon Passmore had been watching coffee cups moving all around the conference room across the way. He had his new buddy and cell mate Marcus look too. Simon screamed loud enough that a guard promised him he would go over and prove to him everything was fine. When the guard entered the conference room, there were three coffee mugs with the handles broken off lying on the table. Everything else looked normal.

The guard went back to Simon and said, "Okay now, describe who you saw in there when this happened?"

Simon was wiping his bangs back from his forehead. They were standing up straight. "I'm telling you man. They were movin' by themselves! There's no people to describe. Just them cups flying all over the room crashin' into each other!"

The guard looked at Simon again, "That's the story you want to stick with, huh? Fine. I think you need a couple more hours in the tank." With that he left.

Simon looked at his cell mate Marcus, "Why didn't you say nothin' man?"

Marcus rolled over on his cot, "I see crap like that all the time, dude."

Ellen joined us in the conference room where we were sitting near the ceiling watching a young patrol officer clean up the broken coffee mugs. Mary spoke first, "We were going to clean it up, but he came in and...."

Ellen interrupted, "It is better to leave it for the mortals. You may have been seen cleaning it up, too." She smiled and said, "I'm surprised Betty didn't need a break sooner."

Agent Dance and Agent Casey came in the room carrying stacks of folders and each with a donut in their mouth. It must be true what they say about cops and donuts. I always thought that was just a dumb joke. Roger finished his donut and asked, "Who all can join us?"

Paul answered, "Just about everybody except Sal and Ed. They are on their way back from Boston, and Detective Taylor had one last interview. Let's see...vic number three, Darla Phillip's employer... shouldn't take that long and then he is coming back here."

Roger was busy comparing a notepad to the one big white board. Then he started erasing everything from that board. "Okay let's tie this up so far. We have Nettie Wilson our number one, eighty yrs. old *(he put a big red circle around her)*, then on the other side we have vic number three, Darla Philips, 32 *(he put a big red circle around her)*, then we have the link. *(drew a long red line between the circles and wrote cleaning gal)*.

A little lower on the board he started drawing, while he continued to speak, "Then we have Karen Smith, 42 vic number two, *(he had her name under Nettie with a big red circle)* and also Valerie McDonald, 33 vic number five, *(he drew a big red circle around her name across from Karen Smith)* and the link *(Big red line connecting)* sorority sis." Roger said, "Let's finish this…we have Burna George, 80, our number four, (*big red circle, and on the far side he wrote Ginger Hall 34, vic #6, big red circle*) We have no link here, yet."

Paul said, "Lets' put in dates," and he took a blue marker and wrote TOD 3-6p.m./ 11-6 under Nettie's name, under Darla's' TOD noon – 3p.m./ 12-6

Roger said, "Put in body found and dates last seen." Under Nettie, Paul wrote: found/niece 11-7, and under Darla he wrote: Last seen 11-11/the date of Nettie's funeral. Under Karen Smith he wrote TOD 9-11 a.m. /11-23 found: 11-25 co-workers, and under Valerie McDonald he wrote TOD noon-6p.m. / 12-21; last seen unknown

They stood back and looked at the board. "The rape victims are being lifted and held somewhere." Roger said.

Paul moved in with the blue marker again. "We have TOD of 10a.m. to 5p.m. / 12-12 on Burna ; found, 12-17 water softener guy, and we only know that Ginger's body was found on 12-23…Yesterday" He sat down and stared at the board with Roger.

"Do you have the coroner's reports for Nettie and Karen?" Roger asked Paul.

"I have copies here somewhere." Paul was shuffling through his papers. "Here they are. Nettie was dead 12 to 24 hours when found, and Darla's estimated TOD was 6-12 hours from when found. Karen had been dead 36-40 hours when found, and Valerie estimated dead 12-18 hours when found. He's keeping them, you're right. He's keeping them from two to three weeks."

Roger asked Paul if he would call the coroner and find out if he has an estimated time of death for Ginger. Roger then opened his phone, dialed, and waited, "John, you guys at the lab have anything for me yet?" He was listening and said, "That was from which scene? Okay, might not mean anything. You know what kind yet? Okay keep me posted." He clicked his phone shut and looked at Paul, who was still on hold with the Coroner. "Our lab has one blonde dog hair from Nettie's foyer." Nettie didn't have a dog. Roger took the blue marker and wrote dog hair under Nettie's name. He thought of Flea Bag.

Paul was talking to the medical examiner, "Hey Sam, any chance you have a time of death for us on this last victim, Ginger Hall?" Paul was listening intently and touched Roger's sleeve, "Sam, say that again, but let me put you on speaker."

The voice on the phone said, "Like I said, I was just getting ready to call you guys. Your girl Ginger had only been dead about an hour when I got her. In fact, she had come in with the car crash victims and because of the ligature marks, etc. etc. I knew she was yours. Here's the thing. Remember I told you there was extensive trauma to the body on this one? I know we all thought your *guy* did it. Now that I have had a chance to look at this *closer*, I think she was hit by the car. There are no strangulation marks, and the only cause of death I can find are consistent with getting hit by a car. Your last vic was *alive* and standing in the road when she got hit."

Paul and Roger looked at each other. Roger asked, "You're sure?"

Sam answered, "Stake my rep on it."

Paul said "Thanks" into the phone, clicked it shut, and asked Roger, "Do we have the accident report here? We need the time of that accident."

"Yes," Roger thumbed through his pile of reports. "White SUV, four women passengers, all dead. Family stated they were on their way to the airport to leave for Hawaii. Swerved and hit a semi head on. Semi driver dead, SUV owner, Teresa Duncan. Accident was about four in the afternoon."

That was us...............

I think we all died, again.

Ellen stood and made a circular motion in the air with her arm that wrapped a heavy gold colored curtain around us. It was instantly warmer and silent. It was like a cocoon. Then she spoke, "Feel like you've been kicked in the gut, huh?" She looked very serious and didn't wait for our answer. She continued, "Granny and Betty called me to a meeting a bit ago which is why I was late getting here. For a while at least, you will all be experiencing some mortal emotions, like now. We can only observe you in this process, we cannot interfere. I am authorized to a much higher level of protocol than Betty, which is why she asked for my help. Granny has the highest level. I believe she told you at orientation you could call on her if needed. Trust me...that should be a last resort."

Teresa raised her hand, "I killed Ginger?" She looked like she was going to cry.

Ellen spoke up, "Ginger died in a car accident. That is why they call them accidents. Technically,

Ginger killed all of you. She made you swerve your car into the oncoming semi."

Mary raised her hand, "Granny said we wouldn't feel grief anymore, but I am feeling something that isn't pleasant."

Ellen paused for a moment and then said, "We thought this might happen, and I have been authorized to teach you how to visit your loved ones, at will, for your comfort. In mortal time you have been gone only one day. The grief angels have been with your loved ones since the actual moments your mortal lives ended. Your visits now will leave your loved ones feeling close to you and feeling like you are still there, even though they will not be able to see or hear you. You will be sensitive to their needs, and you will be able to lend them a small piece of your spirit mind. This will be the way you will know when they need your comfort the most."

I raised my hand, "How long can we lend them this?"

Ellen smiled big, "We don't do little gifts around here. They can keep them their entire mortal lifetime!" Ellen stood and showed us a button on the side of our watches, "When you pull that button out you can think yourselves to the location of your loved ones, any one you choose. When you are ready to come back, or are needed to come back, little button here, see? You just push your visitation button back in, and you can join the group again."

I had to ask, "What if we don't want to come back?" I think I was serious.

"You will." Ellen said, "Remember that the mortal life you just left, is merely one in billions you will experience. Nature recycles, and your loved ones need to live this mortal life of theirs fully, looking forward, not grieving for the past. That is their process at this time." Ellen stood up and said, "Set your alarm to 12-25-midnight. This is Christmas Eve, and you will want to spend it and Christmas with your loved ones. I am going to handle things here, and I will meet you back here at 12:01 a.m. on 12-26...*got it?*" We all nodded and pulled out our buttons.

CHAPTER 8

W hen I got to my house, I saw Kim had a number of paper plates sitting in the snow on the porch with cat food on them, feeding the strays. I was afraid to go in. I stood on the porch and watched the cars going by. Through the curtain I saw a stack of mail lying on the foyer floor that had come through the mail slot. Looked like all cards. We hadn't put a tree up, usually spent Christmas Eve at Grandma's house. Kim's car was still here. It was getting late, so I guess Christmas had been cancelled.

I walked through the front door into the TV room. Kim was curled in her recliner with a blanket over her, balled up tissues all over her and the floor. The TV was on, and her cat Johnny was sleeping in her armpit. He looked at me and didn't even move. Kim is such a beautiful woman with such a big heart, big heart that the wrong kind of men keep breaking. When hard economic times hit, we decided we could just live together. Did a little remodeling to accommodate her closet needs, and for the most part it has worked out great for me. I am sure this isn't what Kim would have chosen for these years. I keep telling her the right man will come around. Kim says she wonders.

I sat on the ottoman across the room from her and just stared. She was so beautiful, inside and out. I was so proud. I hoped I had told her that enough. Suddenly a storybook type angel was standing next to her and talking to me. "She is having a real tough time. I told Granny that I may need help. I think that may be why you are here. I will leave for now and return when I see you have gone. She will be okay. We don't ever give up!" With that she left the room, and I swear she left a trail of golden fairy dust in the air.

Kim started to stir, then sat straight up, looked at me, and screamed!

I screamed back, "Holy Shit! Scare the crap out of me!"

"Not doing me much good either!" she answered. We both sat silently staring at each other.

Finally I spoke, "You can see me?"

She nodded, "And hear you." We both jumped up and hugged each other. She was crying, "It was all a terrible dream wasn't it?"

"Which part?" I asked.

She pulled back and looked at me, "The part where you died."

Hmmmmm, this wasn't going to be easy. I stroked her hair and said, "Have a seat honey, I have a little story to tell you."

* * *

The day before...12-23....

It was Dec 23rd 10:00 a.m., Sandy Devon had loaded up her SUV with an artificial tree kit, Christmas lights, decorations, candles, and her CD player with some Christmas music discs. She had never bothered with Christmas decorations before. She usually spent her holidays away from the apartment volunteering somewhere. It made her feel good about the world to see people helping each other. She was surprised at how much all of it had cost. She had asked the checkout clerk to keep it all on the side of the register bay, so she could run home and get more money. *That* was embarrassing! At the last minute she packed a bag with a pair of sweats, rubber cleaning gloves, and cleaning supplies. Knowing James, this place was probably filthy. She wasn't going to have her first Christmas as Mrs. James Devon in some dirty house. This was a surprise she had been planning for a week!

Her romance and marriage to James had been nothing short of a whirlwind. They had met at the courthouse when she was there to straighten out some legal papers regarding her trust from her parents. She would receive her trust balance with no restrictions on her thirty -fourth birthday which was in ....hmmm, just two weeks! James had come to her rescue with the court clerk who didn't seem to know what she was talking about.

He had introduced himself as an attorney and had offered to take over the conversation for her. He was masterful with the clerk and managed to get everything straightened around using all of the legal jargon she didn't understand. He kept *smiling* at her and even touched her waist as they left the clerk's office. He wasn't handsome by any means, but to her he was a white knight in shining armor. She was pretty sure he was flirting!

She knew that most women she saw seemed to look prettier than her. A lot of people had told her she had a very kind and pleasant face, and that she looked wholesome. That was a good word, wholesome. She had looked it up when she got home, and remembered. He took her to the coffee shop at the Courthouse and talked about all kinds of things that she didn't understand. Things that he said she really needed to do before her birthday. It had been such a stroke of luck to meet him at this time in her life. By the end of their visit he had asked her for a dinner date the next evening. Her first date, ever!

Her mom, when she was alive, always told her what a special woman she was with such a good heart and strong values. Most people were careful not to hurt her feelings, but she had heard a few say that she was kind of 'challenged.' Her Mom had also warned her that she would attempt things in life that seemed too complicated for her to handle, but not to take that as a failure or a shortcoming. It was simply a sign she was needed in other works. She missed her mom and dad and realized if they had not provided for her, she probably would have had a difficult life.

Her trust account had provided her with enough money over the years to live comfortably, but she chose to live quite a simple existence. She donated money to many charities. Her favorite was the Humane Society. She thought animals were the most innocent and vulnerable of God's creatures and needed the most help from humans. Not being able to have pets herself because of her allergies, had been one of life's disappointments. On her thirty-fourth birthday she would inherit the balance of her trust which the man at the bank had said was over fifteen million dollars!

The first thing she wanted to do was give the Humane Society enough money to expand their shelter. Then she wanted to get new boobs. The thought of it made her blush, but now that she had a husband she noticed her body more. James had said that he has seen better. He had a funny sense of humor that way. She was sure he didn't realize that sometimes he picked the wrong words to express himself.

She was smiling as she pulled her car from the apartment building and headed to the address on her note. It was going to be just the two of them for Christmas Eve and Christmas Day. It had required her to play spy. She knew that one of his clients had paid their bill by giving him the deed to some little house in South Bend. He had said it wasn't worth much, but it had potential. He said it was close to everything, but the way it was situated on the land it was impossible to see without really looking for it. After the holidays he was going to have some work done there. The place had become special to him.

His secretary was amazingly unhelpful. Sandy wondered why James kept her. She had eventually found the client file of Nettie Wilson and the invoice that showed attorney fees for estate planning, probate papers, and a will paid in full with a deed conveyance. He must have been right that it wasn't worth that much money because he bragged to everyone how "cheap" he was. Sandy couldn't go into his office because of the dog, her allergies. She had called ahead and told his secretary to meet her outside when she got there. Claudia had seen her pull into the driveway and had walked outside to meet her.

Claudia had been trying to imagine what kind of woman would marry this worm. She was quite surprised. The 'new' Mrs. Attorney James Devon actually looked very sweet and innocent. "Oh brother," she thought, "You know there is a scam going down here." Sandy Devon had told her that she wanted to surprise her husband by arranging a private Christmas party for him. She planned on hosting it at the little house in South Bend he had obtained from some old lady in exchange for her bill to him. Claudia thought it was a stupid idea, but she did have a vague memory of preparing an invoice receipt that looked like that. Also, he had asked her go to the county clerk's office and have it recorded right away. She never got around to it. She thought he was probably worried the family would throw a fit and make him give it back.

She copied the invoice for Sandy and wrote down the address of the house for her. As she handed it to her she asked, "Have you decided on a honeymoon spot yet?" She was hoping it was soon, and she would have a couple of weeks without him around.

Sandy answered, "He just can't get any time away from court these days. Maybe after the holidays we can go somewhere." She smiled, took the paper, got in her car, and left.

Claudia stood speechless. Can't get away from court? I don't think he has gone to the courthouse in a month. Makes me do it. Bastard is probably already screwin' around on her. Shaking her head she walked back into the office. Her last thought of the conversation was that this 'surprise' might not go so well.

* * *

Sandy missed the driveway. Twice. She finally pulled over to the shoulder of the road and studied the mailboxes across the street. Well, her place should be right here. Then she saw it, a narrow dirt drive that angled from the road, and was surrounded with undergrowth and sapling trees. Wow! I guess we will need someone to do a little brush clearing too one of these days. She couldn't imagine how hard it would be to find in the summer and fall with all of the leaves out. She backed up carefully and then angled her SUV into the drive. It curled and twisted a couple of times and opened up to a small, poorly kept yard with a small ranch type home in the middle. It looked as if the drive went around the back of the house and there was no step up to the front door. "Yikes," she said out loud. He thinks this needs a *little* work? She had a sinking feeling that her plans for a party here were going to be scrapped.

She grabbed her purse, and started moving her supplies from the truck to the back door. The big ring of duplicate keys she had made when James fell asleep watching the football game last week, was heavy. She had copies made of all of them since she didn't know which one was which. Now she stood at the door trying keys. She only had three keys left when the one she was trying opened the door. "Oh… not that bad," she thought as she inched her way in. She was in a small, outdated kitchen, but it looked clean and functional. "Nice windows," she thought. She made her way into the living room and saw some lawn furniture set up across from a fireplace, and a small TV with antennae ears. There were Taco Bell bags on the floor, empty pizza boxes and a couple of beer cans on a small TV tray table. "Well, I guess it won't matter where I put the tree." She noticed nice windows in the living room, too. This is a perfect little retreat spot, retirement spot, or starter home. She thought he had really made a good trade to get this place. A little furniture and decorating, she could see why James said it had become 'special' to him.

She went to the back door, carried in her Christmas decorations and the artificial tree kit, and placed them in the living room. She looked around trying to decide where she wanted the tree and noticed a door at the end of the room. She walked to the door and opened it. There was a very nice bedroom with furniture, bedding, and a dresser. She walked around. They must have just *left* the things they didn't need. She thought they could probably use the furniture. It wasn't half bad. There was a nice bathroom off the bedroom. It still had soap, toilet paper, and towels. "Clean it up a little. Could be cute," she thought.

At the opposite end of the bedroom was a door that she guessed was a closet. She walked over and realized it had a lock on the handle. She went through the keys again, trying each one, and found the key that fit. She opened the door, and the light from the room filled the space and revealed a woman sitting in a chair. She had duct tape over her mouth, and her arms were taped to her body. Rope was tying her to the chair. Her ankles were taped heavily, and she looked terrified! Her eyes were bulging and upon seeing Sandy she started moaning and tried to talk. Her fingers, feet, and her head were spastically jerking against their restraints.

Sandy rushed into the space and gently pulled the tape from the woman's mouth. Sandy didn't realize, but she was repeating, "Oh my God, Oh my God."

The woman whispered, "Help me. He will be back! Help me." It was a walk- in closet, but Sandy was having trouble getting behind her to untie the ropes. She managed to untie the woman's hands and noticed they had been bleeding and were bruised.

"Oh my God what has someone done to you? How long have you been in here? Oh my God!" The woman wasn't talking. She had leaned forward when her hands were freed and started pulling at the ropes and tape around her feet. It was a frenzy of hands pulling tape and untying rope. Sandy was trying to help her. The woman looked so fragile and crazed.

When the woman was freed, she lunged forward and fell on the floor. Her legs were weak. Sandy helped her up and walked her toward the bed. The woman screamed, "No...No!" Sandy stopped. She just stood there and didn't know what to do. The woman was hanging on to Sandy so hard it hurt.

"I have a cell phone in my purse. Let me call my husband. He will know what to do." Sandy started to leave the room, and the woman grabbed both her arms.

"Don't leave me. That monster will be back. Where am I?"

Sandy looked around the room. She couldn't help thinking what would a smart person do? Then she pointed out the window. "There is a highway right through those trees, but I don't know the name of it. We are in South Bend. Let me call someone... please...the police?"

Just then a look of horror passed over the woman's face, "Quiet" she hissed. They were silent. "I hear his car motor. He's back. I know that motor. It's the monster!" The woman had a look of terror on her face Sandy had only seen in movies. Not the kind of movies she ever wanted to watch. Sandy was petrified. She heard a car too. Where could they go?

She looked at the window, "Let's open the window. We can run to those trees and get to the road." She couldn't believe someone was using their property for such horror. Sandy's hands were shaking. The window was painted shut. She pushed with all of her might and finally felt it budge. Then she held the window up, and helped push the woman through just as she heard the kitchen door slam.

CHAPTER 9

Roger and Paul had briefed the task force on the new 'linking' developments. Detective Taylor reported that Karen Smith, who had worked at Davis Construction Company, had not reported to work on Friday, November 25th. One of her co-workers had gone to her home to check on her around noon. He had discovered her body by peeking in the window by the front door and had never even entered the house. Killed in the foyer. At her work they had said she was extremely professional and competent. She was the payroll manager for the entire company, and the day after Thanksgiving everyone needed their checks. The consensus was if she had just been ill, she would have come in anyway.

Detective Taylor said no one could think of anyone who was giving her any trouble. Everyone liked her, and as far as anyone there knew she wasn't in any serious relationship. She had divorced about five years ago, had no children, no pets, and was always the first one to volunteer for overtime or to cover for someone who needed a day off.

The construction company, a mid size outfit, good reputation, specialized in remodel and insurance work. They didn't do new construction, and had been around for fifty years. The second generation was running it, and Karen had worked there for almost ten years. Karen was a college graduate in accounting and business from Michigan State and took some heat for being the only one in the office who wasn't a Notre Dame fan. Someone had written ND on her car in soap one time. That was the only entry like that in her file. The company provided a full list of all employees, addresses, and phone numbers. Detective Taylor said he had already sent a copy to the FBI/ IT Department.

Detectives Sal Miller and Ed Parsons had reported that Valerie McDonald's home had only the clue in the mail about her relationship with Karen Smith. They had removed many items for the lab IT department to review, such as her laptop. The crime techs had been called even though Valerie's home was not a suspected location of any foul play. The only curious thing to Detective Miller was she could not find an explanation for how the mail ended up in Valerie's apartment since the neighbor said he knew nothing about the mail and didn't have a key to her apartment. Sal's side comments were that she thought the neighbor was odd and seemed very nervous talking to them.

Ellen had decided to sit in on the briefing and then she followed Agent Dance to his office. Paul Casey came in, "Just got a call from the lab. We got another dog hair, couple of them actually, at Karen

Smith's house. In the foyer. For sure our guy is around a yellow dog of some sort."

Roger was shuffling his index cards and writing on some. "We still may have two guys here," he said without looking up. "Paul, go home. It's Christmas Eve. I'll see you after Christmas." He looked up.

Paul was just staring at him. "I got no plans boss man. Plan to show up here tomorrow."

Roger had a thin smile, "I guess I don't have any plans either. I am going to look over these lab reports a little more and then go to the hotel."

Paul said he needed to swing by the impound and check out something on Karen Smith's car. "You know there is a place called The Pub by my hotel. Neighborhood place, good burgers. You game?"

Roger didn't even have to think about it, "Yeah, about an hour?"

Paul scratched out a little map as he said, "Works for me." Then he left the office.

Roger had his eyes shut and was rolling his head in slow circles. Ellen decided to give him a little Christmas gift. She stood behind him and placed her hand on his shoulder......hmmmm, she thought, a lot of problems caused by stress. Early ulcers, sleep apnea, migraines, high blood pressure, just to name a few. Mortals didn't realize how damaging stress was to their organs. Ninety percent of their medical problems stemmed from it. Ellen 'lent' him a spirit filter for stress, his for this life. "There you go handsome! You will sleep like a baby whenever you want to sleep, and feel better than you did thirty years ago," she said to herself. She knew that he was going to need it. Ellen left to check up on her 'gals' and to perform some required holiday jobs.

Roger made a couple of last minute calls on the case, and phoned his mother in Michigan to wish her a Merry Christmas. Roger had purchased a nice lake house with some acreage in Michigan a few years back and had encouraged his mom to move in. He couldn't see leaving it empty, and his mom loved it there. As little as he was able to go home, the arrangement worked out fine. He knew she had secretly hoped he would come home for the holidays. Not this year, he had told her. She asked if he was dating anyone special. She never gave up.

He consulted Paul's map a couple of times and found the Pub quite easily. There were just a few cars and mostly trucks in the parking lot. Working people vehicles which usually meant good food. It took a minute for his eyes to adjust to the dim light, and he saw a couple of bar stools vacant at the far end of the bar where it made a short 'L'. It was his habit not to sit with his back to a door, and he wanted a view of the entire room. The bartender walked over with a rag hanging over his shoulder, "Can I get you something?" Pleasant enough fella, looked like he had been here for a while.

"What's on draft?' Roger asked. The bartender put a napkin in front of Roger and rattled off a list of beers. Roger picked one and just looked around the room. He found himself doing mini profiles on everyone. Two guys playing pool in the corner, they hate each other. They both want the blonde gal, in the white blouse, sitting in the booth. She is waiting for someone better than either of them. Next booth, yuppie guy. He is trying to make some kind of sale on his cell phone. Papers in front of him suggests disorganized. At first glance he looks successful, but has well-worn shoes and drinking cheap beer. Appears agitated, not making this sale. Snaps his phone shut, gulps his beer, doesn't leave a tip, and gets up to leave.

Roger saw Paul come in the door and head toward him. "Hey, you found my favorite seat!" This was an old joke between them. Whenever they were assigned a case together, they found they always wanted the same seat.

"At least some things never change," Roger said.

Paul looked at the bartender, "Larry I'll take my usual." Larry nodded and pulled a draft.

Roger looked at Paul, "How much time you spending here?" They both laughed.

Paul responded, "One of us has to keep up the image of eligible bachelors!" After ordering their food they settled into some very quiet, cryptic talk about the case. Paul said, "You know when we first got this case, I wasn't expecting it to go like it has. This one is different and not in a good way."

Roger was nodding agreement and said, "I have a very bad feeling about all of this actually. I'm glad you were available to help. We make a good team!" He raised his glass to clink Paul's.

About half way through enjoying their burgers, they both were drawn to a loud voice at the other end of the bar. "Thought you got rid of me, huh? I might just stay the night here tonight! Whew! Crazy night! Crazy!" Judging by the difficulty this fella was

91

having placing his bar stool just right, he had already had too many. Paul noticed that Larry glanced their way. He didn't motion for help, so they just kept working on their burgers.

Larry was quietly talking to the new guy at the bar, "Man, I don't need your shit right now. You don't need any more beer. Come back tomorrow." Larry turned and walked away.

"SCEEEUUZZEEE me?" The drunk shouted.

Larry quickly walked back to Jack and snarled, "You get out of here now, or I will ban you for life!"

Jack straightened himself up, looked at Larry, and said very softly, "This has not been a good day for Jack Simpson. I don't know what I did to make you mad at me. I don't think I want to know."

Larry had lost his patience. He knew Jack, and he knew this little soliloquy could go on for half an hour. "Shut up man. I've got FEDS sitting at the end of the bar. I don't need to serve a drunk right now." When Larry said that, Jack fell forward on the bar and looked toward Roger and Paul. Jack's mouth was open and his eyes were bugging out. Paul pointed his finger at Jack and nearly caused him to fall from his stool, he was so startled.

Then they heard Jack tell Larry, "You know you're right! I better finish that Christmas shoppin'. Seems like time's running short for me." He stumbled his way to the outside of the Pub door and realized he had wet his pants. "HOLY SHIT! HOLY SHIT! First they come to my house, now my bar!" Joy's right. The FEDs want me!" He climbed in his truck and felt the most sober he had been in months.

Roger arrived at his hotel room about 10:30, took a hot shower, got a beer out of the small fridge, and turned the TV on. He watched about half an hour of several news shows. They were all talking about his case. 'Talking Heads' that don't know what they are talking about. "How do they get on TV?" Roger said out loud to himself. He fell asleep with the TV on and had the best sleep he could remember.

* * *

Christmas Eve.......Ho, Ho, Ho. James Devon sat in his office. What a week. That damn bitch got away. Sandy's stupid SUV wouldn't climb that highway incline. Then wham! The bitch is road kill. He couldn't have planned that better, except he really wasn't done with her. Sandy had actually told him to go "save" her! God, she is stupid. Of course he told her his phone wasn't working, and he would need hers to call the cops. Yeah right. He took her car and her keys too, so she wouldn't leave. Sure enough, she was standing there waiting for him when he came back, poor little thing. She didn't like hearing that her new friend was smashed all over the highway. Sandy, Sandy, Sandy. Mrs. James Devon (ugh). Only until her birthday is past. He scratched his dog's head while he was thinking. "What 'cha think Bruiser? Should Daddy go Christmas shoppin'?" He knew the present he wanted. Ashley Tait. A judge. Well, isn't that special? He had her address from Google and her bio as a federal judge in the Grand Rapids, Michigan District. He had his Taser. Mommy would be so proud. She told him he would never have a "Pretty Girl." He'd better make a lot of money if he wanted a "Pretty Girl. He understood right? He was such an Ugly boy."

* * *

Sandy was bound with rope and duct tape in the closet Ginger had just escaped from. Had it only been one day? It seemed much longer. Sandy was cold, hungry, and most of all scared. James was the monster. How had she not seen that? How could she have married him? He was right. She was stupid, but not anymore.

She knew when she saw his face in the kitchen that he was the monster. His eyes were black and piercing. His lips were twitching strangely, and he looked like those people in the movies that are possessed. Yes, that was the look…possessed. That woman knew the sound of his motor. It was his eyes that looked evil. She knew she had to convince him that she thought he was there to save them. How could she do that? Sandy had to act stupid. She had begged him to go after that woman and save her. That some monster had held her captive in their home!

Sandy was proud of the acting job she did to convince him to go after that poor woman and save her. He had told her his phone wasn't working and to give him hers. She knew he didn't want her to have her phone, and he also took her car and keys. She knew he would be asking a lot of questions when he got back. She was pretty sure she couldn't answer them right, so she used that time to prepare. She took the key to the house off the key ring, laid it on the kitchen counter, and hid the rest of the keys in her pants pocket.

She found a nail file in her purse and a pair of scissors in the Christmas decorations bag. She quickly found the tape and taped them to her back under her shirt where she thought her hands would be tied. She ran to the living room, grabbed the cleaning supplies and her sweat suit, and stuffed them in the bathroom under the sink. Surely he was going to let her go to the bathroom. She ran out to his car to see if she could get the North Star person to answer. It wasn't hooked up! She pushed the emergency button anyway, saw his phone, and took it. She just got back in the house when she heard her SUV fly around to the back of the house again. She put his phone in the corner of the closet under some rags and was turning it off as she ran. She didn't need to have it ring at the wrong time. As soon as she came out of the closet and stood in front of the window, he was in the room. "You have been a very naughty girl today."

CHAPTER 10

Ellen checked in on Mary, Linda and Teresa to see how they were doing on their home visits. These gals were pretty amazing, Ellen thought. They will make superior Angels...if we get through training. She had caught Mary in her sister's garage practicing moving objects and nearly causing a suspended wheelbarrow to fall on the hood of a car. Heavy objects were a little more difficult. Mary was playing little tricks on her siblings and having a blast!

Linda had spent a fair amount of time convincing their new puppy she was a "good" spirit, and trying to help season the food on the stove when no one was looking. Her family was feeling her love, and they were managing to have as much of a Christmas as they could.

Teresa's family was having issues, her mother in particular. Teresa had selflessly just planted herself on her mother's lap. It was beginning to work. Ellen made a note to check back soon. Moms can be especially difficult to comfort.

Vicki was another story. Her daughter could see and hear her! This was the will of Granny, so Ellen wasn't real sure where this was going. She peeked in on them, and they were watching TV together and laughing. It looked like any other quiet family moment in the middle of such a bizarre circumstance. Kim was obviously a mortal with exceptional coping skills. Ellen giggled, "That has probably been a saving grace with Vicki as your mother."

Ellen decided to start her Christmas chores and catch up with the gals later.

* * *

Joy had a six pack of beer sitting on Nettie's dining room table that she was determined to finish off herself. No point even puttin' 'em in the fridge, she thought. They are cold, and I am needin' to forget some stuff. The TV news was on, and she listened intently to everything they said about the murders. "How could he even meet this many women?" she asked herself shaking her head. Jack was a loser. She knew that. Hell, she was a loser too. That's how they got together. She started singing, "And the world goes 'round, and 'round, and 'round…"

Suddenly there was a pounding at the door. It was Jack. "Joy! Let me in! You got this all wrong baby! I ain't no killer! Joy let me in. I got you a present."

Oh boy, Joy thought. Gonna be hard to beat last year's nearly empty champagne bottle.

She walked over to the door and yelled to him through it, "Why should I believe your sorry ass?"

Jack was quiet. Then she heard some mumbling. Then she heard, "Joy, I need you."

"Oh shit," she said as she unlocked the door to find him actually standing up straight, freshly showered, clean clothes on. He was holding a new mop with a big red bow on it. She looked him up and down. This was bar time, and he was here. "What's with the mop?" she asked expressionless.

Jack perked up, "You said the other day you wanted a new mop." He was actually proud.

"Not for Christmas you asshole." She moved over, so he could come in. He actually walked to the table where the beer was, sat down, and didn't take one. She waited a while and then said "I'm not real happy with you. What did you mean when you said I best not piss you off?" She was standing next to Nettie's wasp spray, so she felt pretty brave for the moment.

Jack took a minute and answered, "I don't know what I meant by that. You pissed me off accusing me of killin' people, for Christ's sake. I just wanted you to leave me alone. I figured if you really believed that, what the hell. Might as well scare you into fixin' my dinner. I know I ran over here whenever I knew Darla was here. Gave her rides home most times." He waited for Joy to throw something at him. When that didn't happen he continued, "I flirted a lot with her, but I knew she'd never want a loser like me. She was just so pretty; I wanted to be around her. I never even really tried anything. I swear!"

She studied his face. She had known him about eight years and never seen him even raise his voice to anyone. He usually went out of his way to avoid trouble. "Let's say I believe you," she noticed he still hadn't grabbed a beer. "Why do you think the FBI came to our house?"

He looked serious, very serious when he answered, "Why do you think they are at my bar?"

Joy had a sinking feeling. This was not good. Just then the news anchor was showing more pictures of the murdered women. The anchor's voice trailed into the dining room saying, "Karen Smith, the accounting officer for Davis Construction Company, was last seen..." Jack and Joy looked at each other. Joy spoke first. "That's where *YOU* work!"

Jack had his eyes glued to the television. "I know her!" he gasped. They both ran into the living room and sat on the sofa to hear.

The reporter said that of the six women murdered, beginning with Nettie Wilson on November 6th, the only information made available to the public, was that some of the women had been strangled in their homes, and some of the women had been raped. "Who would rape an eighty year old woman? Ugh." Jack looked disgusted.

Joy said, "Nobody ever said Nettie was raped."

Jack was shaking his head, "God I hope not." Jack always got along with Nettie, and she was pretty quick to give him fifty bucks or so for doing handyman work for her. Good source of extra drinkin' money.

The news anchor was still talking about the murders when they heard, "Earlier today, Police Chief Edgar Doyle held a news conference on the case developments. Let's listen to what he had to say." The video of the news conference popped on the screen. Chief Doyle was standing at a podium in the Police Center Conference room with a row of people standing behind him. At the end of the back row stood Agent Roger Dance and Agent Paul Casey.

Jack flipped out, "That's them!" He had jumped off the couch and was pointing on the TV screen for Joy. "That's them two FBI guys that came to the PUB!"

Joy hissed for him to sit down. She wanted to hear. The Chief of Police was moving over, so Agent Dance could speak to the reporters. Now Joy spoke, "He's the one that came here to Nettie's house!" Jack put his hand on her knee to signal her to be quiet.

Agent dance was introducing himself to the group just to be polite. They all knew who he was. Then he spoke, "We do have some positive developments in the case. I would like to assure the public that everything that can be done, is being done, by this task force of your local detectives and the FBI. All resources of the FBI are being utilized to apprehend this individual and bring justice and peace once again to the City of South Bend."

One of the reporters shouted, "Are you saying you have a suspect now?"

Agent Dance took a thoughtful pause and answered, "I am more hopeful at this moment than

I have been since this started that we will be able to announce a resolution to this case soon."

The reporter shouted another question, "Have you developed a profile of the suspect you can share with the public?"

Roger looked at the reporter and answered, "Our profile of the suspect sharpens with new developments, but it basically remains a white male in late thirties, early forties, a job that offers flexibility, arrogance, very intelligent, and certainly a pattern of difficulty with women."

Jack actually looked happy! "That can't be me! He said arrogant, I don't even know what that means, and smart!"

Joy was frowning, "He also said early forties, flexible job, and trouble with women."

Jack looked at her, "I'm screwed."

The sound bite of the news conference was over. The TV news had moved on to national topics, so Joy turned the TV off. "Do you want me to move back home?" she asked Jack. He was looking at the floor.

"You are the most important person in this world to me. I don't deserve to have you in my life the way I've acted. Flirtin' and drinkin' all the time. Lettin' you pay all the bills and never there for you. Hell, I don't even know when your birthday is 'cept in summer sometime." He had tears in his eyes and he still hadn't reached for a beer. He pointed at the television as he wiped his cheek. "This might end up a lot of trouble," he continued, "so I don't know what I should say. I don't want to bring no more shit in your life." His voice trailed off, but he was now looking her straight in her eyes.

Joy saw the Jack she had been attracted to eight years ago flickering back. She was quiet for a minute and said, "Let me pack my stuff to come home. Somewhere around here is a bill from that lawyer Nettie used. I remember her saying he was smart and cheap. You can look for that. I think she also said he was vile, but we can deal with that. You are goin' to need a lawyer. We are going to have to sell this house fast to get some money." She looked at his face and almost cried. He looked so hopeful.

"Are you saying we can go home together?"

She laughed as she hugged him, "Yes, you big fool. I'll start putting my stuff by the door, and you can load it in the truck. Then we'll look for that lawyer's name." She yelled back at him as she went to the kitchen, "Don't forget to pack my Christmas present!" He heard her laughing. She really did like the new mop!

Truck loaded, they found Nettie's little address book with Attorney Devon's phone number and address. Joy looked through Nettie's paid bill basket and found the receipt from Devon showing paid in full. She didn't want some slick lawyer trying to say she owed money for Nettie. "That's funny," she said mostly to herself.

Jack turned around, "I'd like to hear something funny about now."

"Not funny ha-ha, funny weird. You know that shit house Nettie used to rent to that loser Clyde?"

Jack thought a minute, "The one where the garage caught fire and Nettie said he had been making drugs out there?"

"Yeah, Nettie gave that house to this Devon guy to pay for her bill."

"I think she made a good deal," Jack said, "That place was a certified dump, and Nettie said she paid more taxes on that house than it was worth!"

Joy folded the bill and put it in her purse. "I haven't thought about that place in years. Guess I always thought Nettie had just let it go back to the county or something."

They turned off the lights at the front door and stood in the dark in the foyer. "It feels like she's still here doesn't it? She never deserved this. Nobody deserves to be killed." Joy locked the door, and as they pulled out of the driveway, Nettie's recliner began to slowly rock.

* * *

Attorney James Devon prided himself in his ability to manipulate situations. As he packed his car for his trip to South Bend from his office, he made a mental list of the items he needed from Lowes. He wasn't going to want to go to the 'house' any more than he had to now that Sandy was there, instead of one of his Pretty Girls. He decided to board up the window in the bedroom, and devise a long chain and lock that would let Sandy walk around the bedroom and get to the bathroom without him having to be there. Like his own prison. He smiled at the thought of hundreds of women in cages just for his pleasure. His thoughts went back to Sandy. He could just leave food for her on the dresser. He didn't have to spend time with her at all! He only had to keep her *alive* another two weeks and then "Happy Birthday" time! He still hadn't figured out what kind of accident was going to happen to her. It had to look good because of the trust money. This was the only bad part about his new hobby, getting rid of them. There were so many.

He figured if he could get this all done tonight, he would actually have *all* Christmas Day to lay back and enjoy. Think about his new "love", Ashley.

* * *

Ginger Hall's supervising nurse, Jenny Camp, had packed several personal items from Ginger's locker at the hospital and brought them to the police station. Nothing that looked very important, but she didn't know what else to do with them. She understood Ginger had a brother who was making funeral arrangements, but no one at the Hospital seemed to know anything. It was Christmas Eve, and she was already late getting home. This was something she felt she needed to do.

When she walked into the stark building, she was surprised at how many people were there. Of course, she thought, certain jobs have no holidays. It was a fluke she was able to leave tonight, especially since they had been short one RN, Ginger.

She walked up to an officer sitting at a desk and placed the paper bag of Ginger's belongings on the top of the counter. He looked up from his slow typing at the computer and said, "Can I help you?" She told him she had some personal belongings of Ginger Hall, one of the women who had been missing and then was found murdered.

He peered into the bag and then rolled the top of it closed again, and just looked at her. "I was thinking that the detectives on the case would probably want these." She said.

"Oh, yeah, probably," he mumbled as he took the bag and placed in on his desk. "Was there anything else?" he asked her with a look that said, say no.

She looked at him and just said, "No, I guess that's it. Have a nice Christmas." She turned and walked out of the building to her car. She was thinking that Ginger's belongings will be in that bag a very long time. He didn't even ask her for her name. No wonder they are clueless about who is doing all of these murders. She made a mental note to call someone connected to the case after the holiday to make sure they got the bag.

* * *

Paul had stayed at the PUB about a half hour longer than Roger and just watched people coming and going. This could be anywhere in America he thought. It is so easy to read people sometimes. He thought in general people seemed sadder these days. He heard a lot of people talking about the murders, and a lot of them were angry with the police. He couldn't blame them. The killings started in early November and here it was Christmas. The entire community was shocked to the core.

Ellen sat next to him at the bar, but he didn't know it. She was listening to his thoughts and realized that unless something drastic happened, these killings in South Bend could go on for a very long time. She imagined the stress he felt and decided to give him a little Christmas present too. She put her hand on his shoulder and felt almost every health issue she had felt with Roger. One by one she removed them all, and she 'lent' him the same stress screen she had provided Roger. She also assured his mortal mind he could sleep whenever he wanted without fear of past demons entering his dreams.

Paul had been waiting for that slice of onion he had on his burger to start tearing up his stomach and realized that he felt fine, better than fine. When the juke box blasted a good country line dance song, he and Ellen were in the front row. EEE Hah! They danced for about four more songs. Ellen was feeling a little uncomfortable being between Paul and the good looking blonde gal he was slow dancing with, so she decided to leave. Paul couldn't remember the last time he felt so good. The bartender Larry was smiling. That cop had it goin' *on*!

* * *

Mrs. Brooks, Nettie's neighbor, had heard Jack pull up next door in that loud, beat up truck. She had seen Joy over there a lot lately and figured she might have moved in. No respect for the dead, she thought. We just buried poor Nettie, and already using her stuff. Then she heard Jack pounding on the door saying, "I ain't no killer! I ain't no killer!" Now that got her attention! She stood freezing by the window she had cracked open to hear better, but that fool Joy let him in. They were in the house about an hour. She could see them through her kitchen window. Seemed like they were getting along okay, but she knew what she heard. She would wait until after Christmas and let that handsome Agent Dance know about this. She decided she would make some cookies tomorrow for when he visited.

CHAPTER 11

Ellen was expecting the gals to call her. It had not happened yet. She looked at her guide watch and realized they were talking to each other. She went to speaker and heard Vicki, "Kim is asleep. I am bored. Do you guys think we sleep?"

Linda answered, "I don't think so. I am not tired at all. Bob and the boys are all asleep so is Mom."

Teresa chimed in, "I had my hands full with my mom, but she is good now. She always thought she kind of had powers, so I put a special 'angel' necklace on her she has always loved. Now she is convinced I am there and okay. It really helped a lot, but yeah, I'm bored too."

I spoke again, "Mary, are you out there?"

Mary answered with, "Can you hear me now? Hello?" Ellen made a long distance adjustment, and Mary said, "Hey, I can hear. What's up?"

I answered, "We're bored."

Silence, then Mary, "Yeah, I can see that. Nothing ever happens to us." I noted a little sarcasm.

Ellen decided to have a little fun. "Gals?" We all stopped talking.

Finally Teresa said, "Ellen?"

"Yup. Why don't you all meet me at your old bar where you used to have lunch every day?"

"REALLY?" we all said at the same time.

"Yeah. If you get there first, no messin' with people, no moving stuff. You know what I mean."

Linda answered, "I'll personally watch her!" Everyone laughed. Hey, I think they are talking about me!

When we all got to the bar it was about 11:30 p.m. Christmas Eve. The corner of the bar where we all used to sit (the Shallow End) had little napkins laid out just how Carol used to do it for us. The reserved sign was on top of the napkin dispenser and someone had written under reserved, "For our four angels." We all said "Awwwwwwwwwwww" at the same time and sat on our usual stools.

"Gosh this feels good," Linda said as she stretched her neck to see who all was there. Then she pointed her finger at me. "Don't make me come over there." Geesh!

"Are you trying to read my mind again?" I asked her.

"Don't ask me why. You think like an internet search engine, but yes."

"Self-defense," Mary answered. I could tell Teresa was going nuts. The first thing she would do when we got to the bar was move the napkin dispenser and the salt and pepper shakers where they weren't in her line of vision. She was staring at them now.

I looked over at her, "Don't do it. Dooooon't do it." We all started laughing, and Ellen showed up and sat on the late comer's stool next to Teresa.

"Howdy," she said.

We all looked at her. Howdy?

"Been line dancing at the Pub." We all looked at each other. Okay.

"Okay, I have been giving this some thought on the way over here. We can do this a couple of ways. Number one. We can watch everyone and listen and just enjoy the environment and leave when we are ready. Or Number two. We can create a time bubble; no one else can come in or leave. Everyone can see and hear you, but when we leave we pop the bubble. They think they dreamed it all, but they will share certain parts of the dream with each other. This isn't a fine science with the mortal mind involved."

"<u>NUMBER 2!</u>" We screamed at the same time!

Ellen laughed. Then suddenly she was standing on the bar. We were not visible yet. "Hey everybody!" Glasses dropped and hit the floor. Everyone stopped drinking and talking. Ellen stopped the juke box.

Carol, the bartender, asked, "Aren't you Ellen DeGeneres?"

"No, but I have been told I look like her. Ellen is actually very much alive. I am an Angel, and I have brought four Angel buddies here to see you. We can have some fun, but then we have to leave. When we go, you are only going to remember you had a good time, and you may dream a little of this. Are you ready to play?" Everyone was slowly nodding and looking like they were already in a dream. Then we could tell that they could see us.

Carol came running over crying, "Oh My God. You're back! You're back, and you brought Ellen!" She didn't know who to hug first. She had her Grinch costume on, and her hat was falling all over the place and knocking drinks over. Ellen took Carol's Grinch hat, put it on, turned the juke box to a country song, and started a line dance. Four big dudes moved the pool table against the wall and half the bar started dancing with her. The other half were all people we knew. They wanted to hear what it was like to die and almost make it to heaven. Most of them were surprised and kind of bummed out to find out there were classes and stuff.

Every time we looked to the other end of the bar, Ellen was doing something different with people. One time it was magic tricks, then break dancing. Some lady about seventy was doing the splits. Then I think they were playing games like the real Ellen does on her show. They were moving paper wads that were balanced on a spoon to a big bowl on the other side of the room. Ellen was timing them, declaring the winner, and giving a piece of someone else's clothing as a prize.

We were just sitting there talking to everyone when Betty came in.

We all screamed "Betty" at the same time.

"Just look like her, just look like her," Betty nodded and smiled at everyone as she made her way down to Ellen. She whispered something in Ellen's ear then came back to us, "You gals have been busy since I left you."

Mary looked at her, "Are we in trouble?"

Betty smiled, "Oh gosh no gals. Your progress has been unprecedented!" She raised a glass of what I guessed was pretend booze and drank it in one gulp. Then she twisted her head a little to each side and declared, "Now that has been a while." Then poof. A whole bottle appeared in front of her glass. "I don't mind if I do!" she said.

Carol rushed over, "Allow me, Ms. White." Betty winked at her.

When Betty's bottle was about three quarters gone, Ellen danced her way down to our end of the bar still wearing the Grinch Hat. She was being followed by a lady wearing at least five layers of clothing. Ellen looked at all of us, at Betty, and declared it was probably time to get Betty home, and for us to get back to our families. We hated to say goodbye to everyone, but we knew it was part of the deal. As we walked through the door to the outside Ellen said, "That was a blast! I forget how much fun mortals can be."

Betty was hanging onto Ellen's shirt sleeve. She belched and then said, "That one gal is going to wonder tomorrow whose clothes she has, and the others will wonder where their clothes went. At least two people are going to give up drinking after tonight, see? A good thing!" With that we heard her say, "Merry Christmas! Now go home!"

A minute later Ellen popped back. Betty was gone. Ellen said, "Tell everyone what you are thinking Vicki."

I was surprised, but glad she had asked. "I don't see how us being here is helping anything. I don't feel like we have made any discoveries that matter."

Ellen just looked at us. "Do you all feel that way?" Everyone nodded. "This is your mortal impatience. Okay then. Your families will be sleeping for a while. It IS Christmas, so many mortals will totally change their behavior just for tonight and tomorrow. It is a good time to do a little eavesdropping. Are you gals game for this without my help?" We all nodded again. "Split off in pairs. One set go see what is on the mind of Joy Covington's boyfriend, Jack Simpson. Neither Roger nor Paul knows anything about him yet. The other set go to the lawyer Devon's house. We only know a little bit about him, but he was the last person seen with Darla Phillips."

"You are there to hear their thoughts and maybe catch a little of their dreams. If you are lucky enough to catch them dreaming, you may get a peek at their souls. This isn't always pretty. Are you sure you want to do this?" We all nodded again. Ellen looked at us and said, "Be careful, and report to me anything you find out. Tomorrow may be the last chance you have with your families for a little bit, so I do want you to enjoy this time. Okay?"

"Okay," we all said. Then she was gone again.

Teresa spoke up, "Well who wants to go where? Do we even know where to go?"

Linda said, "I have everyone's addresses and phone numbers written down and on lists." I rolled my eyes and she caught me. "Guess I managed to do something at the meetings besides play Frogger." Fair enough, I thought.

Mary said, "I want to go with Linda." (surprise, surprise) Then, looking at me, she said, "You make me nervous." Teresa was laughing and said she and I would check out the lawyer. Linda said fine, she and Mary would check out the drunk. It was settled. We all got our little list from Linda and took off.

Linda and Mary found Joy and Jack asleep at home. Flea Bag was whining under the front porch. Eventually he decided it wasn't his job to be a watch dog and went back to sleep. Mary started tiptoeing through the living room toward the bedroom door.

Linda whispered, "They can't hear us."

Mary looked at her and said, "Then why are you whispering?" They inched their way to the foot of the bed and were straining to hear. "I think I'm getting something," Mary said. "It's more like a mumble. Darn drunks."

Linda was leaning over Joy, "I think Joy is dreaming. She is in a pretty garden somewhere."

Linda looked over and Mary was leaning way over the bed with her ear right next to Jack's. "What are you doing?" Linda hissed.

Mary put her finger to her lips to motion for Linda to be quiet. "He is worried the FBI is after him. Says he doesn't remember doing anything, but he doesn't remember a lot of things. He is worried about what he doesn't remember....ooooooo....He loves Joy....awwwwww....He has a kind soul. I don't think he did it!" Mary exclaimed as she started to get up. Just then Jack rolled over and his face went right through Mary's face! "Eyoooo," she said as she jumped away from bed. "Bad breath!" She adjusted her sensor watch as she shook her head. Jack slowly threw the covers off himself and yup, stark naked, started walking down the hall to the bathroom. Mary looked at Linda, "I am *not* going in there!"

Linda said, "He's awake more now, maybe we can get more thoughts from him. I'll go, I raised two boys." Mary stood outside in the hall whistling. Linda popped her head back into the hall, "What are you doing?"

"Nothing," Mary answered.

Jack started walking back toward the bedroom, Mary put up her hands almost covering her eyes and asked Linda, "Well, anything?"

"Nothing I want to repeat. I think we are done here. Let's go find Vicki and Teresa."

Teresa and Vicki had watched James Devon click on the TV and sit in a dirty recliner. Teresa was closest to him and frowned. "This guy is a piece of work."

"I can't hear anything," I told her.

"You are probably distracted by this pig sty, Miss Clean Freak!" No kidding. The place was filthy. He was filthy. Only one corner of the living room looked tidy. It had a small office desk, computer, and a credenza, holding files and a scanner. It was an island of clean.

I went over, sat at the desk and started quietly looking through papers. I didn't want to get caught moving them around. All of a sudden Teresa said,

"Oh Dear God!" She had her hands over her ears. "You wouldn't believe what this guy wants to do to the girl in the perfume commercial." Linda and Mary materialized in the kitchen and were making their way to the living room.

Linda was the first to speak, "Well, we think that Jack Simpson is not anything." Then she made a face when she saw James Devon sitting in the living room. "This guy is a lawyer?"

I answered from the desk, "Has a secretary, Claudia, who doesn't think much of him either based on the little notes she has sent him on the computer. He isn't very respectful to her either. *Geesh*, you should read this stuff!"

Teresa motioned for us to be quiet. "You guys, I don't know if I can do this." We looked over. James had his eyes closed, and it looked like he was falling asleep. Teresa was making faces. None of us could hear anything, so we didn't know what was bothering her. We all just created our own "clean" chairs and watched her. Now she had her head turned away from him, her chin in the air. Then she looked at us and SCREAMED! We all screamed back! Suddenly Ellen was there with her arms around Teresa, and moving Teresa to a chair. What the heck?

"Oh boy." Ellen was looking at us, "I am so sorry. I had no idea. You are so not ready for this!" Teresa looked like she was ready to cry, but she was listening to Ellen.

Then Teresa said, "I was trying."

Ellen interrupted her and said, "I know, I know, you didn't do anything wrong. Let me just concentrate on him for a minute." Ellen put her hand over James's head and pulled it back like the air was hot or something.

"Okay." She was looking at us. "Stay put. Do NOT get close to this man. I will be right back."

Teresa looked at us, "No way am I going near him. You guys, I can't even describe the evil." She was shaking her head, and I noticed her whole body was shaking. Linda, Mary and I all put our hands on Teresa's hands, and she calmed down somewhat. Shit, shit, shit. Not much gets to Teresa.

Ellen was back, and she brought Granny! UH—Oh

Granny nodded at us and placed her hands firmly on Devon's shoulders. We could see an aura around her, and it seemed like the room started getting very dark. Ellen had kneeled next to Granny, so we did too. There was a silence that no words could describe. More than an absence of sound more like a vacuum. I tried to look at Granny, but my eyes were held to the floor. Then it was over.

Granny was gone.

James Devon was still sleeping.

Ellen told us it was going to be a very long night.

Whoever started the rumor that angels are sitting on clouds, eating grapes, and playing harps, had better get a clue!

CHAPTER 12

"It's him," Ellen said flatly. She held her arm out toward him, "He has killed them all, and he's not done. He won't stop until he is stopped."

"Then let's stop him!" Teresa shouted.

"We can't," was Ellen's answer. "Let me explain. Mortals do terrible things to each other all of the time. Always have, always will. Certain mortals have the task of stopping them. That is the order of things. We cannot alter mortal behavior or manipulate environments to assist these mortals in their goals. What we can do is discover information that is helpful, try to get that information into the right mortal hands, and speed up the process."

"I am going to relay the filtered version of what Mr. Devon here has on his mind, and we are going to begin our own detective work to find information that Agent Dance and Agent Casey can use in the mortal world to stop him. Before we get started, what questions do you have?"

Linda raised her hand, "Can't we just write a note to Roger telling him that Devon is the killer. Leave it on his desk?"

Ellen answered, "Nope. Remember that mortals are working within the constraints of legal systems, proof, evidence, and those things are discovered by mortals. Roger and Paul will only come to the conclusion that Mr. James Devon is their killer when they have had their own mortal discoveries of information."

I raised my hand, "Soooooo, we can discover proof that Devon is the killer, but we have to find a way for Roger and Paul to discover it on their own too?"

"Exactly." Ellen said.

I had another question, "You said we couldn't manipulate environments. Could you get a lot more specific about that?" I was thinking that we may have some wiggle room here based on definitions.

Ellen looked at all of us and then especially at me, "That set of definitions will be my primary assignment. To make sure you girls don't inadvertently break any rules."

Mary said, "I do not want your job, ever."

I didn't want to ask, but I was curious what would happen if you broke an angel rule. I mean, what can they do? You're already dead. Sentence you back to life? Did they have little angel courtrooms, angel lawyers? I could be an angel lawyer! Angel jails, community service? Dust the clouds? Everyone was looking at me but not talking.

That darn mind reading again.

Teresa cleared her throat, scrunched her mouth at me, and asked, "Why did Granny come?"

"Granny came to protect me and to install a filter to enable me to extract thoughts from Devon without causing harm to myself."

I was stunned, "He's that bad?"

"Oh yeah." She answered. No wonder Teresa screamed.

Ellen began the story of what Devon had been doing and what his plans were. We were all captivated by how dark and ugly his soul was. (Linda and Mary took notes.)

"James Devon grew up the ugly son of a truly gorgeous woman who didn't want a child in her life. He was told how ugly he was from birth, and that he would never have a pretty girl unless he was rich. His mother kept him hidden as much as possible. She was ashamed someone would see she had birthed something so ugly and had told him so. She sent him to boarding schools where he honed the dark side of his personality. One Christmas holiday his mother was found in a dumpster behind a tavern where her face had been skinned. The newspapers reported the coroner ruled she had been skinned alive and strangled. Little was mentioned about the young teenage son who attended boarding school. He had become a ward of the state and his file had suggested it was suspected that he harbored some serious personality disorders. He was so bright. Even with that, it was determined he was not involved in her murder. The school master stated he worshiped the ground his mother walked on and did anything he could to please her.

That was his first murder. She didn't look so beautiful when he was done with her. The look of terror in her eyes fueled something inside of him. Pretty girls that know they are going to die. Pretty doesn't solve everything. That power. Each time it was like killing his mother again and again and again." Ellen shuddered.

"He can't get enough. In October of this year he met a woman at the courthouse that somehow means a great deal of money to him. I'm not clear on that. He dated her and married her. He considers her ugly and this triggered something else in him. The fact he married her really bothers him. He also has a place, a cabin or something, he just became the owner of. That sparked his plan to steal pretty women, get rid of them when he was done, or when he saw someone he wanted more. He had decided he was going to live outside of this country, where no one could put him in prison. He has money, and he has an elaborate plan. He even has a plan in case he gets caught. As soon as his wife dies, he is leaving.

Nettie Wilson had some legal papers to sign with him and had her young friend Darla drive her here to his office. That was when James met Darla and decided he wanted her. He prepared this cabin, killed Nettie, expecting Darla to go to the funeral. He took her from the cemetery service to the cabin, kept her for four and a half weeks. He raped her, strangled her, and left her body on the side of the highway.

He wanted a replacement for Darla right away. He was at a grocery store, I think Kroger, and saw two women, one ugly (by his definition) one pretty. This was Karen Smith and Valerie McDonald. He followed them around the store listening to their conversation and surmised that Valerie (the pretty one) was visiting from somewhere. He overheard them say that after they took the groceries home, Valerie was going to use Karen's car to run a quick errand and come back. He followed them to Karen's house, managed to hide until Valerie left, then he killed Karen. He met Valerie in the driveway and said he was a friend of Karen's. He tricked Valerie to get her near his car, shot her with his stun gun, and took her to his cabin. He kept her exactly two weeks and then he decided he wanted someone new. He's been taking women. Oh my...lots of women. He's running out of places to hold them.

On December 8th, Burna George was in the hospital, and Devon took some papers in for her to sign. She was very ill and had her RN, Ginger Hall, witness her signature. He went to Burna's house five days later where she was recuperating and killed her. Then he went to the hospital on the next day, and told Ginger she needed to sign another paper. He told her he was in the parking garage and in a hurry. He asked her if she would meet him there just long enough to sign. He shot her with his Taser gun. He'd kept Ginger for two and a half weeks when she escaped.

I don't know how she escaped. I know he has a woman now, but for some reason she is safe until January 13th. (Ellen was shaking her head). This part is all muddled, but I think he has already decided the next woman he is going to take. He wants to have them both …no…he doesn't want the one he has, but he has to keep her. I don't get that, but he doesn't want to wait to get the one he wants."

Ellen sat down and looked completely exhausted. We all felt exhausted too, just listening. All of us looked at James Devon. He was fully reclined in his chair. Drool ran down his chin, he sputtered out short snores as he involuntarily twitched in his sleep. The soles of his feet were encrusted with filth. He smelled of sour flesh and sweat.

What kind of monster was this?

Ellen said, "We need to really search this house for any document that might shed light on anything we do know, and figure out a way for Roger and Paul to discover it. Somehow we have to get proof to them that Devon is the killer!"

Is that all? I was thinking, there goes Christmas with the family. Ellen laughed for the first time tonight, "We can do this, gals, and still get home for Christmas morning. Let's put a little music on." She clicked her fingers and the song "Everybody Dance Now" started playing. "Now, on your watches you have a small button on the right, see it?" We all nodded, "You usually don't get to use this until your next level. Push that button in and you have photogenic memory. Just look at everything you can, all the papers, everything. We can compare notes later. Ready?" I noticed Linda was still taking notes. We danced around that entire house, office, his car, Claudia's desk, the files, and his computer. Ellen read the mail, and we finished in about an hour.

Talk about a work out! At one point Ellen was break dancing and doing the 'moon walk.' Where does she get this energy? All the while the monster was snoring. I needed a rest, and I wanted out of there.

Ellen said we did a great job and to go home to our families.

* * *

Roger pulled into the parking lot of the police center and noticed the lot was over half full. There was a news truck already there. It was only 7:00 a.m.. He quickly checked his phone to make sure he had not missed any messages. Presumably, there had not been any developments on his case.

He left his car and headed toward the side door. A pretty, young woman holding a microphone ran toward him shouting questions. She was followed by a camera man and a technician. Official policy was to not comment on anything regarding an active case outside of the official press releases. The last question the young reporter shouted to him as he reached the door was, "Special Agent Dance! Isn't there something you can give these families for Christmas?"

Roger stopped, turned around, and saw that the camera was running. He thought for a moment and said, "On behalf of the victims' families and loved ones, especially on this Holy Day, I will make this promise: If you are the monster I am looking for, I will not stop until you have been captured and punished." He hoped his killer was watching the news and would find him intimidating.

Roger went inside and heard the reporter, "There you have it, and the FBI is calling in the Heavens to help them capture this monster!"

Roger was shaking his head, "That is not what I said." Little did he know the Heavens were already on the case.

Roger greeted several now familiar faces as he headed to the little office that had been assigned him during his stay in South Bend. As he passed the Information Desk, a young patrolman stopped him, "Merry Christmas, Sir." Roger returned the greeting and the patrolman reached behind him and pulled out a paper bag. "Night Officer said someone dropped this off at the station last night for you, some lady. Left before he could get a name or anything."

Roger looked in the bag, "Did he say what this is?"

"Yeah, something to do with that nurse that was murdered. He said he thinks it was her boss that brought it here. Sorry I don't know more, Sir." Roger thanked him and took the bag as he continued toward his office.

Near the conference room he could hear voices. He popped his head in the door and saw the entire task force set up in groups, busily reviewing piles of papers. He walked in and most of them stopped talking. "Isn't this Christmas morning?" Roger looked at their faces and knew exactly what they were feeling. Their Christmas would come when this case was solved. While they were told to take the day off, he knew they would be here. He was glad he had arranged for a local deli to stop in with a big breakfast. He turned around, and the deli staff was already in the hall with a steam cart piled high with everything he had ordered. He moved aside so they could set up, and received a big cheer from the people in the room.

Paul came into the conference room and saw a line at the buffet cart and several people eating at the tables. He saw Roger across the room talking to Chief Doyle, and he got in line to get some breakfast. He was ravenous! Slept like a baby, and that blonde, whew!

There was plenty of food to go around, and Paul walked the halls encouraging people to come down and have some. Roger made his way to his office, set the paper bag on his desk, and turned on the small TV that had been set up for monitoring the news. He made a pot of coffee at the credenza and stood looking out the window. Another Christmas hunting a monster. The holidays brought out the best and worst in people, like a seasonal full moon.

Paul knocked on the open door as he came in and took a seat across from Roger's desk. "Merry Ho Ho. I hear we have called in extra troops?" Roger looked at him puzzled, and Paul turned the channel on the TV. Using the remote as a pointer, he directed Roger to listen as he turned the volume up.

"This morning, SSA Roger Dance promised the victims' families that he would call in the Heavens to catch the killer." Then they ran the short clip of Roger.

Paul laughed, and then said, "You know if they are going to distort what you said, they shouldn't play the actual statement right after."

Roger answered, "Probably don't want the FBI after their collective asses."

Roger sat down and looked at Paul. "We have a Christmas present this morning." He started unrolling the paper bag again to dump the contents on his desk. "Someone, the officer didn't get a name, don't look surprised, left this bag at the front desk for the FBI. Presumably, it was Ginger Hall's boss and these are items that were at the hospital. I haven't confirmed anything yet. Shall we open our present?"

"Please do," Paul said as he lifted his coffee cup from the desk. Roger dumped the bag and a small notebook fell out, a folded paper, some personal hygiene items, and a uniform blouse.

Roger got himself a cup of coffee and came back to his chair. He took out a clean index card and started writing a heading on it. *Ginger Hall:* Items from hospital. He added a question mark and looked to Paul to start describing items. Paul began, "Let's do the big ones first, we have a (he sniffed her blouse) fresh uniform blouse, size 10, white, looks freshly pressed, unworn, slight wear around pockets. Pockets empty. I see a couple of hairs and looks like a smudge on the button here." He was holding it out for Roger to see.

Roger reached in his desk drawer and pulled out an evidence bag, some gloves and tweezers. Then he said, "We have no chain of evidence here, but the lab boys may find something." After bagging the blouse Roger went back to his index card, and Paul picked up the personal hygiene items. They bagged them too.

Next, Paul put on gloves and unfolded the paper, "This is a medical Power of Attorney form, for Burna George!" Roger and Paula looked at each other. Paul continued, and he laid it out flat on the desk for Roger to read along. "Prepared by Attorney James Devon, and witnessed by Ginger Hall."

Roger said, "Isn't that the attorney for Nettie Wilson, the one that gave Darla Phillips a ride to the cemetery?"

Paul had flipped out his notebook from his breast pocket. "Yeah, I have a note from yesterday to call him and see where he dropped her off after the funeral." They both sat silent for a moment.

Roger was tapping his pen on the corner of the desk and swiveling his office chair. "This attorney must have a good size practice to coincidently represent two of our murder victims and be seen with a third."

"Four, if you count Ginger Hall." Paul was thumping his index finger on the bottom of the form where Ginger had witnessed the signing of the document.

"Four," Roger said slowly.

"Have our guys check out this Attorney Devon." Roger was writing down the dates on the document, "This was signed about a week before Burna George was murdered, so we know Ginger Hall was alive then. Do we know when Ginger was last seen?"

Paul looked at his notebook, "Hospital Supervisor, Jenny Camp, probably the one who dropped this stuff off last night, said Ginger had put in for holiday time off. Didn't expect to see her for a while. Last day at work was December 13th."

Roger was flipping through his index cards, "Day after Burna George was killed." Roger was talking again, "Can you contact this Jenny Camp and just verify she is the one who brought this stuff here? I don't think she will mind a quick phone call on Christmas."

"Will do," Paul said as he watched Roger place the paper into another evidence bag.

"We also need to get updates from task force members. I plan on doing that as soon as we are finished here." He was basically just talking out loud, and Paul was carefully opening the small notebook and thumbing through.

"Looks like her version of a day planner. She has little notes about groceries, doctor appointments, etc. I will go through each one later." He was still thumbing, reading. "Not seeing anything that really jumps at me." His voice was trailing off, "*except*...pick up flowers for Burna. No date, but it is toward the end of the notebook."

Roger was thoughtful, "What do we know about her personal life? Not much as I recall. Can we get someone on the task force to work up the local on that? Our boys didn't have anything helpful that I remember."

Paul looked at his notebook, "Single. She used to be a model for a while out in LA. She moved back to Indiana when her mom got cancer, took care of her until she died. Decided to go to nursing school about six years ago. Been an RN at Memorial since 2008. She lives in the house she inherited when her Mom died. Dates some, nothing serious according to girlfriend, fellow nurse, Rachel Morse. That's it. All I got." Paul stood, "It's a little early for calls. I think I will check on what the guys in the 'room' have got going."

Roger said, "Later," and went back to his index cards. He reached into his desk drawer and got out a blue marker pen. On the top right corner of Nettie, Darla, Burna, and Ginger he put a big blue dot. He was thinking this lawyer Devon was a very busy man.

Roger heard a commotion in the hall and looked around just in time to see a black cat run into his office, jump up, and sit squarely in front of him on his desk. He slowly reached out his hand to pet it, and it rubbed into his hand and purred. "Nice little kitty. What are you doing at the police station?"

A short stocky patrolman slid into the doorway opening, "Grab it! I've been trying to catch that thing for twenty minutes! Sucker is fast!" He was out of breath and hanging onto the door frame.

Roger laughed, "I don't think it's hurting anything for a minute. Go about your work and I'll put it outside soon. Hey, see if there is any sausage left in the 'room'. I'll feed the little guy before I put him out. It is Christmas." Roger was scratching the underside of the cat's neck. The patrolman shook his head and left returning about five minutes later with a small paper plate of sausage and eggs and a little dish of milk. He seemed to be in the spirit now. Someone had put a Grinch hat on him, and he was smiling. "Well, Grinch", Roger said. "Where'd you get the hat?"

The patrolman proudly modeled it for Roger and said, "It just showed up! I don't know where it came from!" Roger laughed and looked at the cat now licking its paws, and he could have sworn it winked at him.

Roger sat the cat on the floor and started spreading FBI reports across his desk. The cat jumped up on the credenza, rearranged a pile of napkins next to the coffee pot, and went to sleep. There was a light snow coming down and a Christmas parade on the TV. He could hear the cat purring from across the room. About an hour later Paul stopped in and sat across the desk. Roger wanted to give him a minute to notice the cat, so he pretended to be engrossed in a report.

Seconds later Paul jumped, "Shit! You know you have a cat in here?" He was backing his chair up, "I am not a fan of cats. Especially black ones!"

Roger laughed. The cat stood up and stretched, turned around and lay back down with his back to Roger and Paul. "It doesn't look like he thinks much of you either!"

Paul opened a file, "Well, speaking of animals, lab says the dog hair found at Nettie's and the dog hair found at Karen Smith's house are from the same dog. Got doggy DNA in yesterday. Guess it has to be sent to some special lab somewhere. Both hairs found just inside the homes, foyer areas, may be from our guy. As far as I know this is the only link between Nettie and Karen."

"You're right, we don't have anything between *these* two." Roger answered. Then he said, "Didn't the crime techs note a bunch of groceries sitting out, still in bags, at the Karen Smith house? Seems I saw they found a receipt," he was shuffling his index cards. "Yeah, Kroger. Have they produced any security film yet?"

"Not yet," Paul answered.

"I have a couple of things from the tip line that might be something." Paul held up a stack of pink phone notes about four inches thick. Roger moaned. Paul volunteered, "You should see how many are in the 'room.'"

"That is pretty much what everyone is doing today. I think Detective Sal (what Paul had started calling Detective Sally Miller) has about thirty names she would like our guys to check if we would." He fumbled through his file, "Here it is. We have DNA on that piece of duct tape you and I found at the Hall scene."

"Yes, but remember that was quite a distance from the actual scene," Roger stated.

Paul replied, "Well the Lab is running the tests *now*, so we should see if anything clicks."

Roger got up to get another cup of coffee and looked to Paul, "Want some?"

The cat raised its head and looked at Paul. Paul shifted in his seat, "No, thanks anyway."

Roger scratched the cat's head and gave its back a long stroke on his way back to his chair, "You know, I used to have a black cat when I was a kid. Well, I called it mine, but actually it just had a way of showing up. It always made me feel better when it was around." He smiled as he said that. The cat stretched out, so it was facing him as it slept. "I think it likes us."

"Did you do anything after you left the Pub last night?" Paul asked Roger, still watching the cat out of the corner of his eye. The cats' eyes looked closed, but Paul could see tiny slits watching them.

"Went to the hotel and slept like a baby. I think I am going to ask the manager what kind of mattresses they buy."

Paul got up to leave, "You know I slept well last night too, and my headache is gone. I've had that thing for three days now, non-stop." With that he left the office. Roger turned his attention to the TV and the latest news report. Paul stuck his head back in the door, "I am going to take a ride by that lawyer's office. I know he probably isn't anywhere around today, just curious. Maybe I can get a feel for him."

* * *

Sandy Devon knew it was Christmas Day. Yesterday, after James had nailed boards over the bedroom window both inside and out, he had attached a type of ankle bracelet to her with a chain long enough she could walk to the bathroom and shower. He had told her not to worry. Now that he didn't have to screw her, he certainly wasn't going to. She shuddered at the thought of him touching her.

He had also moved the TV and remote in for her to watch and had brought her food. Only three channels could come in, but she appreciated the company. He told her what he had done to all of those women. He seemed to enjoy talking about them, like he was re-living their horror. She had asked him why. He had shrugged and said, "I guess because I wanted to." He obviously figured she wasn't a threat. He was going to kill her after her birthday. He had told her that. The more he confessed to her, the more she believed him. She had seen him walking around outside through a small crack in the boards on the window. He was looking for something, and she figured it was probably his cell phone. The phone she had hidden in the closet. She discovered it didn't get a signal where she was, but it was working.

She had asked him if he wouldn't please bring her clean clothes from the apartment, at least underthings. She couldn't tell from his attitude if he planned to or not. He had brought a small cooler that had some lunch meat and a few cans of pop in it. She couldn't help but wonder what kind of a messed up mind strangles and rapes women, imprisons his own wife, and makes sure she has TV and food? She also didn't know when he was coming back, so she had to be careful to keep her projects hidden.

She changed the channel whenever the news came on. She couldn't stand to hear what he had done to all of those women. She knew that there were many more. The families of women that had been missing were begging for someone to tell them 'anything' that might help them find their loved ones. How could he have managed to do all of this and not get caught? Of course, she married him and didn't have a clue.

She had started writing on the wall behind the headboard by carving into the plaster with one of his keys. She had his name, what he had done the whole story as he told it. If they ever found her dead, at least they would catch him. She also was saving food wrappers, so she could use the lettering some-how. She wasn't sure yet what she was going to do, but anything she might be able to use was being stuffed between the mattress and box springs. She hated that bed, knowing what he had done there. Last night she had soaked the linens in bleach in the bathtub, and they were now hanging on the shower doors to dry. Those poor women. Sandy wiped her tears and turned the channel, again.

CHAPTER 13

Ellen wanted to look at the papers on Roger's desk. When he prepared to leave the office and tried to pick her up, she acted like she was totally dead weight and fast asleep. He laid her back down and went down the hall. When she was sure he was out of sight, she went over to the door and pushed it shut with her tail. She jumped onto the desk and thumbed through his index cards he had stacked by the phone. These seemed to be his "hint" cards. She wasn't impressed with where he was yet. She heard him coming, jumped back to the credenza, and assumed her sleeping position. Roger grabbed his jacket off the back of his chair and started to put on his overcoat. He looked at her and said, "Okay little buddy, hate to do this to you on Christmas, but it's time for you to go back to wherever you came from." He picked her up, carried her outside, left her in the snowy parking lot, and drove off.

Roger had decided to stop in at the Hope Rescue Mission and volunteer about two hours to help them get ready for their Christmas lunch crowd. Since he seldom was able to go home for the holidays, this had become a ritual for him wherever he was working. The volunteers welcomed him with open arms, had him in an apron, and slicing vegetables within fifteen minutes. He knew his television coverage in the community had ruined any hopes for anonymity, but he found that few people mentioned who he was or what he was doing in South Bend.

A couple of the characters that he served were not as passive. One gentleman gave a salute to him and a big toothless smile. Many reached over and patted his hand and said, "God Bless you for what you do." All in all it was what his soul needed. When twelve noon came, he decided they had enough volunteers. They wouldn't miss him, and he said goodbye. He headed over toward the PUB for a burger. He was hoping they were open, and they were. A big sign on the door said, "Food and soft drinks only on Christmas."

He saw there were only a couple of cars in the lot. One was Paul's. Roger nodded to Larry and went down to the end of the bar. "You're in my seat," he said to Paul.

Paul grinned, "Yup."

Larry came down with his rag over his shoulder and smiled at Roger, "You missed your buddy line dancing last night."

Roger was taken by surprise, "Really?"

Paul was grinning again, about to take a bite of his burger, "Yup."

Roger ordered a cola and a burger with everything and looked at Paul, "Anything good from the tip line yet?"

"I was going to call you. Nettie's neighbor, Mrs. Brooks, says for you to call her tomorrow. Doesn't want to bother you on Christmas, and she's going to her son's house today. She says she made you cookies." Paul had a big grin, "Anything 'special' you want to talk about there?"

"Anything else?" Roger asked.

Paul looked up and wiped grease from his mouth, "God these things are good. No, I think just the usual crackpots, but Detective Sal and Ed are making a few home visits this afternoon, just in case. Hate to bother people on Christmas, but at least they are usually home." Paul finished his burger in one last big bite and looked at Roger, keeping his voice very low. "Our attorney friend? I went by his office, some kind of home/office setup, not so fancy. Old Buick in driveway. Thought I saw a TV on through the window, but I stayed in my car out at the street. A real dump actually. If he has a lot of clients, they are not paying him much, or he does something else with his money. I think tomorrow I am going to call him for an appointment. Maybe our guys will have something for us by then." Paul meant the FBI researchers would scour every record available on Devon.

Roger said, "I think our guy is smart. A lawyer would know the odds of getting away with this shit in a community where you are known and do business. To openly drive one of the victims to a cemetery service in front of witnesses, in broad daylight, kind of redefines arrogance."

Paul looked up, "Almost as arrogant as leaving them dead next to the highway in broad daylight."

Roger nodded, "Yeah, good point. Maybe there has been a trigger. He's out of control, or plans on leaving the area soon."

Roger worked on his burger. He and Paul agreed. Either forensics gives them something fast from Ginger Hall's scene, or they might have to wait for another murder. Roger spoke first, "Ginger Hall was different. He let her loose. She was alive when that car hit her. Why would he leave her as a witness?"

Paul was stroking his chin, "I have been giving that a lot of thought. Maybe he liked her? Dumps her and leaves the area. He must be sure she couldn't describe him, or it wouldn't make any difference if she did. He's gone."

Roger nodded, "That is exactly what I have been thinking, and I don't like it. Or, we do have two doers and the one in charge of dumping got sloppy."

Paul stood up from his stool to leave, "If we only have one, and he left Ginger alive because he has split, we are screwed. If he has cracked and just doesn't care about getting caught, and he's still here, then he's still killing…and we are really screwed."

Larry came over to cash out their bills, and they each gave him a $20.00 Christmas tip. Larry said, "Thanks guys, I know you guys are working on this serial killer thing. Man, I don't know how you do it. I got to tell ya, it's causing a lot of people to act crazy. I have a beautiful wife. I mean beautiful! My wife looks like hell lately, on purpose! She quit wearing make-up, wears this ugly scarf everywhere. Says that guy wants to kill pretty women. I hope you catch him soon!"

Roger and Paul laughed when they got outside the PUB. "Now there is a consequence I didn't expect to hear," Paul said.

Roger was staring at a billboard across the street advertising BMW. "Start your new life today." He pointed to the billboard and then said to Paul, "As far as we know, our guy 'started his new life' with *Nettie's* death. Somehow, maybe she was a trigger. She had to die for his new life to start."

Paul was nodding, "It seems like that. I will go over her finances again, and I know our boys have searched public records. Found nothing, but we'll look again."

Roger asked, "Do you have the address for that senior center Nettie was going to?"

Paul shook his head, "Probably get it from somebody in the 'room'."

Roger watched Paul drive off as he waited for someone to answer the phone at the task center. The tip lines had been keeping everyone swamped. They hardly had time to *take* all of the calls, let alone follow up on them. He and Paul knew that seventy percent of the time when a case like this is solved, there *had been* a tip leading directly to the killer, that hadn't been acted on. Finally, Detective Ed Barnes answered, "Hey Roger."

Caller ID, he loved it, "Ed, can you get me a phone number and address for the senior center that Nettie Wilson used?" After about two minutes he was writing down the information and dialing the senior center. "Hello, I was calling to see if you were open on the holiday."

A small, high pitched voice answered, "Why of course we are honey. You just bring your little self-down, hon." Roger said thank you and thought of his mom, again. He noticed that everyone's voices start to sound the same after a certain age. Last time he visited his mom her recliner area in her TV room was beginning to get that 'senior' look.

He called his mom again while his car was warming up, "Hey there pretty lady, Merry Christmas!"

He pulled into the senior center parking lot and noticed quite a few cars. Usually seniors car pooled, so he expected a pretty good sized crowd inside and wasn't disappointed. He was met at the door with a mix of smells, good food, Ben Gay, perfume, and a lot of voices singing Christmas Carols around an old piano being played by a rather young man.

A little blue haired lady ran to greet him, "OOOH! You must have been the young man that just called me. I told the girls we had a live one headed this way."

Roger laughed, "And you are?"

The lady made a short courtesy and said, "I'm Maribell, the Director of the Center. Are you here to visit anyone in particular?" She was scanning around the room to see if anyone had noticed her talking to this handsome young man.

"Well, Maribell I think I'm probably here to see you." Roger flipped open his badge and introduced himself.

Maribell looked like she was going to faint. "Oh my. I don't remember doing anything wrong. I did borrow some of the extra paper plates from the kitchen, but I.."

Roger stopped her confession before it got too far, "No Ma'am, I am here to ask you some questions about Nettie Wilson." Maribell was noticeably relieved and motioned for Roger to follow her to her office. She led him there telling everyone they passed to leave her be, she had important business with the FBI.

He learned that Nettie used to be a volunteer at the center, but as she got older she just came for the special events. She usually had her neighbor, Mrs. Brooks, bring her or that nice young girl Darla Phillips. Roger could tell that Maribell didn't know Darla was one of the victims. He didn't want to interrupt the interview, so he didn't tell her. He asked Maribell if she thought Nettie had a lot of money.

She was thoughtful, "You know, you can't tell with these old people. Some of them act like they are home eating cat food, and then they die and leave the center a hundred thousand dollars. We had that happen back in 1959."

Roger got her back on track "Nettie had a niece, Joy Covington. Did you know her?"

"Oh yes! Didn't come here very often, but she's a professional cook you know. When our cook was sick last year, Joy came over one night and helped us out. We had already advertised a spaghetti dinner and everything. Oh Dear, we were in such a mess! She really saved the day!" Maribell continued, "You know it is hard to keep places like this from just dying off, literally. We lost three people in just the last two months, Nettie, Phil, Burna...."

Roger spoke, "Are you talking about Burna George?"

Maribell lit up with the question, "Well yes, did you know Burna? Poor thing was really quite ill there at the end."

Roger didn't think Maribell knew that Burna had been murdered too. "Were Burna and Nettie friends?" Roger asked. Maribell said it was important to remember that your real friends talk nice about you when you are not there. She didn't think Burna really had that many friends anymore. Roger thought that was kind of a nice way to say that. He was thanking Maribell for her time outside of her office when he noticed the event calendar on the wall. January 9th speaker: Attorney James Devon.

Roger was tapping the calendar where January 9th was, "Do you have many attorneys that come here and speak?"

Maribell rolled her eyes, "The good ones don't have time for the likes of us." She had her mouth crimped tight. "Now Nettie really pushed this guy on all of us, knowing we are old and all, needed wills, etc. I heard her say he gave her money for every new client she could push his way, but I do have to say he was fast and cheap. He would come to your house with his paper work, and not make you drive to his office."

Roger thought he probably didn't want people to see his office, "How often does he speak here?"

Maribell looked thoughtful, "I'd say about every other month for about the last couple of years. He does all the funerals too, doesn't miss a one. Hands out his cards like it's a political convention or something. I don't know, guess even lawyers have to make a livin'." Roger thanked her for her time, wished her a merry Christmas, and went to his car to write down some notes. Attorney Devon is looking more like a predator type lawyer than a killer, he thought as he left to return to the police center. Too bad, Devon's was the only name that seemed to touch more than one victim.

Roger parked in the assigned space at the police center and noticed the snow was coming down steadily now. Huge fluffy flakes, the size of quarters, they called it lake effect snow. It was beautiful. It was a white Christmas after all. He felt something at his feet, looked down, and there was that black cat again. "Whoa there fella, didn't you go home? Maybe you don't have a home?" He reached down and stroked the cat's back. It was rubbing up against his pant legs.

He walked to the door and held his foot out for the cat to stop. It did. When he shut the door, it was looking at him through the glass with snow piling on its head. "God what have I started," he mumbled to himself. He opened the door, and the cat came in and waited for him to walk. As he neared his office the cat rushed ahead of him, assumed its position on the credenza next to the coffee pot, and lay down. "What is it with me and cats?" he asked it. He could have sworn it winked at him. Again.

145

Paul walked into Roger's office, "Got a minute?" Roger looked up and saw Paul looking at the cat and shaking his head. "Got a guy at the front desk wants to know if we are going to charge him with the murders, or not. He doesn't want to pay an attorney unless he has to." Paul was grinning.

Roger sputtered, "What?"

"I told the desk guy to put him in the interrogation room with the observation window. Care to join me?" Paul started laughing. They both knew this was probably some crazy confessor, but at least it provided a little humor to break up the day.

They waited in the observation room and soon the door opened. A man came in and was told to sit and wait. Roger spoke first, "Isn't that the loud mouth from the PUB?"

"I think you are right Sherlock. Well, you or me?"

"By all means Dr. Watson, you," Roger smiled. Paul grabbed a yellow legal pad, entered the interrogation room, and sat at the corner of the table, so Roger could clearly see their mystery man.

Paul started, "I need to get a little information from you before we can start, is that okay?" The man nodded. His shoulders were all hunched forward and his eyes kept darting around the room. He was void of the arrogance Roger and Paul had witnessed at the Pub. Paul smiled, and positioned his paper to write and asked, "Your name?"

The man looked at Paul and said, "Oh come on man! Let's not waste time, okay? I know you know my name, where I live, where I work. Hell, even my bar!" He had put his head into his hands.

Paul looked sideways toward the glass window and raised an eyebrow. They didn't know anything about this guy.

Then Paul spoke again, "Well this is for the official record sir, so I have to ask these questions."

The man sighed and said, "Okay....Okay...My name is Jack Simpson. I am Joy Covington's boyfriend. I knew Nettie like a Mom, and I flirted with Darla, a lot, and I work at Davis Construction and I know, knew, Karen Smith...and she probably didn't like me...that is three of your dead women by my count! I'm thinkin' I best be talkin' to my lawyer maybe?" Paul pushed his chin forward in his thoughtful tick, he wanted to keep Jack talking, but he had already mentioned a lawyer.

Paul asked him if he would like a soft drink, and Jack said "Sure." Paul excused himself and went into the observation room where Roger was waiting. They just stared at each other.

Roger handed Paul the pop can he was carrying. He hadn't opened it yet, "Ask him if he has a dog."

Paul went back into the interrogation room and handed Jack the pop. He opened it, took a big gulp, and shook his head. "Never really liked this stuff," he said. Paul asked him if he had a lawyer. He had mentioned a lawyer to the desk sergeant. Jack took a minute to answer, "In a way I do, and in a way I don't. If it wasn't Christmas, he would be here right now." Jack thought that was probably true. He wasn't sure, but he had heard if you give the guy money he would do anything. Paul was concerned about questioning Jack without his lawyer present. They couldn't risk getting any of this statement excluded as evidence in the event it really was something.

Paul decided to play it safe, "You know Jack, under the circumstances your lawyer may be willing to come in today. What is your lawyer's name?" Jack pulled a paper out of his breast pocket and handed it to Paul.

Paul looked at it and said, "Let me get you a phone, so you can call him. See what he wants to do, okay?"

"Yup," and Jack put his head in his hands again.

Paul came in where Roger was waiting. Roger said, "Let me guess, Devon."

"Yup." Paul was shaking his head, "This should be interesting."

Roger touched Paul's sleeve and said, "Wait, he isn't confessing to anything. He is asking if we are looking at him in this. I think we can ask him a few questions without his attorney. Why don't I call the D.A. real quick." Paul heard Roger apologizing on the phone. By Roger's facial expression he didn't like the answer. Roger came back to where Paul was waiting. "D.A. says we'd better be careful, reminded me it was Christmas, said to let him go."

Paul looked through the observation window and said, "Look at that!" The black cat was on the table, and Jack was rubbing its back and talking to it. Roger rolled his eyes.

Paul went back in the room with Jack and said, "Looks like you found a new friend."

Jack answered, "Animals like me. I've got a great dog, Flea Bag." Roger had said the dog's name in his head at the same time Jack said it out loud.

148

Paul said, "Well Jack, you are not here today to tell us you killed these women are you?"

"Oh, hell no!" Jack said. "I come in because everywhere I turn is you guys, and I wanted to let you know I ain't done nothin'! I figured you came to my house, and my bar! I'm just here to tell ya you are wastin' time on me."

Paul looked sideways at the observation window then said to Jack, "I think that we will ask you to come back and answer some questions. Not today though. You make sure your lawyer knows you came here, and that we will be calling him tomorrow."

Jack sat up straight, "Are you saying I am not a suspect in this shit?"

Paul answered, "Let's say you are now a person of interest."

Jack thought a moment, "I can live with that. Yeah, that's not near as bad as being a suspect." Jack stood up and asked, "Can I just leave now? Go home?"

"Yes you can Jack. Just don't be leaving town without letting me know." He handed Jack a card.

Paul noticed the black cat ran out of the room. He watched Jack strut down the hall, saying 'bye to everyone he passed, and then he was out of the building. Paul watched him get into an old Dodge pickup and drive off. When Paul got back to Roger's office, the cat was back on the credenza, and Roger was sitting at his desk.

Paul spoke first, "What was that? Do you believe this guy? Thanks to your cat we found out he has a dog without having to ask the question."

Roger raised one eyebrow, "I have met Flea Bag. He is a very unusual dog, and he is yellow."

Paul's smile went away, "Yellow dog, huh?"

Roger brought out his notebook and told Paul everything he had found out about Attorney Devon. After a minute Paul said, "So you think our lawyer friend is just a funeral chaser, and not our doer?"

Roger answered, "I think we need to get a lot of information on both of these guys, fast. Either the world's smartest lawyer is soon going to be representing the world's dumbest drunk, opportunity there. Or the world's smartest drunk is about to suck in the world's dumbest lawyer, opportunity there. Either way, we are going to be severely hampered by attorney / client privilege."

Roger told Paul to brief the task force on what had developed, and remind them that it was imperative to the investigation not to leak to the press they were looking at anyone. The rumor would already be flying around the station that some guy came in and confessed. Roger called the FBI Data Agent assigned to the case, Agent Ray Davis. He instructed him to start sending anything he could find on Mr. Jack Simpson and Attorney James Devon. It was probably going to be a very long night. While he was on the phone, Ray told him he had just sent over the security tapes from Kroger for the entire day of the 23rd of November. He also instructed Roger on how to freeze frames and zoom, on the new software. Roger swore they changed the software they used for this stuff every time he figured it out. Ray sent him photos and stats of Devon and Simpson from DMV records.

Roger walked over to the window, leaned against the wall, and pulled his wallet out. He flipped to a well-worn picture of a beautiful woman sitting at the edge of a canyon, blowing a kiss. Sharon. It had been five years now and his heart ached like it was yesterday. He looked out at the snow, remembered their first snow ball fight, and how he had let her win. He had tackled her and kissed the snowflakes from her face. On Christmas he proposed to her, and she had said no. Her doctor had just told her she had cancer. A bad one. There was nothing that could be done. In her eyes that night, he saw himself dying too.

He had taken a family leave from the Agency to be with her. The cancer had eaten her alive. It was like watching her vanish from life, a little piece at a time. Roger took care of all of her needs. Near the end he stayed in bed with her as much as he could. He read to her, sang to her, and brushed her hair. She was so brave. She had held him in her arms, on her bed, to comfort him, and she had whispered, "Promise me you will love again."

He had promised, even though every cell of his being was screaming, "How?" He had felt the warmth of her last breath on his cheek. It was another six months before he returned to work. He thought he was ready. He talked to people who had lost loved ones who said they were empty, hollow, just going through the motions of living. He *envied* them. He had a burning sword piercing *his* heart. He returned his wallet to his pocket, poured a cup of coffee, stroked the cat's back, and downloaded the files from Ray. Roger wondered if he would ever keep that promise to Sharon.

He had been reviewing the Kroger tapes for an hour in fast speed when Paul came back into his office. "How can you see anything that fast?"

"This is now about noon on the 23^{rd,} and I was just getting ready to slow it down," Roger hit pause and turned to look at Paul. "Anything of interest in the 'room'?"

"Yeah, we have a couple of tip line calls that might pan out. Detectives are on them now. I think a couple of guys think we messed up bad letting this Simpson guy go home. Just getting tired of the hunt, you know?"

Roger nodded, "Wait 'til the Captain hears. He is the one getting heat from the press."

Paul asked, "Mind if I watch with you?" Roger turned back to his monitor, adjusted it so Paul could see better, and set the video for normal speed x two. Fast enough not to take all day and yet slow enough to catch something. They watched the store fill up with customers, and they went to a split screen showing four camera views at once of different aisles. After about an hour of viewing, Roger reached over and hit the stop button then backed up about six frames. He pointed to the top right view. "Who does that look like there?"

Paul squinted, "Maybe, let's follow that camera a few more frames". They watched two women walk through the front door, grab a cart, put their purses in the cart basket, and start walking through the store. One looked like the right description for Karen Smith, and the other fit Valerie McDonald.

Paul was tapping the screen on another camera view, "Go back to the front door." A man in a long dark trench coat had walked in, grabbed a cart, and moved up fast behind Karen and Valerie. He had the right color hair and body shape for Devon. They watched as the three progressed through the store. The man who looked like Devon put a few items in his cart, but most of the time just looked at items and put them back on the shelf. As the three turned the aisle corner there was a full face shot of them all from the third security camera. Paul leaned forward, "There! Freeze and zoom on that!"

Roger looked at his notes, and Paul just hit a couple of keys on the computer. They were look-ing at Karen Smith, Valerie McDonald, and with the aid of the pictures sent by Ray, a perfect shot of Attorney James Devon. "What do you know?" Roger said, "Let's keep going." They watched about ten minutes more when Roger said, "I don't believe it!" He hit stop, backup, stop, and zoom. There was Jack Simpson putting a case of beer into a cart, obvi-ously saying something to Valerie and Karen as they passed by him. Devon was close behind.

"Are we back to two doers again?" Paul looked at Roger. They watched as Karen and Valerie stood at a freezer case. Jack went past them, through the check out, and out the door. Devon was across from Karen and Valerie and picked up items on an end cap dis-play. He put the items back and moved toward the check out right behind the girls. Karen and Valerie went out the front door no more than two minutes before Devon. Reviewing the checkout again, Devon had pushed his cart to the side at the last minute and just walked through without making a purchase.

Roger called Agent Smallwood back, "Yeah, Ray, do you have parking lot video for around 12:45 p.m. on the Kroger? Great. Send it now would you?" Paul and Roger watched the store video again while they waited for the parking lot video. A pop-up told them the video was there, so they brought it up on the screen. It clearly showed Karen and Valerie walking to Karen's car, unloading groceries, and pushing the cart to a bin. Karen drove. As they backed out, they saw a light colored Buick slide in behind them and leave the lot. "Didn't you say you saw a Buick at Devon's place?" Roger asked Paul.

"Yup, and I think that was Simpson's Dodge pickup. Right at the beginning, at the top of the screen, leaving the lot." They played it back, and it did look like Jack left the parking lot about when Karen and Valerie were coming out of the store.

Roger was back on the phone to Agent Smallwood, "I want every traffic camera from the Kroger to Valerie Smiths house from noon to 3:00 on the 23rd. You know, get me the camera at the corner of Lincoln and Michigan too for that time." He clicked his phone shut and looked at Paul. "Gut?"

"Devon," Paul answered. "And he is going to have a late Christmas gift when Jack calls."

Roger looked at his watch, "What are the odds we call Devon at 6:00 p.m. on Christmas, he's home, and he lets us come up and talk to him?"

Paul said, "I like the odds better, we just show up." Roger nodded agreement, pet the cat, and grabbed his coat. Paul said, "You leaving that cat in here?" Roger reached around the back of his desk and pulled out a bag that had a travel litter pan in it. He peeled the cover off and put it in the corner, took out a small paper plate, and emptied a can of cat food on it. Pulled out a small plastic bright blue bowl, and emptied his water bottle. Paul was laughing, "Always prepared, my man, always prepared."

Roger said, "That cat has been bringing us good luck." They turned off the office light and shut the door. Ellen walked over to the litter and rolled in it for a while. She sniffed the food and almost threw up. She knew she had to make it disappear, so she buried it in pieces in the litter. She did get a drink of water then she vanished. She had to beat them to Devon's place.

CHAPTER 14

Ellen was glad to see Devon home watching a football game. This was going to be tricky. She couldn't remove things, but she could move them to where Roger and Paul would see them. She went into Devon's office at the end of the house. Oh whew! It stunk....wet dog, cigars, filth.....geesh. She adjusted her sensor and pretended she was Roger and Paul. What could they see from where they would sit? There was a metal in-box type file sitting on the far right hand corner of the desk. Ellen turned it around, so the open side faced the "company" chair. She started looking for documents of interest for Roger and Paul. She went through her notes from when they were there before. All of the photogenic memories of the girls were there. Lowes receipt Christmas Eve day, she put that with a piece of tape right on the front. She found the trust account notice for a Sandy Nelson and the marriage certificate for Sandy Nelson and James Devon, Oct 28, 2011. She went over to the dog bed in the corner.

The dog was outside, and she scooped up a big ball of dog hairs and put it on one of the seats.

On Devon's computer she pulled up his web browser history and hit print. It printed his favorite porn sites and a couple of Google searches. Might be something. She was really moving fast. She went back to the secretary's desk in the living room and tried to just look at what was lying on the surface. She had to be careful. Devon was watching TV, and his recliner was only about nine feet away from her. Unfortunately, his secretary was very neat, and the only things showing were phone message receipts and some billing folders. There wasn't any way to move those without Devon seeing.

Just then he shot up from his chair and went to the window, "What the Hell?" He was thinking, "Shit, I bet it's the damn IRS! Bastards come on Christmas." He grabbed a shirt from the couch, shook it out, put in on over his dirty tee, slipped his filthy feet into some loafers, and headed toward his office door on the other side of the house.

Roger and Paul had knocked on the door a minute or so before Devon got there. Devon opened the door and was about to speak when Paul flipped opened his badge and said, "Attorney James Devon?" Devon nodded. "I am Supervisory Special Agent Paul Casey, and this is Supervisory Special Agent Roger Dance, FBI. We apologize for bothering you on Christmas, but we are working a very important case in South Bend. We need your help."

Ellen could hear Devon's thoughts, "FBI...not IRS...cool." Man he is arrogant Ellen thought.

Devon was opening the door wide and smiling, "Not a problem guys, just watching the game. Come on in." Devon's' office was very small, so it didn't take long for him to be at his side of the desk. Roger and Paul took seats across from him. Devon noticed his computer screen on and excused himself for a second while he closed it down. Roger motioned for Paul to look at the documents next to him. Paul was doing a good job of speed reading when Devon twirled his chair back to face them. "Okay, what can I do for you?" Roger noticed Devon's shirt was buttoned wrong. He must have dressed in a hurry.

"We are working the recent murders in South Bend. I'm sure you have been reading about them. We have noticed that you have connections to four of our victims."

Devon didn't bat an eye, "Yeah, I was thinking the other day you guys might want to know how I knew these people." He started an obviously well-rehearsed version of how he had known Nettie for years, met Darla through her relationship with Nettie, dropped Darla off at her home after the cemetery, handled the estate for Burna, and had Ginger witness a document for him at the hospital. All very innocent.

Roger asked, "Just for the record, I have a couple of dates if you could check your calendar and tell us where you were. Then we can finish this up and let you get back to your game. The first one is Sunday, Nov 6, afternoon?"

Devon looked at his calendar, "Really didn't need to look at that because Sundays I am always home in the afternoon. You know day of rest and all."

Roger continued, "Okay, the day before Thanksgiving, Nov 23rd."

Devon looked like he was thinking hard about that, "Day before Thanksgiving. I don't think I had any court cases that day. Let me look at my calendar here…. I think I was just working here in the office all day."

Roger gave him another chance, "Didn't do any shopping for Turkey Day? A lot of the stores are closed on Thanksgiving."

Devon laughed a little, "I don't do Thanksgiving. What makes it a holiday for me, is I don't get any crazy clients coming around. I think I just stayed here that day. Yeah, I was here all day. Anything else?"

Ellen was starting to panic. She went outside, turned herself into the cat, and got Devon's dog worked into frenzy. Devon got up, went to the side door, and looked out of the small window. "Damn black cat out there teasing my dog! Sorry about that." They could hear the dog yelping.

"What kind of dog do you have?" Paul asked trying to sound casual.

"A Golden," Devon answered. He wasn't going to sit back down, which was his signal for them to leave.

Paul's arm accidently hit the metal in-box on the corner of the desk and sent the papers flying. They all bent down to pick them up as Paul was saying, "I am so sorry."

Roger stood, holding a Certificate of Marriage form, "Hey, looks like there is a new Mrs. Devon. October 28th. Congratulations. Is she home?"

James Devon, clearly angry, took the paper from Roger. "Newlywed spat. She went on the honeymoon without me."

Paul asked, "Where to?"

James Devon was not as good a liar as he thought, and when he answered "Jamaica", the hairs on Rogers arms stood up.

Roger asked, "Are you going to be joining her soon, in case we need you again?"

Attorney Devon was holding the door open for them to leave, "That's the plan. I will call you before I leave. Does that work for you?" He shrugged as he said it. Roger gave him a card, and they went to their car.

Roger got into the passenger seat, put on gloves, and pulled an evidence bag from his pocket. When Paul got behind the steering wheel, Roger said, "He'll be watching us. Go slow behind that Buick. I want to write down the plate." Paul watched as Roger used tweezers to put a large ball of golden dog hairs in a bag. Then Roger pulled out his notebook and wrote down the numbers of the plate.

Paul pointed, "He's got the curtain pulled a little there. He is watching us."

Roger gestured as they got to the corner, "Head north here, and we'll circle back around to this back street." They drove a few minutes to get a clear view of the Buick and the side door, and parked in the driveway of an empty home for sale.

"If we put eyes on him, and they're seen, we'll spook him," Roger said.

Paul was staring at the Buick and said, "I'll run tags and call for flight information from the US to

Jamaica from say Oct. 28th, to now for Sandy Devon. Did you see her maiden name?"

Roger answered, "Yes, it was Nelson. I am going to call Ray in Intel and get phone records, background, and financials."

Paul's voice boomed, "Oh Jesus! Look who just pulled in."

Roger looked to Devon's driveway, and Jack Simpson's Dodge pickup had parked next to the Buick. "What is he doing?" Roger's view was obstructed by a small tree. They both had their binoculars.

"Looks like he is putting a note on the windshield," Paul answered. Just then they saw Devon step outside the door and walk towards Jack. They talked for about ten minutes. Jack was waving his arms and shifting his weight from one side to the other. Devon was standing like a statue. Then Devon put his arm around Jack's shoulder and walked him back to his office. "Did you see Devon's smile?" Paul asked Roger.

"Yup," Roger answered. "Devon just got his Christmas gift, and we just got screwed." They both knew they would have a rough time getting a subpoena for a phone tap and office bug on an attorney with no real evidence. Add to that, another suspect has retained him for counsel. "We still can't be sure these guys aren't working together. We can put a tail on Simpson." Roger's voice trailed off.

"That's probably the only thing we can do."

Roger called and made arrangements for the tail on Jack, and they waited until the unmarked car arrived. Ray called and said he was sending feed to Roger's computer unfiltered. Roger preferred to get unfiltered info. More than once some tech thought something wasn't important, and it was never shared. Ray also said it would be the next day before they had all of the airline info requested. The holiday had the airlines all short staffed, and his people were not even there. Roger had him pull anything he could get on Sandy Nelson Devon also. "I need cell records on all three of these people and place a tracer on them all...24/7...auto feed copy to me." Roger clicked his phone shut. He spoke out loud to himself, "How did we ever do this job before technology?"

Ellen had been in the backseat of the car, so she could pick up on what Roger and Paul were thinking. Then she left to go see Betty.

CHAPTER 15

Sandy was sitting crossed legged on the bed using a key to dig into the wood at the top of one of the footboard slats. Her eyes stung from her tears. She couldn't believe that poor woman had been hit by a car after finally escaping. Monster. That had been the woman's word, and it was true. His parting words to her had been that he brought extra food, should do her a couple of days. He had plans for Christmas. He was going to get his Christmas present. She knew that meant he was going to kidnap some other woman. She had to keep herself focused, so she could stop him.

Sandy was making some progress, but it was going to take a long time. Her hand was getting blisters. She had wrapped some tissues and toilet paper into a bandage and held it together with a strip of sheet she had torn. She changed position to get more comfortable and started using her left hand. Then she heard a little rustle by the TV. She stopped sawing with her key and saw a little mouse walking on the empty grocery bags by the cooler. "Oh, I have company!" she squealed. She quickly went over and made up a plate of some cracker crumbs, a couple of grapes she pulled apart, and a small piece of cheese. She put the plate on the floor in front of the TV and got back onto the bed to wait. She waited quite a while, and her eye lids were getting heavy. She ended up taking a nap.

She must have slept for a couple of hours. She peeked outside through the small crack in the boards on the window. It looked like it was starting to get dark. When she looked at the plate on the floor, she saw that most of the food she had set out was gone. "You sneaky little thing." she said. She made another plate of food for her little mouse friend, ate a sandwich herself and got back to work on sawing. She would saw all night if that is what it took. She wiped her cheek with the back of her bandaged hand. Somebody has to stop him.

* * *

James Devon was humming Jingle Bells as he made a ham sandwich and poured a small glass of milk. He couldn't believe his luck again! First, Ginger gets hit by a car after escaping, and now this Jack Simpson is who the cops think is killing all these women. He wants ME to represent him. This could actually be fun. In fact, if he can help the cops with their case against Jack, he might not have to leave the States after all. Devon couldn't stop a giggle from escaping. Actually, it even works out that Sandy is his prisoner at the 'house.' He doesn't have to screw her anymore, just keep her alive 'til after her birthday. He balanced the milk glass in his elbow while he opened his bedroom door. He sat the sandwich and milk on his night stand and looked at the woman handcuffed to the headboard and footboard. Her eyes flashed sheer terror as he ripped the duct tape from her mouth.

He snarled, "Merry Christmas, my pretty Ashley. Let's get you some food, a nice shower, and then Daddy gets his Christmas present."

* * *

Joy watched Jack's pickup pull into the driveway. He got out of the truck carrying a bag of something and a big red poinsettia flower. He made his way over to the porch and sat everything down. He loved on Flea Bag for a while then he went in. Joy met him at the door. "Where in the hell did you go? It's Christmas! I get up, and you're nowhere."

She didn't look very happy, and all Jack could think to say was, "I got you a flower."

Joy took it from him and said "Thanks." He didn't sound drunk, and he didn't look drunk.

Jack took his coat off and said. "I think I am going to treat myself to a Christmas beer. I haven't had a beer since yesterday." He walked over to the fridge where Joy handed him a beer and got one for her.

Jack pulled a kitchen chair out for her and said, "Wait 'til you hear the good news!" Joy's eyebrows went up, you never knew with Jack. "The POlice do not consider me a suspect in these murders!"

Joy nearly choked on her beer. "What makes you think that?"

Jack leaned back in his chair, "Because they told me that today. I went to the police station and asked them why they were following me around."

Joy couldn't believe her ears, "You did what?"

Jackspokeslower, "I-went-to–the-police-station…"

Joy smacked his head, "I know what you said you crazy fool! What happened?" He told her about his meeting with Paul, and Paul had said he wasn't a suspect. He was just interesting. He went to leave a note at that lawyer's office she told him about. It turned out the lawyer was home, and said that he didn't have to give him any money yet. If the police talked to him again to give him a call. He would help.

Joy looked at him for a minute, "Jack did the police officer say you were *interesting*, or a person of interest?"

"Yeah, I think that other way is the way he said it. But I'm telling you Joy, he was real nice. I think all of this shit is over, for us anyway." As he said that, Joy noticed a dark sedan park down the street facing their house and turn its lights out. Jack unpacked the grocery bag, "Hey, I picked up some stuff for making chili dogs. You hungry?"

"Yeah, I could eat something. I'll make 'em in a minute."

Jack stood and took a bow, "I'll cook tonight. Another Christmas present for you, my Lady." He made his way over to the stove, found a large fry pan, and turned to Joy. "You know the last time I saw this thing, it was flying at my head." They both laughed.

Jack fell asleep watching TV, and Joy decided to take a walk. She got up next to the parked car and knocked on the window. The black glass slowly lowered, and Joy saw a man in a suit looking back at her. "I saw this on TV once," she said. She handed him a couple of chili dogs wrapped in foil. "They're chili dogs, good ones too. I warmed 'em up for you. I know you have to do your job, but Jack is not your guy. He has a way of being at the wrong place at the wrong time. I just wanted to let you know." Detective Ed Mars watched her walk back to the house and turn the back porch light on. He ate the chili-dogs. They were great. He called Roger and told him what had happened. Roger told him to stay put. He would call him back in a couple of hours.

* * *

The entire task force was carefully sifting through all of the data being printed out from Roger's computer. Roger had to change the ink cartridges twice and had gone around stealing paper from everyone else's printers. Paul and Roger both were worried about fatigue and told everyone to cross review. Select fifty pages of data, finish reviewing, highlight items in question, and pass it on to the guy on your right. They announced that everyone had to leave at 10:00 p.m.. Their families needed them, and they needed a night's sleep. There was going to be a lot of work to do tomorrow.

Ten o'clock came, and everyone honored the order to go home. It had been a long day for them, and it was Christmas. Earlier Roger had called Chief Doyle to update him on their new suspicion. The Chief had started his detectives gathering everything they could on both Simpson and Devon. He thought they had amassed a lot of data until he saw the reams of paper coming from the FBI. That didn't count the stuff being sent for scan viewing only. He had his best computer guys on those. By 10:00 they all needed the break.

The halls were almost silent as Roger and Paul stood looking out the big window toward the parking lot watching the huge snowflakes. There wasn't a lot of accumulation, just enough to call it a white Christmas. Paul noticed he hadn't seen the cat. "Where's your buddy?" he asked Roger.

"I haven't seen him for a while. Must have slipped out when someone came in. I'll keep my door open in case he needs the box." Roger smiled, and then said, "I think this day is over. I'm ready to make the call to Ed and pull him off Jack for the night."

Paul looked thoughtful, "Your call."

Roger snapped his phone open and dialed, "Ed, can you be back on it about 5:00 a.m.? Yeah, thanks." Our manpower on this is thin as it is, Roger thought.

Paul said, "I'm heading to the hotel. See ya in the morning." Roger nodded and walked to his office. He watched the steady stream of e-mails coming from Ray, put his coat on, and headed out the door. In the 'room', lights out, papers were flipping and a marker pen occasionally made a mark. Ellen was working as fast as she could and watching the clock. The gals would be there at 12:01.

* * *

12:01 in the conference room at police center, the gals had arrived and were talking about their visits home. I could tell from what everyone was saying that their loved ones couldn't see or hear them. Maybe it was some kind of mistake or fluke that Kim saw me. Maybe she won't ever be able to see me again. Teresa looked at me, "You are being unusually quiet." I wondered if she could read my mind. Teresa's hair is on fire! Nothing, I'm still safe.

"It is not," Mary said. "Safe from what?"

I might as well spill the beans, "Kim could see and hear me this whole visit." Everyone looked shocked. I was afraid they would be mad at me. Then Ellen and Betty appeared at our table.

171

Ellen spoke first, "Betty and I have been told that Granny arranged that. We have to assume she has her reasons."

Then Betty spoke, "You girls will not believe how much has happened since you went home on your visit. Ellen and I are going to bring you up to date with a knowledge tent." She stood and made a circle with her arm in the air and there was that gold curtain again. Betty said, "Just rest your eyes for a moment, and then we will talk." Again, it felt warm and quiet. We opened our eyes, and the curtain was gone. Ellen showed us the piles of papers she had been working on, and we all knew what we had to do. Find connections in these documents that could prove Attorney James Devon was the killer.

Ellen agreed with us that Jack was just a lost mortal. Betty was flipping through those pages when I spoke to her, "Betty?"

She didn't look up, "Yes dear." She just kept on flipping papers.

"If Ginger died at the same time we did, why wasn't she in this group with us?"

Betty looked up, "Well dear, I think she actually died a few minutes before all of you. She would have been in the class before you." Then her eyes got big, and we shouted at each other, "MAYFLIES!"

Ellen looked startled. "What?"

I couldn't control myself, "Betty, you said that either as a group or as an individual, someone in that class would not let go of their mortal memories. What if it is Ginger?"

Ellen was looking at Betty, "Mayflies?"

172

Betty was excited, "Oh yes dear! We have to make a quick trip back, and you (she said pointing to me) are going to have to ask Granny for a favor."

I was almost speechless. Actually I went into super speed talking. My mouth was on auto-pilot, "Can't we do this as a group? After all we are a group. You guys said, you- are- a- group." I was wildly pleading my case.

Betty smiled, "Of course dear, we shall talk to Granny as a group." I sighed with relief, Mary kicked me. Linda and Teresa didn't look very happy either. Oh well, it's not my rule. A group is a group, is a group, is a... "We get it dear," Betty said. We all took off for the park with the mayflies.

CHAPTER 16

I t was nice to see the park again. Betty had left her hammock out for us to see. I doubt if she really got much of a nap. Teresa and Linda were on a bench, and Mary was looking at the massive cloud of mayflies. Mary turned to me, "Please don't tell me we have to figure out which one of these is Ginger?"

Teresa spoke, "Oh, this is going to be good. I suppose we will have to get little nets. Do little DNA tests. We should be done about…NEVER!" She frowned at me.

Linda said, "Look and see if any of them are just sitting somewhere. Maybe after the accident she doesn't feel like flying." Mary started walking really slowly looking at the mayflies, and then Linda said, "I was just joking!"

Mary said, "You might be right though." She was still looking when Ellen and Betty appeared with Granny. Mary's head was covered with Mayflies, but she didn't move. She just kept blowing them away from her mouth.

Granny looked at me, "Do you have a favor to request of me?"

I summoned my courage and said, "I believe that the woman who died in our car accident, Ginger Hall, might remember something that can help us in our assignment. I was hoping there was some way you could find out." I swallowed hard and tried to remember what I had just said to her. Did it sound stupid?

Granny put her arm in the air and made a circular motion. There was that gold curtain again. Only this time what looked like a big movie screen was at one end. Granny said, "Ginger *has* been hanging on to her last memories. Understand, she is not capable of filtering any of them. She also may not remember as much as you need, but she wants to help." With that Granny was gone.

We were seeing a dark space… then a burst of light from a door opening and a woman came into the area crying and tearing at ropes and tape and suddenly a vision of a floor up close… I think Ginger fell, and then it looked like Ginger had gotten up… now she and the other woman looked really scared…they kept looking around the room and at the window… Ginger and this woman were pushing open the window. The woman lifted Ginger into the opening and pushed her. Ginger turned back to look at her and the woman's face on the inside of the house looked terrified…it looked like she was saying "go —go". Ginger had turned and was running toward a line of trees…we could see a highway on the other side of the tree line…it was daylight, and there was a lot of traffic. Ginger looked behind

176

her, and there was an SUV barreling toward her.....she was crawling up some gravel, her hands were bloody, and then she was standing on the road, she turned and then...black. Nothing.

The gold curtain was gone. We were still in the park, but there were no mayflies. Betty spoke, "Oh Boy! Well, we have a lot of work to do, but I want you girls to notice, no mayflies. This class is now at peace. Ginger was holding on to those memories in order to help that woman."

Ellen stood tall and thrust her right arm out straight, "Now we have something to work with. Let's go kick some mortal butt!" Angels do that?

We were back in the conference room and had sorted through most of the papers. We found little bits and pieces, but I was worried they would never piece it all together in time to save this other woman.

Teresa asked Betty, "Don't you already know who this woman is, and where she is?"

Betty looked at her, "What I may know isn't helpful. A mortal must save a mortal. The mortal mind is constantly questioning, seeking Truths, aware that only a small percentage of their potential is utilized. Which explains the constant search for mind expansion. The spiritual mind knows Truths. It isn't cluttered with quests for truths. For the spiritual mind to second guess the mortal mind is an exercise not deemed valuable. Therefore, the most we can do is point them to inevitable mortal discoveries. Perhaps a little sooner than they would have made on their own. We cannot manipulate their environment."

Wow, I remember that. This is really tricky, how to help without helping. Ellen said we would work through the night, and then see what Roger, Paul and the team needed. There was another way for us to help, if needed. Ellen had a sneaky look on her face. We all looked at each other. What other way?

I had a thought, "Couldn't we just fly over the place we had the accident, turn around, go through the trees, and find the house where Ginger had been and the other woman was?"

Ellen said "Did that. I know where the house is, and there is a woman there right now." We all looked at her with our mouths open. Ellen said, "Mortals have to discover this house." Geesh.

"Is the woman okay?" I asked.

Ellen said, "She is holding up, but she is in great danger. She fed me grapes."

Mary asked, "What?"

Betty smiled, "Ellen was a mouse." She giggled while still flipping through pages and marking occasionally. Is it me? This was not making any sense anymore.

Ellen looked at Linda, "If a house is sold, what kind of papers are we looking for?"

Linda looked thoughtful and answered, "If it is a straight sale, there will be a deed."

Ellen spoke again, "I have looked through land sale documents, and there are no deeds from Nettie Wilson to James Devon. We saw the receipt. She gave him that house."

Teresa spoke up, "I saw that deed at Devon's house. It was original signature, but it didn't have a Recorder's Stamp on it. He hasn't recorded that deed yet."

I spoke, "So the only proof we have, is that receipt in Devon's office."

Ellen spoke, "I went to the tax office and the December tax bill was paid by a Clyde Jones. The form says he was the land contract owner and to send the bills to a different address than Nettie's...... AH-HAA! Guess what address was given to the tax office?"

We all answered, "Devon." Yes!

Betty asked, "Do we have a copy of this tax bill?"

Ellen answered, "No." We all looked stumped.

Mary said "Soooooooooo, a mortal has to get this, right?"

"Right," Betty and Ellen answered at the same time.

"The mortals are going to eventually discover that the woman being held is Sandy Devon, James's new bride." Ellen paused for a minute and continued, "They will be getting some information that will lead them to that conclusion, but maybe not soon enough. I have been trying to find something to prove she is missing in this information. It is not here. There *is* someone who knows a little about Sandy Devon that Roger hasn't talked to yet."

We all said at the same time, "Who?"

Ellen answered, "His secretary that he fired Christmas Eve. She was the last person to talk to Sandy from what I could get from Sandy's thoughts." Ellen threw her hands up, "I think we have to go another way here."

Betty looked at her with her eyebrows raised and asked, "Are you sure?" I was not following this conversation well at all. Here we go again. I don't have a clue what they are talking about.

Ellen looked at me, "This is going to be your call."

I know I had to look like the picture of stupid. "My call? I can't even figure out what we are doing! What are we talking about?"

Ellen took a deep breath and said, "I need a mortal that can be trusted, to relay information we know as true. A way to steer the police in a more efficient manner otherwise this could take months." She had waved her arms over the piles on the table.

"Why is it my call? Just pick a mortal.....Uh oh. You want Kim?"

"Yes, I want Kim. I will get permission from Granny to do whatever it takes to protect her. I will keep the police from thinking she is guilty or crazy and protect her from Devon."

Whoa. There is no way I would have Kim put in danger. She is at a very vulnerable time right now, "This is the only mortal in the World that you think could do this right now?"

Ellen smiled, "Of course not. We have mortals we have used for centuries. I think Granny saw this as an eventuality." Oh, pulling the Granny Card. I looked at Linda, Teresa and Mary. They clearly were leaving it up to me.

"You guys, what are you thinking?"

"I'm thinking we should trust Ellen and Betty," Mary said.

Betty laughed, "This isn't our first rodeo girls."

I looked at everyone and said, "Well, she always accused me of meddling in her life. Maybe this will just seem normal?" I had a very low expectation of that.

CHAPTER 17

We were all on my front porch. A stray cat had been there eating the food Kim had put out. It hissed at us and bolted away. Hope that wasn't an omen. "I think we should knock on the door instead of just popping in. She's watching TV and reading a book." I was getting worried we would cause her to have a heart attack.

Ellen laughed, "It won't be any less of a shock having us knock."

True, I thought. "Well, how about I go in and kind of break the ice. Then you guys can come in?"

Teresa shrugged and said, "Whatever."

I walked in. Kim jumped up, "I didn't think I would see you again so soon!" She had her long hair twisted and held with a clip on top of her head and a big oversized hockey jersey on. We hugged. She sat back down on her chair, and I sat on the oversized ottoman across the room.

"Well you know me, always with the surprises. Remember how you always *said* you liked my surprises?" I eagerly looked at Kim.

She had a deadpan look on her face, "I never said that." I was looking around the room. "Oh." I figured I might as well blurt out why I was there since Teresa had her face pressed against the front window. "Well, remember how I told you that Teresa, Linda, Mary, and I were a special 'group' going through 'almost' heaven classes?"

Kim still looked unimpressed. Then she raised one eyebrow and blurted, "You got kicked out." I couldn't believe she said that!

"No. We have hit a snag of sorts, and our 'boss', so to speak, thinks you can help us." I waited for her reaction....waiting for it...waiting for it...

"You're going to kill me?" she asked wide-eyed.

"What? NO!" Geesh. "Can the other gals come in and explain this? I need help."

Kim was looking around, "The other gals?" All of a sudden they were all in the room with us.

Kim could see Teresa, Mary, and Linda. Ellen wasn't there yet. They all started jumping up and down and hugging each other, a little crying. Kim sat back in her chair and asked Linda, "What is Mom talking about?" Kim always had Linda translate even when I was alive.

Just then Ellen popped into the room, "TAA DAA!"

Kim looked like she was going to faint, "Ellen DeGeneres? Ellen's dead?"

Ellen ran over to Kim's chair and sat at her feet. "I just look like Ellen to make your mom and the gals more comfortable. Ellen is very much alive." With that Ellen jumped up and started dancing to music from nowhere. A big disco ball appeared on the ceiling. "But I've got her moves!"

We all laughed and I looked at Kim who was giving me a deadpan stare. "I am pretty sure this is some kind of bizarre dream." It was 10:30 at night and about when Kim would be going to bed.

Ellen stopped the music and sat at Kim's feet again, "No dream, Kim. We need you to go to the police station and give some information we know, but cannot prove, to the FBI Agents working the South Bend murders." Ellen stopped to give Kim a moment to absorb those thoughts. Kim was waving for Ellen to continue. "Your mom and I will be there, but of course they won't be able to see us. We will protect you from them thinking you are guilty of anything, or crazy. Oh, and we will also protect you from the murderer." Kim's mouth fell open, but she waved Ellen to continue. "We know information the agents will discover in time, but that is the problem. We are running out of time. We need a mortal to communicate, and the decision was made you are that mortal. Well, what do you say?"

Kim swallowed hard and gave me a 'look.' Uh oh. "Let me re-cap this. You want me to go to the police station, (Ellen inserted 'tomorrow') *tomorrow*, talk to the police, (Ellen inserted 'The FBI') the *FBI*, about this serial murder thing in South Bend. Give them information they don't know, and tell them I am getting this from my 'almost' angel mom and her boss, Ellen DeGeneres."

I nodded and said, "Yes! You got it!"

Kim dropped her head to one side and looked at me, "I think I would rather you just kill me."

"Yeah! She'll do it!" I screamed.

Mary looked at Linda, "Did I miss something?"

Linda said, "No, that's the way they talk."

Ellen told Kim to be at the Police Center at 9:30 a.m. exactly, *not* Kimmy time, (Kim gave me a dirty look...I just shrugged) and to ask for SSA Roger Dance. Ellen told her we would meet her there and tell her what to do.

Kim gave me a parting hug and said, "Mom, what if they *arrest* me for knowing stuff I'm not supposed to know?" Kim was not wearing a happy face.

I tried to reassure her, "Honey, trust me, or trust Ellen."

Kim scrunched her mouth, "She's not Ellen."

"Oh yeah.... Don't do your mouth like that! You'll make wrinkles!"

Kim's eyes opened wide, "Mom, wrinkles are the least of my problems right now!"

Fair enough. "All I can say is that an angel has promised me you will not come to harm and promised you too."

Kim rolled her eyes and said, "Okay. Is this going to happen a lot? I need better clothes." That's my girl! As we left, I saw Kim looking out the window. I knew she couldn't see anything. I knew this was a bad time for her, and I probably wasn't making things any better.

Ellen touched my arm, "She is doing fine. This is actually helping her, by helping us." That made me feel better.

* * *

Ellen told us to help her go through documents in the conference room. When we got there, Betty was still flipping through papers. "You gals might want to look at the computer data. I am just about finished in here." Betty had at least forty stacks of papers filling two of the tables.

I looked at Ellen, "Aren't these guys going to wonder how all of this work got done?"

Ellen shrugged, "My experience with mortals is that they are just glad it was done. They will have plenty more to go through."

Ellen and I went to the computers and couldn't believe the amount of data still being transmitted. Data is fine, but if you don't have the time to read it all, it's useless. I think calling Kim in was a good idea. It was 9:15 a.m. the day after Christmas. I heard Roger and Paul walking down the hall toward the conference room. We all vanished as they turned the corner. They started reviewing the piles and the highlighted markings. Paul said, "I have to give it to this task team. I have never seen a group go through this much data this fast...look at this! I just hope we find something useful."

Just then the patrolman who had been wearing the Grinch hat on Christmas Eve popped his head around the corner. "Agent Dance, you've got a pretty redhead wants to see you."

Paul raised his eyebrows a couple of times, "Hey, hey! Didn't you used to have a thing for redheads?" Roger just made a face and walked toward the information desk. He saw a tall, beautiful redhead, about forty, smoothing out her skirt. She looks nervous, he thought.

She watched him walk toward her, and he noticed what a beautiful blue color her eyes were. Her skin looked like porcelain. Her long red hair fell in waves well below her shoulders. He couldn't help it. He felt himself being drawn in.

"I am Agent Dance, you wanted to see me?"

Kim looked at her watch, again. It was 9:25, she was early, had to wing it. This is why she preferred Kimmy time. "I was hoping there was somewhere private we could talk. I may have some information for you about the murders." She could hardly bring herself to say that word. Roger noticed she was uncomfortable and six feet tall. Wow.

Roger pointed toward his office, "We can go in my office down here." They started walking. Kim was close to having a panic attack. What if Mom doesn't show up, what if this was some stupid dream? What do I say? Oh my God!

They got to Roger's office and he directed her to a chair and closed his door. He sat across from her and began twirling a pen. Those eyes. "Tell me what information you have." He was looking intently at her. She didn't know how to start. All of a sudden up near the ceiling her mom and Ellen were sitting in chairs.

I said, "Tell him who you are." Kim started, "My name is Kimberly Troutman and my mom was one of the four women killed in the car accident on December 23rd, the one where one of the kidnapped women was killed." She waited for Roger to say something. He didn't, so Kim continued, "This is going to sound strange, but my mom, her friends, and her "boss" in heaven want me to tell you things to speed up your investigation." Kim exhaled. At least she got that much out.

Roger said, "What kind of things?"

Kim looked at him, "Did you get the part where they are talking to me now, dead?"

"I got that part," Roger was laughing to himself. The beautiful ones are always nuts, he was thinking.

Ellen told Kim, "He thinks you are nuts. No worry, we will offer proof if he gets Paul in here too."

Kim looked at Ellen, "Paul?"

Roger turned around to see who Kim was talking to.

Kim said, "My mom's boss said you think I'm nuts. They will give you proof, but she wants Paul in here too."

Roger was clicking his pen, "How do you know Paul?"

Kim answered, "I don't. They want him." She pointed at the ceiling.

Roger looked behind him again, "I think Paul would like to meet you." Ellen told Kim Roger thought she was certifiable...not to panic...she could fix this. Kim wasn't so sure, and she really didn't like the look Roger was giving her now. Sort of a pity look. Roger opened his phone and punched a button, "You in the building? Can you come to my office? Good."

Paul had been around the corner in the conference room and knocked on the door as he opened it. He saw Kim and his eyes twinkled. Roger introduced him to Kim and told Paul to just have a seat. Roger told Kim to tell Paul why she was there. Paul pushed his chin out in his nervous twitch as he looked at Roger. Kim exhaled and rolled her eyes. Roger said, "Kim says her mom, and her mom's boss are here in the room with us. They have information that can help us with our case. They are going to prove to us that Kim is not nuts."

Paul was thinking this should be good. Kim said, "Have both of you felt better and slept better since Christmas Eve?" Paul and Roger looked at each other and then back to Kim. She shrugged and said "I'm just saying what they are telling me to say." Paul looked around the room....nothing. "Okay, here is another one. Roger, when you were at Joy Covington's house the dog, Flea Bag, was barking up the tree. My mom and her friends were up there." Roger laid his pen down. "Here's one for Paul. You knocked over the out box on an attorney's desk, so you could read the papers. My mom's boss put those papers there for you to find. That is how you found out he was married." Paul stopped smiling.

Ellen said, "They need more." The black cat appeared on Roger's desk, winked at Roger, looked at Paul, winked at Paul, and then disappeared.

Both Roger and Paul jumped up. Roger said, "Whoa!" It looked like he was going to pull his gun. Kim covered her face and said, "Don't shoot me! I've never seen that cat in my life! I don't even want to be here!" They both slowly sat down again.

Paul said, "How did you do that?"

Kim looked at him, "Trust me, I didn't do that."

Then Ellen told Kim, "Ask Roger about his good luck cat, the one that got Devon's dog going, and Jack to admit he had a dog."

Kim looked to the ceiling, "Slow down, I can't talk that fast." Paul and Roger looked at the ceiling. "Mom said to ask Roger about his good luck cat that got Devon's dog barking and Jack to admit he had a dog."

Roger said, "Is that the cat that was just here?"

Kim said, "Yes, that is mom's boss. She can only show herself in certain ways to mortals. (Kim rolled her eyes) She said you can quit buying cat food. She doesn't eat it. She buried it." Kim shrugged, I can't believe I just said that… it's hopeless now. She couldn't believe she was in a police station telling two F-B-I agents this crap. I'm going to jail.

Ellen spoke up, "Tell them they will never sort this data in time. Sandy Devon, the attorney's wife, is being held hostage by him. They can confirm this by talking to Devon's secretary that he fired on Christmas Eve. He only married Sandy because she is coming into a bunch of money on her birthday, January 13, and then he will kill her." Kim relayed the message, and Paul started writing it down.

Paul asked Kim, "Do you have a name for this secretary?"

Kim looked up, "Claudia something. She was placed there by a temp service in October. She spoke with Sandy, in person, on Christmas Eve morning. She will confirm Sandy is not in Jamaica faster than flight records."

191

Roger looked at Kim, "How do you know about Jamaica?"

Kim answered, "You don't get this. I don't know anything. Think of me as a human telephone. I am just telling you what they are saying." She looked up at the ceiling, "Mom, can't you do something?" Roger and Paul looked at the ceiling.

Ellen said, "Tell them to look at the TV. These are Ginger Hall's last memories."

Kim swallowed, "Mom says she is going to play you Ginger Hall's last memories on the TV." They all looked to the TV and the gruesome film played out just like I had seen it before. Kim started to cry, "That was mom's crash wasn't it?"

Ellen said, "They believe you now. They just don't know what to do with it. We will get them more as soon as we have it. We are working on a couple of things for them. Just see what they say."

Kim told them what Ellen said. Roger looked at Paul then back at Kim, "Could you, all of you, (he looked behind him) give Paul and me a minute to digest this, alone?"

Kim stood up, "Thank God you believe me. I'll just wait in the hall." Roger helped her out the door and then sat back in his chair.

He looked at Paul, "I have to tell you my knees are weak."

Paul was as pale as a ghost. "No shit!" They sat for about five minutes. Each time it looked like one of them was going to say something, they stopped and shrugged.

Finally Roger said, "Let's check it all out. Maybe we did call in the Heavens."

Roger and Paul walked Kim out to her car and asked if they could call her later. She said fine and gave them some background information on herself. As she got in the car and started it Roger tapped on her window, "It took a lot of courage for you to come in today. You have to be still grieving the loss of your mother."

She thought he looked like he really meant it. "I am." She answered. "If you had known mom and her friends in life, this wouldn't be as shocking." She tried a small smile.

Roger watched her drive off. He turned and Paul looked at him, "Uh Oh…I have seen that face before." Then he laughed so hard he lost his balance and started slipping in the snow. Roger caught him. He was laughing too.

Ellen and I were in the back seat of Kim's car, and I said, "That went okay."

Kim slammed on the breaks. She was still in the parking lot, "Don't do that when I am driving!"

"I'm sorry, I thought you saw us."

Kim was frowning into the rear view mirror, "Is this what it's going to be like Mom? We need some rules."

Ellen was laughing, "She's right you know. You just can't be popping in and out of her life without warning. How 'bout when your mom is going to talk to you, most of the time, your cell phone will ring with a special tone?"

Kim was looking at Ellen in the rear view mirror. "She couldn't figure out her cell phone when she was alive! I know I am going to regret this, but what ring tone do you have in mind?"

Ellen thought for a moment and said, "How about 'I am woman'?"

Kim said no. I said, "I know, 'Help me Rhonda. Help, Help Me Rhonda'."

Kim laughed because that song had a story with us. "Yeah, I guess that will do." Ellen looked disappointed, but Kim's phone rang with "Help me Rhonda."

Ellen said, "Just testing."

Kim asked, "So if that happens, do I answer my phone or just talk to air?"

Ellen was really laughing now, "Oh gosh, I love this girl! Whichever suits your situation will be fine. If you need to speak to us, just concentrate on that. You don't need to talk."

Kim looked horrified, "Mom can read my mind?"

Ellen answered, "We have disabled her from being able to read your mind."

"Good," Kim said relieved. You could see the strain on Kim's face from the morning.

Just then Betty popped into the back seat with us, "Hi dear. I figured I should introduce myself before you get into traffic."

Kim turned all the way around to look into the back seat, "Betty White?"

Betty laughed, "No, I just look like her. I'm kind of like Ellen." They elbowed each other giggling. This isn't happening, I heard Kim think. I looked at Ellen, and she winked at me.

Betty was speaking, "Kim, I think Roger or Paul will probably call you later today. One of us will be available to help you, but in the meantime we have a great deal of work to do. Are you going to be alright dear?" she was patting Kim's head like a puppy.

Kim looked at me in the mirror, "Mom, are you sure they don't think I'm some kind of nut?"

Ellen answered, "They believe you Kim. They just have never had something like this happen to them before."

Roger and Paul had walked back into the building to the conference room which had now pretty well filled up with people. Detective Sal came up to them and said, "You guys must have worked all night to get through all of this." Roger and Paul glanced at each other and shrugged. The paperwork stacked on the tables was formidable.

"Not really. There is still a lot that has come over since last night," Paul answered.

Sal said, "You must have angels working for you after hours," and walked away.

Roger just cleared his throat and said, "Let's make a couple of calls real quick." Paul nodded his approval.

When they got to Roger's office, Paul said, "I am going to start calling temp services in South Bend. Why don't you take Mishawaka?"

Roger asked, "Claudia, right?"

"That's what your girl said," Paul answered smiling.

Paul got a hit with the first temp agency. He was given Claudia's full name and telephone number.

195

She had just called to let them know she had been fired. Paul felt that creepy shudder again. "This is spooky," he said as he punched in Claudia's number. She answered, and after Paul told her who he was, he told her he was putting the call on speaker phone, so his partner could hear her too. Paul asked, "Have you ever met the new Mrs. Devon? Sandy?"

Claudia answered, "Yes."

"When was the last time you saw her?"

"I saw her Christmas Eve morning. She was going to surprise Attorney Devon for Christmas by decorating this little house he has. She wanted to have some kind of a private Christmas party or some dumb thing like that. She said he was working so hard, she never saw him. Humpf."

Paul asked, "Is he a hard worker?"

Claudia responded, "Not that I ever saw. Just goes to funerals and swindles old ladies out of their last dime. He is a vile man. I wasn't around anymore than I had to be. He's a creep, and I am not saying that because he fired me."

Paul asked, "Can I ask why you were fired?"

"These are his exact words, on the intercom mind you. Your fat ass is no longer needed here. I have just inherited almost enough money to make even you look good, so I'm going to retire. Consider yourself unemployed. He was laughing." Paul and Roger looked at each other.

Roger said, "Claudia, this is Agent Dance, do you remember the address you gave Sandy when she came to see you?"

There was a long pause. "No. It was written on a receipt for legal services. Who was that? Oh Gosh, I can't remember." Roger told her to take her time. "I know! It was that Nettie Wilson. She had paid him for legal services by signing over some little house in South Bend. I think it had been a rental. I bet the niece knows, Joy, something. I gave her the original receipt." Roger asked Claudia to come in and give a formal statement, and she agreed.

Paul was the first to speak, "We caught him in a lie about his wife being in Jamaica, and we caught him lying about the grocery store. Not exactly enough to go to a judge."

Roger said, "I wish I could see that TV thing again. There is probably something in that background." He no more than said it, and the black cat appeared on the credenza.

Paul sat up straight, "I take back what I said about cats." Ellen made the TV come on, and the memories of Ginger Hall passed over the screen.

Roger looked at the cat, "Can we do a real slow frame by frame of this?" Ellen was licking her paw and looked at the TV. It was now playing again very slowly. When it finished, Roger looked at the credenza, and the cat was gone.

Paul spoke first, "Can we work like this, and not go nuts? I mean, it's great —it's just...I can't wrap my mind around you asking a cat to turn on the TV!" Paul looked serious.

Roger was rubbing his chin and got up to look out the window. It was still very early in the day, and he had a feeling it was going to be a very long one.

He turned to speak to Paul, "Do you consider your-self to be a spiritual man?"

Paul didn't hesitate with his answer, "Very much so. We see the worst mankind is capable of. I couldn't do this if I didn't believe in something. I don't think it is logical that spirit or souls just die with the human vessel. There has to be a greater meaning in the scheme of it all."

Roger thought about Paul's answer and decided that was probably why they worked so well together. Paul's views mirrored his own. Roger said, "I think what I find most difficult about all of this (he waved his arm toward the TV) is being faced with what appears to be Devine Truth. I can't explain what happened in here this morning, but I feel extremely privileged. I don't want to mess this up."

Roger looked at Paul who simply said, "Amen."

Roger's phone rang and he picked up and said, "Send her in." Paul almost looked afraid. "It's not Kim." Roger laughed, "It's Ginger Hall's supervi-sor from the hospital. I think she is the person that brought us the paper bag."

Paul just nodded and said, "I am going to make some calls to get the address of Nettie's old rental, starting with Joy, just in case." He left Roger's office as Jenny Camp got to the door. Roger rose to meet her and introduced himself. Jenny started with how terrible this had all been for the staff at the hospital. Ginger was thought well of by everyone.

Roger said, "I am assuming that you are the per-son who left Ginger's belongings here for us?"

Jenny nodded, "Yes, I don't know if anything there will help, but under the circumstances, well, I know the police are really stressed over all of this." Roger thought she seemed like a very warm and caring person. Exactly what he would expect from a nurse.

Roger got his notes out on Ginger and said, "We are still working on determining the last time Ginger was seen. A Mr. Davis at the hospital said she had put in for Christmas time off, and the last day he knew anyone had seen her was December 13th. Does that sound right to you?"

Jenny got a small calendar out of her purse. "No, actually I called Ginger in to work on Friday, Dec. 16th for a few hours because we were shorthanded. I did let her leave before shift end though."

Roger was taking notes, "Was there any particular reason, or do you remember, why you let her leave early on Friday?"

"I know exactly why I let her leave. She had grown pretty close to an elderly woman who had spent quite a bit of time with us over the last year, Burna George. She didn't have many visitors at all. Anyway, Ginger got some great news on Friday from Mrs. George's attorney. Burna had left Ginger a bunch of money. She asked if she could leave to meet the attorney in the parking garage to sign some papers."

Roger looked at his notes from a couple of days ago and turned his big calendar around for Jenny. "This Friday, the 16th? You are positive about the date that Ginger got the news about inheriting from Burna George?"

Jenny looked puzzled by Roger's reaction. "I *am* positive. I took the call at the nurses' station myself. That lawyer identified himself and asked for Ginger. I got her, and she started crying. I asked her what was wrong, and she said Burna had died. Then Ginger got excited and said Burna had left her money. Ginger asked to leave to meet the attorney in the parking garage. I even noted in my little book here that Ginger earned five hours for Friday, left at 4:30." Roger thanked her and asked if she could please furnish a formal statement to one of the detectives before she left. She said sure. He walked her to an empty office to have an officer take her statement and went looking for Paul.

Roger found Paul in the conference room surrounded by a couple of detectives pouring over a large map. Paul looked up and declared, "I've got an address!"

Roger said, "I've got Devon telling Ginger that Burna died a day before her body was found." Paul and Roger stared at each other and smiled.

Just then Roger's phone rang. It was Detective Ed Mars, "Roger? I've got something here. I am not sure what to do."

Roger asked him to wait while he put him on speaker. Roger asked the 'room' to be quiet, and then said, "You're on speaker in the 'room'."

Ed resumed speaking, "I followed Jack Simpson to his worksite this morning, and a neighbor let me park in their driveway. I had a great view of his truck and the door to the building. Lots of construction vehicles there. A black Lexus 430 pulls up next to Jack's truck, and some guy in a hoodie reaches in the cab, takes out some papers, and throws some junk in the back of the truck. I got a plate number. Then I walked over. Because of the light snow last night, everything in the back was snowy except a roll of rope and a partial roll of duct tape. I bagged 'em, but I think you want them. Oh yeah, I ran the plates on the Lexus, and it belongs to Judge Ashley Tait."

Paul straightened up, "Ashley?" He and Ashley had a 'thing' a couple of years ago that just died out because of work. He still cared a great deal about her and always thought someday they would try it again.

Paul looked at one of the detectives in the room, "Call her home, the courthouse, her family. Anybody! Find her." He looked at Roger, a look of urgency and shock was etched upon his face, "*He has her.*"

Roger put his hand on Paul's shoulder and said, "Let's find this house," as he bent over the map. "Maybe she is here." One of the local detectives came over and pointed to where he thought the house would be based on the address. Roger asked him to locate where Ginger Hall's body had been found. This took a little longer because they had to get a highway mile marker map. Finally, the detective placed a red dot where Ginger had died. It was a straight shot of about 200' from the house. Roger and Paul were shouting orders as they checked their weapons and Roger said, "We are going in quiet, unmarked." Roger pointed at the map, "Use four wheelers, and position here and here. Work your way to here on foot. No weapon discharging without authorization. Paul and I are going from the front. Use the x frequency. Ready?"

CHAPTER 18

Sandy thought she would probably see him today because she was running low on food. He was making sure she stayed alive. Bless his little black heart. She was being careful to wipe away all traces of saw dust from her sawing on the footboard slat. She thought she was starting to see real progress now. She was about halfway through the thickness of the slat and about three quarters of the way across it. She had bandaged both of her hands now because of the blisters, and was trying to think of a way to hide them from him. She heard a strange noise from the back door area; she turned the TV down low. She hadn't heard his motor. Then she heard fast moving footsteps, lots of them, running through the living room, and then her door burst open!

Roger was in the doorway with his gun pointed straight at her, and two men behind him came forward to flank each side of him. Roger lowered his gun and slowly walked toward her. She was the woman in the TV video they had watched with Kim. Roger felt a spooky shudder creep through his body. "Is he here?" he asked Sandy quietly.

She answered quietly, "No." Roger was looking her over for signs of torture.

He yelled, "I need cutters!"

Sandy threw herself over the lock on her ankle and said, "NO! You don't understand. You can't save me! I won't go! He will kill those other women!"

Roger tried to comfort her, but she was having no part of it. It was now Roger, Paul and Sal in the room with her. Paul looked at Roger and said, "Ashley isn't here."

Roger yelled out, "Don't disturb anything. Fix that door. Check out the grounds, basement... Report." He looked at Sandy, "Can you tell me your name?"

He was startled when she giggled, "Of course I can. I can tell you your name. I have a TV." She pointed to the television that was on, but the volume was very low. "My name is Sandy Nelson, well technically Sandy Devon, but I am going to fix that as soon as I get out of this mess!" Sal cracked a smile. "Special Agent Dance you have to really listen to me, and I don't think we have a lot of time. He should be coming here fairly soon." Roger nodded agreement. She continued, "James is a monster! He had that poor nurse a prisoner here, in that closet. (She pointed to the closet.) When she escaped, he decided to keep me here until my birthday on January 13th. I will be coming into the remainder of my trust money which is about fifteen million dollars." Roger whistled. Sandy continued, "Being that James only married me for my money, as long as he feels safe, and can keep me alive until the 13th, probably 14th to be sure about legal stuff, I am perfectly safe. He brings me food, clothes, I have the TV, I have a hidden cell phone, his, but it doesn't work here." She took a big breath. "I have thought about this. At first I was praying for someone to save me, and now, I want to save the other women. I know there is at least one besides me, and I think he has 'picked' another one."

Roger understood what she was saying. "I cannot leave you here chained to the bed. It isn't going to happen. We are the FBI. Our primary goal is to protect. I believe James is in what we call frenzy mode. He isn't thinking right, even for him."

Sandy interrupted him, "Protect? If you want to protect someone, it's those women he is raping, and he will strangle! He's scared to death I'm going to catch a cold!" Roger couldn't help but smile. This was certainly his day for strong women.

Roger looked at Sal. She was smiling ear to ear. "Don't even have to ask boss."

Roger looked at Paul, "Can we erase we were here?"

"I'll go check," Paul answered, and he was gone.

Roger looked back at Sal, "I saw a deli type place about a mile down the road. Can you get some provisions for say a day? I will get relief here for you, but…"

Sal interrupted him, "I'm already gone." She popped her head back in the door. "You play cards?" she was talking to Sandy.

"Oh yes, and get some Ho Ho's!"

Roger had a staff paramedic they had brought with them look at Sandy's palms, and he had another detective saw through the remainder of the slat. They tested that it would give away with pressure. He also gave Sandy a Taser gun she swore she wouldn't touch and made him put it under the mattress. He gave her a company issue phone in exchange for Devon's phone she had hidden in the closet.

Sandy reached in her bra and brought out a big ring of keys. "I had these made from his key ring on December 23rd. I didn't know which one, so I copied them all."

Roger threw his head back and laughed. "They have been in your bra the whole time? You are one smart gal!" Sandy was still beaming when Sal returned a few minutes later.

Sal told Roger, "I parked just off the street and gave my keys to one of the guys to drive back."

In Roger's entire career in law enforcement, he had never left a victim at the scene knowing the captor would return. He and Paul talked about how to station personnel so they were invisible but useful. They also had to consider the weather. It was freezing, and they couldn't expect anyone to be outside without any shelter.

Detective Sal joined them, "May I interrupt a minute?" They both stopped talking to listen to her. "I only need a guy that will stay close to the basement, in case he comes, and help me watch the driveway. I think she is right. He's just going to drop off food and go. I can hide in that closet when he is here and hear everything." Two people might not be enough, Paul was thinking.

206

Roger said, "I concur for now. Sal you report to me hourly."

"Got it," she answered.

Roger looked at Paul, "We'll have to come up with something for tonight."

Sal interrupted, "Jammies. Just switch out my bodyguard. I'm here for the duration." She was holding an oversized T-shirt she had bought at the deli.

Paul's phone rang as he and Roger were driving back to the police center, "Casey….damn…have you reached family? Okay, be there shortly." He clicked his phone and without looking at Roger said, "Ashley missed court this morning." He put the red light on the dash, and they sped back without talking. Roger could only imagine what Paul was feeling.

After a couple of brief updates to the team, Roger went to his office to call one of Ashley's friends, a guy he knew Ashley started dating after Paul. "Dan, Roger here, have you talked to Ashley Tait lately? Do you know who she is close to? I need to reach her and just trying to take a couple of short cuts. Can you spell that? Oh really? What was that number? They were going to go together? Uh huh….. Well thanks Dan, you've been a big help." He hung up before any more conversation could take place.

Roger was dialing his phone, and Paul came in and sat across from him. Roger whispered "Anything?" Paul shook his head. Then Roger was speaking into the phone. "Is this Darlene? This is Special Agent Roger Dance, a friend of Ashley's. I understand you went to a Christmas Eve Party with her? Yeah. Have a good time? Good. Say, I need to reach her, and she doesn't seem to be answering her cell. Would you know where she might be? Uh huh. You think she might have gone to family after all? Yeah, that's true. What time was that call? She wasn't there? Huh. Well you have helped Darlene. Happy Holidays."

Roger hung up and looked at Paul, "She went to a Christmas Eve party, bunch of law types, with her friend Darlene. Said she was going to have a quiet Christmas with a good book. Darlene got a call at 8:00 a.m., caller ID said it was Ashley. No one was there, and she couldn't get an answer later. Figured she had been calling just to say Merry Christmas and never thought about it again."

Paul was up pacing. He spun around and declared, "8:00 a.m. Christmas Day? He had her when we were at his office!"

Roger cringed, "More than likely."

Paul slammed his fist on the door, "Son of a bitch! I'm sorry, I just..."

Roger held up his hand, "I get it."

Roger's phone rang, "Dance.... wait, let me put you on speaker." Roger said, "Go ahead Al."

Detective Al Watson came on the line. "We are at Judge Tait's house now. No sign of anything in the house, but looks like the service door to the garage was tampered with. Her purse is on the garage floor. Car is gone. I've called CSI. I already checked, and GPS is not operating in her car. It's been manually disabled. Last known signal came from 2700 area of County Rd 6, this morning about 10:30, what now?" Roger told Al to have CSI report ASAP. This was now abduction of a federal judge, and for Al to report back to center.

Roger looked at Paul and said, "That location and time matched up to where Jack Simpson was working."

Paul said, "If he took her at 8:00 a.m. Christmas day, and took her car…We were at his house at 6:00 p.m. and the only vehicle was his Buick. We've had eyes on that house since we were there. He's driving her car the next morning, today, at 10:30 a.m., Where's he keeping these cars?" Just then the cat jumped onto Paul's lap.

Paul started stroking its fur without thinking, and Roger smiled, "Maybe your new friend can help with this one?"

Paul looked down and managed a half- smile. Then he looked at Roger, "This is personal for me now."

Roger said, "I know. Do you want off?"

Paul said, "Hell no." Just then the TV came on with a Santa sitting in the middle of University Park Mall telling the viewers they could already take advantage of post-Christmas sales. Santa was still talking when Paul asked, "You think he's parking cars at the mall?"

Roger reached for his phone to place a call, "We'll soon know." The TV went off, and the cat was gone.

Paul looked at Roger, "I could get used to this."

* * *

Ellen had told me to stay with Kim. Linda, Teresa and Mary had been busy at the county clerk's office with Betty. They were going through documents that had been filed but not yet recorded. Linda had pointed out that especially during property tax season, the county staff gets behind. The FBI will only be pulling items already recorded. They had thought it was worth a shot, and they were right. Betty and Mary stayed busy "breaking" office equipment to keep the county staff busy on the other side of the room, so Linda and Teresa could move paper without being seen.

Mary had tucked an employee's sleeve into the fax machine while she was using it. That was good for about twenty minutes, and kept two employees busy. Betty had the toilet overflow and the power go out. When they finished going through the entire pile of unrecorded deeds, they found seventeen unrecorded deeds to James Devon since August. Some of the deeds were part of estate filings and some were just warranty deeds. They also found two property tax bills in his name that were not the address of his office. Linda asked Betty if they could fax the documents to Roger. She said yes. The documents would have been eventually found, and they were not altering them. Linda had received the fax number for Roger's computer from Ellen, and she began sending them. The cover sheet said, "To: Roger, From: Kim." As soon as all of the documents had been faxed, Linda put them back into the piles in the same order they had been. Then Ellen called for a meeting at police central.

Kim fell asleep shortly after returning home from the police station. She had not slept well, worrying about how it was going to go with the FBI. I decided to do a little housework for her while she slept. Even the sound of the vacuum upstairs didn't wake her. I made some brownies and was just putting the foil over them when I got the call from Ellen for a meeting. I blew a kiss to Kim and left.

Five minutes later Kim's cell phone rang. She looked at the caller ID, and it said Govt.....okay. "Hello?" It was Agent Dance.

"Kim, I need your help with this fax you sent me."

Kim was puzzled, "I didn't send you a fax."

Roger was smiling, "Yes you did, about five minutes ago. I can see it is from the county clerk's office. Didn't you say that you worked with your mom and another gal doing mortgages, in addition to your job at the casino?"

Kim answered, "Yes."

Roger continued, "Looks like a bunch of deeds, but our guys have already searched public records."

Kim asked, "Do you see Register of Deeds Stamp on these deeds?"

Roger answered, "Where would I find those?"

Kim said, "Real big, right on the top of the page, stamp says Register of Deeds, will have the signature of the clerk and a date?"

"Nope."

Kim thought for a moment, "Okay, I think if you check the dates of the deeds you will find they are all recent, meaning they have not been recorded yet. They wouldn't show up in a public records search."

Roger then asked, "I don't see addresses on these, just legal descriptions. What is the quickest way to get addresses?"

Kim thought a moment and said, "If your people can access the tax rolls for the counties showing in the legal descriptions, they could match even a partial description to an address. The tax computers at the county level are more accurate than the other data bases."

Roger said, "We had a break this morning after you left."

Kim answered, "I know. Mom told me."

Roger added, "We also had a setback."

"I know, Mom doesn't know anything, but she says they are trying to do anything they can." Kim said, "Agent Dance?" Roger told her to call him Roger. "Roger, Mom says this guy is real evil. Her word." Coming from Kim this may be more than just an expression.

Roger was careful in his response, "Your mom and her friends have already helped a lot. I just hope we prove ourselves worthy."

Kim liked him, and she said, "Did you need anything else?" Roger answered no, and said goodbye.

Paul was excited as he pulled papers off Roger's printer. "I count nineteen properties, all in St. Joseph County, all since October 1. There must be a *reason* he held up on having these deeds recorded."

Roger was on the phone to Ray in IT. "Ray, I have been meaning to call you all morning…busy here… Yeah thanks. Look, first I'm going to scan you about nineteen legal descriptions in St. Joseph County.

Can you access the property tax data base and get me addresses? Well try hard. Also cancel the airline info…don't need it…and cancel the phone trace on Devon's phone. He is using Sandy's. I sent Devon's phone to forensics to get his info. They should be contacting you."

Paul had started scanning the documents to Ray and said, "If he owns these homes he could be keeping the women at any one of them. He may have Ashley at one of these! Do you realize it is already 3:00? We need the clocks to stop." At that, they both looked up to the wall clock which was steadily ticking away the seconds. Then they both started laughing. It must have been tension relief because neither one of them could stop.

Paul was wiping his eyes when the stocky patrolman knocked on the door and said, "Your line has been tied up. Just got a call, we have another body." Paul went pale.

Roger asked, "Our guy?"

The patrolman answered, "The detective there thinks so. This one's in a house. Found by a HUD inspector." He handed Roger a slip of paper with the info on it and said to Paul, "The Chief is looking for you guys."

CHAPTER 19

Paul and Roger drove together to the location. The flashing police lights could be seen from three blocks away. Troopers were redirecting traffic and had taped off the entire block. People were standing in their front lawns and in the middle of the street trying to see what was going on. Paul ran up the driveway and slowed only long enough to hear the detective on sight say, "M.E. is in there. I've kept everyone else out." Roger followed Paul into the house noting there was an SUV in the garage. He heard voices from down the main hall.

Paul was quickly walking back toward him. "It's not Ashley," he kept walking. Roger saw him throwing up outside in some bushes.

Roger walked into the room where a young woman had been bound to a chair with duct tape and ropes. She had obviously been dead for some time. The medical examiner, Dr. Ross said, "Been dead at least a week."

Roger asked him, "Strangled?"

The M.E. shook his head, "This one starved to death, rough way to go, one of the worst." Roger

215

called CSI and looked around the room. There was an inflatable bed, deflated in the corner. The windows were boarded up in the bedroom. There was evidence rats had been in the room and feeding on her. The rest of house was empty. In the kitchen there was an empty beer bottle and a Menards' receipt from about a week ago, charged to a Visa, signature unreadable.

Roger opened his phone, "Ray? I know they are killing me too. I have to pass it on. We have another one. Run this Visa number for me." Roger read off the number and waited. "Thanks, I had a hunch. Send that to me, would you? Thanks." and he snapped his phone shut. He was calling in the plate number as Paul walked into the garage. The voice on the other end of the line gave him a name and address, he wrote it down. Roger looked at Paul, "You okay?"

Paul nodded, "What you got?"

Roger answered, "Visa receipt in the kitchen belonging to Jack Simpson and a beer bottle that probably will have his prints on it. Car belongs to Sara Huffman, Notre Dame student, and student housing address. I'll send officers there now and have the family notified."

Paul went into the house, looked around, came out, and asked the detective to point out the person who found the body. The officer pointed to a man near the street holding a laptop and a small stack of file folders. Paul introduced himself and asked him to repeat what he had told the detective. Roger had joined them and was taking notes.

"Well, like I told that officer, when a house is in foreclosure, if it was an FHA mortgage, and the asset manager is ready to put the house on the market, I get called to do an appraisal for the lender. I got the call this morning to do this appraisal, but the HUD key box lock wasn't on the door. I had to jimmy the garage service door there. That happens a lot lately. Anyway, I saw this car in the garage which is really unusual. When I opened the kitchen door, …the smell…. Anyway, I thought an animal or something… I just called the cops. Never even went in the house."

Roger and Paul thanked him and walked away, so they could talk. Roger dialed Kim, "On a fore-closed home the asset manager is usually what?"

Kim answered, "Usually a law firm, sometimes a local attorney"

Roger interrupted her, "Would a HUD appraiser know who the asset manager is?"

Kim answered, "Yes, the asset manager would actually order the HUD appraiser to go to the house and report back to him." Roger hung up.

Kim sat looking at her phone, "Goodbye to you, too. Geesh."

Roger walked over to the appraiser and asked, "What asset manager ordered this appraisal?"

He looked annoyed at Roger, but looked at his phone for an Internet App. "Here it is," he said, "Law Firm of James Devon." Roger said thanks and walked away.

He looked at Paul and said, "I have a real bad feel-ing. There are a lot of foreclosed homes around here. If Devon has control over when they can be entered, he could stash women for months, and no one would know. He wanted this one found to set up Jack."

Paul was nodding and said, "You know the Chief is looking for you, but I am about to pass out from hunger here. Pub?"

Roger looked at his watch, "It is 4:00 already, and I haven't eaten yet either. Good call."

Roger remembered that Detective Ed Mars had been watching Jack Simpson since 5:00 a.m.. He dialed him as he drove, "Ed, I'm sorry, I just left you out there hanging. You wouldn't believe the day we are having...oh, you heard, well...just got another body...really. Look, if you can get someone to relieve you, I still want eyes on Jack but more for security than surveillance. It looks like Jack may have a target on his back. Thanks Ed." Paul had his eyes shut and his head back against the headrest. Roger glanced over, "We'll find her."

They were at the Pub and found their favorite seats at the end of the bar. Larry came over for their orders, "You guys have a good Christmas?" Then he lost his smile and said, "Of course not. Sorry guys, I wasn't thinkin'." They each ordered two burgers and soda.

Paul looked at Roger, "You know I have felt better and slept better since Christmas Eve." They both chuckled. That was the last they spoke until the burgers got there. Paul said, "Remember earlier today when you said you felt privileged?" Roger nodded. Paul continued, "We wouldn't have found Sandy in that house for at least another week."

Roger said, "I was thinking that."

About five minutes later Paul looked at Roger and asked him, "Why us? There is so much going on in the world."

Roger took a drink of soda and answered, "Kim says our guy is evil, her mom's word, not hers. Maybe they know we need help."

Paul looked serious and then smiled, "You know that last time you called her, you didn't say Hi, Bye, nothing; just hung up. Got to work on your technique there buddy." Roger shrugged and kept eating his burger.

Roger looked at Paul, "If Devon is an asset manager for HUD, using foreclosed homes to stash women, your guess where this may end up?"

Paul answered, "That doesn't count the fax from Kim of all the properties Devon owns." Roger said he was going to call headquarters and get more agents on this. Paul just shook his head, "You know the headaches we're going to have with new guys."

"Yup, let's start with the Chief." Roger put money on the bar, and they left. On the way to the center Roger called Ray again, "I'm surprised you are still taking my calls." Roger chuckled. "One more favor, get someone at HUD. I need to know how many properties, and the addresses, of foreclosed homes that Attorney James Devon is the asset manager on. I am serious. Yes, HUD, Ray. I'm sure there is one brain there somewhere….. There isn't another way." Roger hung up.

Paul looked at him, "Like that, no goodbye." Roger shrugged.

They were about a block from the center and Roger's phone rang. It was Detective Sal. "He just pulled in. I will call you when he leaves." Roger clicked the phone shut.

Paul said, "I'm afraid to ask."

"That was Sal. Devon just got to the house. She'll call when he leaves. I think we should be in the neighborhood."

"Right," Paul said. Roger put the light on his dash —no sirens.

* * *

Betty and Ellen had a short meeting with all of us to give us our assignments. Ellen told Teresa to go stay with Sal and Sandy at the house. She told Mary and me to go to all of the houses on the tax list from the county clerk's office.

I raised my hand, "What are we supposed to do at these houses?"

Betty answered, "Look for dead mortals, dear."

Mary and I looked at each other. *This can't be right...*EEE GADS. Mary asked, "What is Linda going to do?" I think she was hoping for a trade.

Ellen answered, "Linda is going to be with me watching Devon." I read Mary's thoughts. She was thinking for once she would rather be with me. Huh.

* * *

Teresa was outside the house checking things out when Devon pulled in the driveway. He sat in the car a couple of minutes and then got out carrying a paper bag. He went into the house through the back door, and Teresa went into his car to see if she could find anything useful. Lots of garage door openers, a whole bag full. The rest was trash, used food bags, a couple of pairs of shoes, maps. She went inside to watch over Sal and Sandy. Devon had come into the bedroom where Sandy was and just stood in the doorway. "I'd like to say you are more trouble than you are worth, but that's not actually true is it wifey?" Sandy had her bandaged hands hidden under the blanket.

There was such a sneer in his voice it made Sal's skin crawl. She was in the closet with her gun drawn. She had loosened the trim around the door just enough to give her a sliver of a peep hole. She could see most of the left side of his face, ugly bastard. Teresa was smacking him on the back of his head, but he couldn't feel it. It made Teresa feel better though.

He dropped the paper bag on the floor next to the TV. "Sorry I can't stay and chat. Got a date!" He walked over to the window by the bed and tested the boards. They were secure so he left the room. She heard the kitchen door shut and the lock click. A minute later his car started, and he was gone. Sal came out from the closet and checked out the kitchen and living room windows. She didn't see a car.

She yelled, "All clear" for the benefit of Patrolman John Douglas who was in the basement. She then called Roger, "He's gone. Dropped off a bag of food and said he had a date. Sandy was right. He doesn't even come near her."

Roger said thanks to Sal as he and Paul watched Devon's Buick turn onto the highway. "We can't risk him spotting us," he said to Paul.

Paul was grinding his teeth, "I know." Roger called to the center and spoke with the team leader. Roger instructed him to have observation points between the exit Devon just entered and Devon's office at home, and to report. No tailing, just observation. Teresa was sitting on the bed watching Sal and Sandy play cards. She kept yelling out moves, but no one could hear her.

Ellen and Linda were in the backseat of Devon's car. Ellen was sending Linda filtered thoughts from Devon. They were already filtered for Ellen from Granny. This was one sicko. The first thought Linda heard was "Fine...Just let them starve", and he was laughing. "Bored. I'm Bored. Where are you pretty girls? Where are you? At the mall? Should we go shopping?" He was laughing. Then it sounded like he was talking to someone, "You didn't think I could do it did you? BITCH!" He slammed his fist on the dash and screamed, "BITCH! PRETTY MOMMY! UGLY boy! PRETTY MOMMY! UGLY BOY!"

Yikes! Linda was looking for a seat belt, every time he said pretty mommy he was banging his hands on the steering wheel. His eyes looked crazed. He reached into his glove box and laid a Taser gun on the seat. Then he started giggling like a child.

Linda was in full panic mode and looked at Ellen, "We can't just watch him do this, can we?"

Ellen looked back at her, "We'll do what we can." He made a sharp turn on to an exit ramp, and they saw a sign for University Park Mall, next exit. Ellen winked and a tire blew, and then another. She looked at Linda and said, "Let's go to police center. He is going to be at least two hours getting back on the road, and he will probably go home." Ellen said, "You might call Kim and have her let Roger know where Devon is."

Linda was grateful for a chance to talk to Kim. "Yes," Kim answered.

"Did the ring tone work?" Linda asked.

"Yes, but I thought only mom was using it?"

Linda said, "Guess not…Ellen just told me to call you. Why do you sound funny, are you at work?"

"Yes, what do you need? It's okay." Linda told her what she wanted, and she said she would call Roger in about five minutes. She had a break coming up.

In addition to being a mortgage loan officer, Kim was a dealer at the Great Lakes Casino. The Gaming Commission probably wouldn't be thrilled if they knew she had 'spiritual' friends. When she heard the "Help me Rhonda" ring tone she just started talking. She was dealing Black Jack and the old guy at her table kept thinking she was talking to him. He kept saying, "Yes, what?" "What? What did you say? Who's mom? Do I need something? What's okay?" She convinced the old man she hadn't been talking, and he left for another table. A couple of minutes later Kim was tapped off to go on break. She called Roger and told him what Linda had said. He thanked her and called to stop the observation points. No sense wasting manpower. There were thirty people dedicated to this case and calling in more. Not to mention the staff of back office people running data checks, etc. .... unbelievable.

* * *

Mary and I arrived at our first address. The house was dark and didn't look like anyone had been there in a long time. I said, "Cool, nobody here, let's go!" Mary frowned at me, no sense of humor. We walked through the garage door, our way, and — yup, a car....not liking this. We walked into the house, adjusted our sensors to "high," something didn't smell right. We walked down the long hall to a bedroom where the door was cracked open a bit. We both peeked in and saw a body of a woman. She had been bound with duct tape and rope to a chair, tipped over and her skin and body tissues were oozing out everywhere. I looked at Mary and screamed, "Meet you in the garage." I took off.

In the garage we spent about five minutes holding up the walls while we hyperventilated and eventually composed ourselves. We made note of the vehicle type, plate number and connected it to the address in our memory guide. I looked at Mary; neither of us looked very chipper.

"One of us should go back in and see if there is a purse or anything that says who she is."

Mary looked at me with one eyebrow up and her hands on her hips, "One of us should probably do that." She wasn't moving, and her chest was still heaving.

I said 'fine' and went in. One minute later I was back. "No purse," I exhaled as I got back to the garage. I was leaning on the hood of the car trying to get that image out of my head and asked Mary, "Well, where do we go next?"

Mary took out her copy of the list, and like a sick version of "Trick or Treat," we made our way around South Bend.

We called Ellen when we were done, and she told us to meet her at the Police Center. Ellen asked me to call Kim and give her a message for Roger about what we had discovered, ASAP. I called Kim and gave her the message. She wrote it down and said, "I don't think Roger can take this Mom."

"Roger has to know. We'll do everything we can honey."

Kim called Roger just as he and Paul reached the parking lot of the police center.

"Hi Kim," it was Roger answering.

Kim said, "I am feeling like a stalker, but Mom said I had to get this information to you ASAP. She and her friends are doing a lot of work trying to cut through red tape to make it easier for you."

Roger paused and said, "It sounds like you are trying to prepare me for bad news. Paul is here. Can I put you on speaker?"

Kim said yes, and Roger told her to go ahead, "Mom says that the fax you got today with the nineteen legal descriptions, you really wouldn't have mortal knowledge of those addresses until tomorrow. So there is no way you can pass on this information until they think up something."

Roger said, "Okay." He had a bad feeling in his stomach.

"Mom says of the nineteen houses they went to, thirteen have dead women, been dead a while, starved, and ten have cars in the garages. They have the addresses and vehicle info they will get to you somehow tomorrow morning. Mom said to tell you the houses that have utilities turned on are the ones they found the bodies in."

Roger and Paul were speechless. Finally Paul spoke, "Did you say we have thirteen more bodies?"

Kim answered, "Yes, Roger, does it make sense to you that you would have no mortal way of knowing this tonight? Mom said it was crucial that you understood how important that was."

Roger answered, "Yes. Tell your Mom thank you. I have a lot of decisions to make in a very short time."

Kim said, "I'll tell her, and no offense, but I hope I don't talk to you again for a long time." Roger said goodbye.

Paul said, "I think I could cry."

Roger looked thoughtful, "Do you remember that conference we went to last year in Arlington?"

"Yeah."

Roger continued, "They had some pretty ridiculous statistics, we thought, about how the average serial killer victim numbers were increasing. Unprecedented, and would keep getting worse. Today's serial killer was so much more driven. Remember? We thought they were grand standing."

"Well, Devon will be a great example for the next conference."

They were walking toward the building. Roger asked Paul to keep the Chief busy about fifteen minutes, and then he would deal with him. In the meantime, he was going to call headquarters and try to get some people here by tomorrow morning.

Roger went into his office, shut the door, and dialed FBI Central Headquarters in Quantico. When he was connected to the Director, it appeared from Roger's expression that he had gotten what he wanted. He walked into the room where Paul was speaking with Chief Doyle. Roger could tell the pressure had pushed the Chief to his breaking point.

Roger felt bad for anyone in the Chief's position because the law enforcement side of this kind of problem was equal to the political pressures. They seldom played out without casualties. Roger explained to the Chief that he had just hung up from his Director at the FBI, and additional resources were being brought in tomorrow. This should give his people some much needed relief. He also explained to the Chief they had positively identified James Devon as the perpetrator, and their goal was to keep Devon under control until they could safely extract the location of his known live hostages, one of which was a federal judge. He hoped the situation would play out in about two days and be done, except for cleanup.

Roger wasn't sure how up to date the Chief was. Things had been moving pretty fast. He was inserting as much information as he could without risking insult. He told the Chief about Devon planting evidence against Jack Simpson in his truck and at the last crime scene. Roger's plan now was to contact Jack and bring him into the plan as a Person of Interest to keep Devon feeling like he was winning.

The Chief said, "Hardly seems fair to ask this Simpson guy to ruin his life to help us."

Roger said, "This is where I really need your help and that of your people. I want to keep his name off the radar. I want everyone to refer to him as POI. He may not cooperate, but that is my plan."

Chief Doyle said, "So my homework assignment is to explain to the DA and the Mayor that we know who the bad guy is, but we don't want to arrest him. Instead, we want to hold a guy we can prove is innocent? Have I got that right? How do you propose to word this to this press?"

Roger looked thoughtful, "I want to talk to Jack Simpson myself tonight and make sure we can trust him to contain the plan. He has a history of having drinking issues."

The Chief rolled his eyes and said, "Oh great."

"I will get back to you yet tonight or first thing in the morning. Are we good?"

The Chief looked at him, "You boys have done an unbelievable job since you've been here, so yes, we're good. I just hope my heart holds up 'til this case ends. I'll call the DA and the Mayor." With that he left the room, noticeably tired and feeling more than a little out of touch.

Paul said, "How many guys are we getting tomorrow?"

"I'm not sure, but I tried to make it sound bad. I'm supposed to get a call back." Just then his phone rang. It was the Director. "Yes Sir? Thank you, Sir. Exactly who is coming? Good. Do my best Sir." Roger looked at Paul, "Didn't hurt that Notre Dame is his alma mater. We'll have five guys from Indy, three from St. Joseph, Michigan, and there are three more that can come from Chicago if we need them. They'll report here at 8:00 a.m. sharp. I'm still lead." Paul was relieved and said he would go update the Chief in person.

* * *

Ellen had Linda, Mary, and I meet her in Chicago in the space station type office of Agent Ray Davis, Roger's Information Tech, to make sure the documents Roger needed in the morning would arrive at the right time. She had Teresa stay with Sandy and Sal. We all sort of floated around his desk and watched Ray's fingers fly across the keyboards. There were eight monitors in total making a semi-circle around his desk. He was amazing. He had a phone cradled between his shoulder and his ear, and he was pleading, "Please, I know HUD is a large organization. I'm FBI. *I get it*. It is urgent I speak to someone immediately who can get me the asset manager information I need. There are lives at stake here! Do not put me on hold again! Damn! Damn!"

Ellen said, "Watch this!" She jumped up behind Ray's computer monitor and said, "Everyone give a warm welcome to Dotty, the Director of HUD Asset Management!" Ellen was taking a bow.

Just then Ray's other line rang. "Yes," he answered. Then he sat up real straight and repeated his request to the caller. "Oh thank you so much! Your direct line? Yes, I'm ready. Thank you!" and he hung up.

He was looking at his monitors and in two minutes they started streaming all kinds of data, line after line rolled down his screens. Ray started rocking in his chair laughing, "There is a God!"

Ellen said very deadpan, "Computers always bring out the religion in mortals. Let's let Ray take a little nap." She placed her hand on his head, and it looked like he passed out. He actually slid off the chair. Ellen said, "I guess he was tired." She moved him to a small office sofa and made a chair for each of us.

Mary said, "I am not the world's best computer guru."

Ellen said, "You don't have to be. I am going to color code the information that has come in with one thought, (she was bragging), and all you have

to do is press select on every item that is that color."
She looked at us, "Well? What color?"

Linda and Mary were fighting over red or green.
I have always liked the purples. Ellen had curled up
next to Ray on the couch. "I don't know how Betty
did it so long," she said, "When you guys decide, just
type in the color, and hit enter. Nite, nite." It looked
like she was sleeping.

I looked at Linda and Mary, "You know, that
brings up a good point. Do we sleep?"

Linda looked at me, "Have you pooped yet?"
Huh? Oh. Wow, that seemed like years ago! Mary
typed in blue and hit enter. Linda and I looked at
her. "Blue? Nobody said 'Blue.'"

Mary looked authoritative, "That's why I picked
it."

Within minutes we were scrolling away, hitting
'enter' when we saw the color blue. This went on
for hours. Wow. The government has its fingers in
everything. Linda came to a screen that said County
Tax Data. She scrolled down a little, looked at Mary,
and said, "I think I'm in a different thing now. This
is the County Tax Data. What do I do?"

From the couch Ellen rolled over and threw her
arm over Ray's chest, (he was snoring) "Just type
another color and continue," she said never opening her eyes. Linda typed red (her original choice)
and the data started running again. At about 8:00
p.m. we were done. Mary tip-toed over to wake
Ellen. Ellen popped up and said "Boo! I just loved
that didn't you?" Mary was still holding her chest
from shock when Ellen said, "Let me encrypt this

with a time pause and a "special" Ellen command. Regardless of when Ray sends this, it will not appear for Roger until the time is right. Okay, let's wake up Ray, make sure he thinks he did all of this, and head back to the police center."

Ray woke up and noticed he was on the couch. "Shit! Why did I do that? I don't have time for a nap! Shit!" He walked over to his monitors and was rubbing his chin. He remembered getting the top gal at HUD. He remembered the data stream. Wow, he had compiled the filters for HUD and the County? Damn, he was so tired he didn't even remember. Well, might as well get it to Roger. He hit a couple of keystrokes, and his computer said, "Data Sent." Ellen smiled; she knew it wouldn't be received until the time was right. She set his computer to give him a message tomorrow morning that the data had been damaged, and his system restored and batched it for future transmission. When Ellen was ready, it would look to him like it just happened. She couldn't take the chance her "manipulation" could appear as anything but mortal or machine error.

* * *

Teresa had been watching the evening news and a couple of sit coms with Sandy, Sal and John (the basement cop). Sandy started to sniffle a little. "I always wanted to do something important with my life. My mom always told me I could make a difference if I gave things enough thought. I look at what you guys do every day. How can I ever do something more important than that?"

Sal said, "You know Sandy, you are going to inherit enough money that if you can find someone you trust to help you manage it, I bet you will think of a lot of things you could do to make this a better world. Things John and I could never do!"

Sandy gave Sal a big hug, "You are right! Here I sit feeling sorry for myself, and I could be thinking about how I can make this a better world! For real!" They decided to play some more cards for a while and eat the last of the Ho Hos.

* * *

Roger asked Paul to get the white boards ready for tomorrow morning. Things had been happening so fast that the boards didn't even resemble their case anymore. Paul agreed, "We don't want our new visitors thinking we are slackers."

Roger said, "Right."

He went to his office and dialed Jack Simpson. He was surprised when Jack answered, "Howdy."

Roger said, "This is Special Agent Dance. Is this Jack Simpson?"

Jack almost choked on his food, "Yeah, this is me." He was giving a questioning look to Detective Ed Mars who was sitting in Jack's truck with him, eating chicken Joy had brought to the job site. Jack was done working now, but Joy had to go back and cover for the dinner cook who had called in sick.

Roger said, "Jack, we have had some developments here that are unusual, and we are thinking you may be able to help us. Would you be willing to come to the police station and give me a listen? I promise I won't take much of your time." Roger waited for the answer.

"Absolutely, Sir! I can be there in ten minutes!" and he hung up. Jack looked at Ed and asked, "Are you sure they know I'm innocent? They want me to come to the police station."

Ed thought a minute and said, "Last I heard you were one of the good guys." Jack beamed.

Roger sat the phone down with serious misgivings. This may not work.

The black cat was on Roger's credenza looking at him, "I hope this isn't more bad news." The cat leaped over and sat on his lap. Roger started petting it, and it fell asleep on him.

Paul came in and said, "Not more bad news?"

Roger looked up smiling, "No, just a cat."

Paul shook his head and continued, "I just wanted to let you know I am going to be a while getting that board right. Do you know where the forensic reports are?" Roger said the last he saw them, someone had them in piles on the corner desk, organized by victim, type of evidence, and date received. Paul pulled his head back, "Wow, aren't we good?" and left the room.

CHAPTER 20

J ack entered the building through the main entrance and told the desk officer he was there to see Special Agent Roger Dance. Roger quickly arrived and walked him to his office. Along the way he popped his head into the 'room' to notify Paul. When the three of them were seated, Jack said, "You guys still think I'm one of the good guys, right?"

Roger didn't answer that, but he said, "Jack, I have a very important decision to make tonight, maybe the most important decision of my career. I am, maybe, going to ask you to make the most important decision you will ever make." He waited a minute to see Jack's reaction. None. "I know in the past you have had a problem with drinking. I am not saying this to make you feel bad, but we have lives at stake here. I have to be able to trust everyone involved."

Jack looked at Roger, "I don't know what you want from me, but I guess it's fair to ask me about my drinking. I *have* had trouble with drinking. *Lately*, but I'm not sure why, I haven't wanted to drink that much. I think I have only had two beers in three days." He looked at Roger, "*The old me could do three beers in two minutes.*" He continued, "I think it happened when Joy got so worried about me after you talked to her. I saw the look on her face when she looked at me, and, you know, there was no *respect* there. I didn't like that. I am trying to win her trust back. Does it make sense that *before* I didn't see a reason *not* to drink, and now I do?"

Roger took a deep breath, he decided to trust Jack. He almost didn't have a choice. "We *know* who the guy is that is doing all of these murders. He has hostages now that he is holding, and one of them is a federal judge. He will kill them if we don't find them soon." He let Jack soak that in for a minute. Jack's eyes were wide open, but he wasn't saying anything. Roger continued, "Our only hope to save those women is for him to think his plan is working. We think we know what his plan is. We need to buy enough time for ourselves to locate where he has these women hidden, and we are close."

Jack still wasn't saying anything but he was shaking his head. Roger said, "This monster's plan is to frame you for these murders. He has been planting evidence that points directly at you." Roger leaned back in his chair, and Jack jumped up from his.

"Me? Why the hell me? Out of this whole world, he picks me?"

Paul put his hand on Jack's shoulder and pressed him back into the chair, "Jack can I ask you a question?" Jack slowly nodded. Paul continued, "When you went to your lawyer's office two days ago, did he get you a beer?"

Jack looked surprised at the question, "Yeah, not my brand but…"

Paul interrupted, "Did he ask you many questions about how you spent your time. The places you go, work, stuff like that?"

Jack was sitting up straighter. He leaned forward toward Paul and whispered, "Are you telling me my *LAWYER* is the monster?" Paul looked at Roger.

Roger said, "That is exactly what we are saying. That beer bottle with your prints and a Visa receipt from Menards with your signature and account number were found this afternoon with the body of a dead woman." Jack went pale, his jaw dropped, and his eyes were wide open. "Detective Mars saw a man take papers out of the cab of your truck at the worksite earlier and throw a rope and a partial roll of duct tape into the back of your truck."

Jack was on his feet stomping. "No way! Are you shittin' me? No way!"

Roger continued, "The man that put that stuff in your truck was driving the car of our missing judge."

Jack was back to sitting but shaking his head and moaning. Then he looked at Roger, "Now what?"

Roger smiled at Paul and spoke to Jack, "We need him to think his plan worked. He knows we found that body today if he watches the news, and I'm sure he does. He is going to expect that eventually you will be arrested. That is the only way he will feel safe and not kill these women. He knows forensics take a little while, but…"

Jack swallowed hard, stood up, and put his wrists straight out in front of him. "We don't have a choice man. Arrest me!" He turned his head, but Roger could see the tears on his cheeks.

Paul said, "Sit down Jack. You need to tell us if Joy can be trusted to be made aware of our plan. If one person says the wrong thing, those women are dead." Paul got very close to Jacks face and said, "We are naming him the monster for a reason. One word will *kill* these women."

Jack was waving his arms in front of him, "I get it, I get it!" Jack continued, "I know in the big picture this is just a teeny tiny problem, but ...if, when I get arrested for this, won't I lose my job? The whole world will hate me. I know it sounds selfish."

Roger spoke up, "That is precisely why we almost didn't ask for your help, Jack. Those things could happen if your name gets out, and I'm telling you it is easy for that to happen. You also have Joy to think about. She may not be willing to have her life turned upside down. This thing has dominated the national news every night for over a month."

Paul quickly added, "The good news is we think we are within days of getting him. When it's over we can get your job back, if that happened, and you will probably be a hero."

Jack wasn't talking, and Roger thought he might have to arrest him for something just to keep him from talking to anyone for a couple of days. When Jack said, "I think you are right that Joy should know what is going on and have a vote. She doesn't get home from work tonight for another hour. Can I call you and tell you what she said?"

Roger and Paul both said, "Certainly."

Jack was in the doorway, "He is going to have to think I am in custody, right?"

Roger answered, "Right"

"Do I have to stay in a prison cell this whole time?"

Paul said, "I think we can work out something more comfortable than that."

Jack looked scared, "Are you guys going to call me a suspect on the news?"

Paul answered, "We will probably release a statement that we are detaining a person of interest. A POI."

Jack looked at Paul, "You called me that before." Jack smiled. "Can I have a beer when I tell Joy?"

Paul laughed, "You better have *two*."

They watched Jack walk slowly to his truck. His head was down, and the snow was piling on his shoulders. Paul said, "This is no little thing we are asking of him. I hope he's tougher than he looks."

Roger said, "That's what I'm counting on. Let's get that board looking something like this crazy case." The black cat was lying in a chair watching Roger and Paul piece the case back together on the white boards. The night shift guys were coming in and applauding at the sign that said, "New Troops Arriving in a.m.!" They congratulated Paul and Roger on finding Sandy.

One detective walked up and said, "You know, if I were him, this Devon, when I saw on the news we had a POI, and I knew it was Jack, I would be moving the wife real fast. He knows Jack has a connection to that house." Paul and Roger looked at each other. They hadn't even had time to think about that.

Roger said, "Very good point." The detective walked out of the room smiling.

It took Roger and Paul three hours to reconstruct the boards. They had just finished and decided they needed to get a bite to eat when Jack stood in the doorway of the 'room' with a duffle bag on his shoulder, and a huge tray of something covered in foil. "Can I sit this down? It's hot!" Roger pointed to a long table next to the wall, and Jack took the foil off. It was a huge platter of fried chicken. "I got mashed potatoes and gravy in the truck if somebody will give me a hand."

Paul said he would help. Then he looked at Roger, "This is one crazy case!"

It didn't take very long for the room to fill with everyone that worked in the building. The smell of that chicken swept down the halls and brought them running. Jack declared with a big grin, "That's my girlfriend Joy's special recipe! We're gonna own a restaurant someday!" People were picking the little pieces off the bottom of the tray. When it looked like everyone had eaten, Roger asked the room to be cleared of everyone except the task force. Jack walked over to Paul and asked, "Am I on the task force?"

Paul realized he was serious and answered, "No Jack, you are a civilian. We have a conference room around the corner if you want to wait in there. Remember not to talk to people about why you are here, even if they look official. You are top secret."

Jack got a very serious look on his face, nodded, and walked down the hall looking for the other conference room. Paul walked over to Roger who had just finished talking to Chief Doyle. "Got a minute?" he asked. They walked over to the corner to talk away from everyone. Paul relayed the conversation he had with Jack and ended with, "One wrong word to Devon and this whole thing ends up in our face. I'm still not sure he *gets* that."

Roger said he had the same concern. "Maybe we need a little fear injected before we put him with Devon in the morning. Go tell him we want him in here for some of the meeting. We'll get this out of the way before the new guys get here tomorrow."

While Paul went to get Jack, Roger went back to Chief Doyle to explain the concern about Jack. Chief Doyle was nodding as Roger spoke, and then the Chief said, "Well, the way I see it, there are downsides both ways. You are going to take heat for letting him see and hear official information during an investigation and prior to an arrest, particularly knowing he will be in contact with the actual subject. On the other hand, if he isn't fully prepared before he talks to this guy, those women are dead. Devon will smell a trap a mile away."

Roger made a quick call to Detective Sal telling her they were thinking that after Devon saw the news tomorrow he would be moving Sandy. He told her to send him a text as soon as he showed up there and to instruct Sandy on things she might be able to do to stall him as long as she could.

After Sal talked to Sandy about her call from Roger, Ellen called Teresa to let her know what might happen tomorrow. Ellen told Teresa to follow Devon and Sandy after they left tomorrow in case the police lost them. Teresa said okay and went back to watching John cheat at cards. Even cheating he couldn't beat the girls. Sandy was smiling. John made her feel smart. Of course he was trying to.

When all the members of the task force had arrived, Paul started the meeting with, "We see the end to this!" The room broke out into cheers. In the back of his mind he was thinking, except for the 13 bodies we are going to find tomorrow. He continued, "I would like to introduce everyone to Jack Simpson. He has been chosen by Devon to be the fall guy, and he has volunteered to pretend to be our POI."

Jack stood up, waved at everyone, and then sat down. Paul noticed Jack had taken out a little notebook and a pen. He was going to take notes. Paul walked over and took Jack's notebook, "Nothing said in this room, leaves this room. Clear?"

Jack was stunned, "Yeah, sorry, I …never mind."

Paul continued, "For the benefit of Jack, I am going to review what Devon has done, that we know about. Some of you have been in the field and have not been briefed on all of today's news. One big item is that the FBI Lab has DNA from Ginger Hall. She escaped, and he did not have time to clean her. This is a huge break because other than the wife, who is living at least for the moment, we have no direct evidence on Devon, only on Jack. We are working on getting Devon's DNA, but he will be extremely careful. Roger is going to do the first presentation. Then we will have Jack leave, and we will go into tomorrow's assignments."

* * *

Jack sat in the extra conference room in shock. "Oh my god!"

Joy had listened to his story earlier and said, "Most men would not risk getting involved in this." Jack had told her he had made up his mind, but the final decision would be hers. It was her life too. She had answered, "This Monster already put you in the game. I would want to be on the police team when the uniforms are passed out." Then she had said, "Let's go back to the nursing home, so I can use their kitchen. We'll stop at the store first. These guys will need some protein in their guts to catch this guy. How 'bout my famous chicken?" Jack gave her a big hug, and she saw tears on his cheeks. Joy squeezed his hand and said, "I am proud of you Jack."

He had answered, "I'm scared."

Joy said, "I know. You need to be. It will keep you careful."

He wondered if she would still feel that way if she had heard what he had just heard. Especially this last woman that was just used up and left to rot, all taped and bound to a chair. They said she probably died over a week ago from starvation, and it probably took a couple of weeks to die that way. He couldn't imagine. She was a young, beautiful student. Her family was *just now* finding out. He was wiping tears. They had been on TV yesterday asking people to help them find their missing daughter. How is he going to be able to talk to this man and not let on he knows what kind of monster he is? Could he act that well? Devon had set him up to get blamed for all of this, and he was Jack's lawyer? Oh my God! Agent Dance was right, this was the biggest decision he had ever made.

* * *

Ellen told Mary, Linda, and me to take a copy of the list of foreclosed HUD homes Devon was the asset manager of and start doing checks. She looked at me, "Calling this Trick or Treat is just a little "Mortal" at this stage don't you think?" She was smiling, but I got the message. I think I do that to keep from thinking of it for what it really is. "You do," Ellen said. She told us that it would probably take us most of the evening. She was going to divide her time between Agents Dance and Casey, and she wanted to try to enter Devon's dreams later. She told us that he would be most vulnerable when he was dreaming.

CHAPTER 21

T he meeting in the conference room ended at 9:45 p.m., and the task force people were noticeably happy to hear that reinforcements would be there in the morning. Maybe at least *some* of them could get a day off. They were all asked to be there for a 9:00 a.m. briefing at which time Chief Doyle would issue assignments. One officer had a baby due any moment, and Paul was hoping he would be the first to get some time off. Roger had put in a call to the local medical examiner to see how he was holding up. He knew that he was probably still there. "Sam. Dance here, what do you have there for me?"

Dr. Samuel Frost spent about twenty minutes going over some of the latest results from autopsies and finished with a few quick observations on the new one brought in today. He ended with, "You know I called in the medical examiner from Indianapolis to help with this. Just the job of getting our findings to your boys takes a lot of time, and we are short staffed under normal conditions. This isn't an excuse, but an explanation. I'm thinking if we don't get any more bodies in here for the next two days, I can start to finish up some of this for you."

Roger asked, "The M.E. from Indy, what's his office situation?"

Sam answered, "We were lucky to get him, from what I understand, and mind you we haven't had a lot of time to talk. He is short staffed there too. They had that stadium collapse, remember. They were hit hard." Roger said thanks and hung up. Tomorrow was going to be an impossible situation for the medical examiner's office.

Paul was in the office doorway, "Jack is settled in the little apartment off the kitchen. He has TV, bathroom, small fridge...he'll be fine. I told him in the morning to just let Officer Ames know what he would like for breakfast, and we would get it to him. His little apartment is within eyes of the prisoner lock up. We should be able to keep him okay." Then Paul said, "I can't think anymore. I'm not sure what I should be doing right now."

Roger looked at his watch. It was 10:00 p.m., and he had been there since six in the morning. "We've been here sixteen hours. Why don't you get some sleep?" Paul nodded agreement and walked away.

Paul stood in the vestibule area by the back door waiting for the snow plow to finish the parking lot, so he could leave. As he watched the huge snowflakes drift from the sky, he thought of Ashley. They had been good together, they had cared about each other, and then, like the snowflakes hitting the window glass they had just melted away. The thought of her being in the hands of Devon had his blood pounding in his temples, his heart was fisted in panic, and he was helpless.

Roger thought he would say goodbye to Jack before he left. He noticed eight post-it notes on Jack's door thanking him for the chicken. Roger laughed to himself. Who brings chicken to the cops that take you into custody? Jack said, "Come in." When Roger opened the door, he saw Jack returning the Bible to the nightstand.

Roger asked, "Getting some fortitude?" as he pointed to the Bible.

Jack looked at him. "If I tell you something, don't think bad about me, okay? That is the first time I ever opened a Bible." He looked scared, and Roger felt bad about the position he had put Jack in.

"Well, now that you opened it, what do you think?"

Jack thought for a minute, "Well, the words are funny; you know, hard to read. And I didn't start in the beginning. I just opened it and pointed to some words and read them. You know, like maybe that was what I was supposed to read."

Roger nodded, "I've done that before."

Jack looked surprised, "I thought there were rules about how to read it."

Roger thought about that for a minute and said, "To me, it is supposed to be messages from God, lessons, I guess. So I think it is more important that you pay attention to what you have read, than the order you read it."

Jack looked thoughtful and said, "These aren't the exact words, but I think what I read said that if my actions came from purity of heart, then they were the right actions to take."

Roger smiled and said, "That sounds to me like you found a fairly pertinent quote for today."

Jack said, "Yeah, I thought so too." Roger told him he was going home and would see him in the morning.

He handed Jack the post-it notes, "Looks like if you ever do open that restaurant, Joy's cookin' will be a big hit!"

Jack smiled, "You said you are going home, but it's a hotel isn't it? Man, I never thought about how much you guys give up." He was shaking his head.

Roger got to the hotel, took a shower, and warmed up some soup in the microwave in his room. He had the urge to call Kim. He looked at his watch and decided it was too late.

* * *

Linda, Mary, and I had decided that even though we were capable of splitting up to do the foreclosure house check quicker, there was no way any of us wanted to do this alone. We decided we would rather take the whole night. The first house we went to did not have a garage, so we were hopeful. The electric meter wasn't running, so it looked like this one was going to be a piece of cake. We walked into the house through the front wall and stood silently listening. Mary said, "I don't smell anything." Linda started walking cautiously down the hall from the living room. There wasn't any furniture or anything in the house, but we looked in closets and in the shower stall trying to be careful. We all went to the basement at the same time, and there was an older man in a fetal position in the corner.

Linda whispered to me, "Is he dead or sleeping?" I told her I thought he was sleeping.

We moved in closer, and my heart just went out to him. Here it was December, he had a couple of jackets on, but he was shivering. There was a cart next to the wall piled high with junk. Probably everything he had in the world.

I said, "I wish he had a warm blanket." Suddenly there was a down comforter on him. Linda and Mary looked at me.

Mary asked, "How did you do that?"

I was as shocked as they were. "I don't have a clue!"

Mary said, "I wish he had some food." Poof! There was a little table set up with a big bowl of stew and a glass of milk!

Linda was squealing! "Let me, let me! I wish he had new clothes and good boots!" He was now wearing new clothes and new boots. We just stood there looking at each other. This is too much fun.

I finally said, "I think we are evolving, and they just haven't told us yet we can do this stuff."

I guess we just went nuts. There is no other explanation. Our mortal minds were in complete control. By the time we were done, about five minutes later, there was a bed, a stove, a refrigerator full of food, a working TV, and a closet full of clothes. I put a chandelier on the ceiling, Mary was steaming drapes, and Linda was putting up wallpaper when Ellen appeared.

We heard, "Ah-huh!" We stopped and saw Ellen on the bottom step with her hands on her hips. "Vicki —define manipulation of mortal environment."

Me? Oh yeah. Well, humm. Then I just held my hands out and said, "This?"

Ellen explained to us we could only leave the clothes we had put on him, some of the food, and the blanket. Everything else had to go. Then she said, "Okay, you put it there, you fix it!" Oh, it's going to be like that. Okay, I concentrated on the refrigerator. It didn't disappear, but it nearly ran over Mary as it shot to the other side of the room.

I looked at Ellen, "Do I just wish I hadn't done it?"

"If you do that, it all goes. He doesn't have a blanket, food, or clothes anymore." Ellen was sitting on the bottom step smiling. She was enjoying our stupidity. Mary started frowning at the chandelier. It started shaking, and the old man woke up.

He started looking around, then he looked at his blanket and clothes, then he ran over to the table, and started eating. We looked at Ellen in desperation, "What do we do now?"

Ellen was shaking her head, "Now you know that rules are imposed for reasons. Have you learned this?"

We were all nodding, and Ellen winked. Everything was gone except the food, the blanket and his clothes. The old man stopped chewing for a minute and then just continued as if none of it had happened.

We all met outside of the house, and I was thinking, I bet if I had *winked*....Ellen looked at me, "We just won't know for a long time if that would have worked, now will we?"

"No we will not!" I answered. EEE GADS.....I was actually looking forward to going to the next house.

Mary frowned, "We're going to flunk this class aren't we?" as she looked at me.

"Hey! You did it too!"

Ellen said we were developing faster than expected. Some things would happen. She was on her way to Devon's house and hoped that she didn't have to leave before she was ready. We get it.

After Ellen left, Linda said, "You notice she really didn't answer Mary's question? We had better straighten up!"

I looked at Linda and Mary, "It was fun though wasn't it?" We all laughed as we headed to the next address.

* * *

It was 7:00 a.m. and Roger, Paul, and Chief Doyle were standing by the whiteboards changing a few forensic notations. The FBI Lab had sent confirmation that the dog hairs from Devon's dog were a match to the hairs found at Nettie's and Karen's. Also a few hairs that matched had been found on the duct tape piece Roger and Paul had found at Ginger Hall's site. Flea Bag was off the hook. There were also fingerprints on the tape that were being run this morning. Jack had provided fingerprints and DNA for them last night, and his prints were confirmed on the beer bottle and Visa receipt.

They still wanted DNA from Devon to tighten the forensic part of the case. Roger looked at his watch and said, "I want to meet the new team in the other conference room first. Can we get a sign on that door and maybe a coffee pot or something? I've ordered enough breakfast from the deli for everyone, should get here at 8:45. We better make sure everyone has a good breakfast."

Chief Doyle said, "The DA is with us in this plan, but the Mayor is giving me grief. He's worried this won't work, Jack will screw things up, and he will look like a fool. He is up for re-election next fall, and this case is a thorn." The Chief shrugged, "I'm happy just having *one* of them on our side." He looked at Roger, "I know you have eight guys coming. How many of my guys can I let go home today?"

"I think it's safe to let at least six of them stay home today. I think tomorrow will be an all hands on deck type of day. Maybe you want to call them before the new guys see them. Just tell them to stay home." Chief Doyle looked satisfied with Roger's answer and left.

Paul noticed the black cat sitting in the middle of the hall making people walk around it. "Uh-oh," and he pointed. "Should we grab a cup of coffee and meet in your office real quick?"

Roger was rubbing the back of his neck and thinking about what he knew was going to happen today. "Looks like the day is getting started."

Roger closed the door after Paul and Ellen were inside. Ellen jumped up on the credenza. Roger sat at his desk and looked at her. "Should I call Kim?" he asked Ellen, and she winked at him. Paul looked at Roger, and shook his head with a facial expression that said, "Do you believe this?" Roger dialed Kim, and she answered right away even though she sounded sleepy. "This is Roger. Did I wake you?"

Kim answered, "No, Mom did about five minutes ago. I've been reviewing my notes and getting ready to call you. It's not good…"

Roger's heart sank, "Can I put you on speaker? It's just Paul and the cat."

Kim answered, "The cat's name is Ellen. Don't ask! Yeah, speaker is fine."

Roger laid the phone on his desk and said, "Okay, I think I am ready."

"Mom and two of her friends went to all the foreclosure homes Devon is the asset manager for. Ray is still working on getting you addresses for those houses. Mom thinks Devon will get spooked if you guys find the bodies in the homes he owns first, so she thinks you should do the foreclosures first….."

Roger said, "Are you saying there are more bodies in the foreclosure homes?" He and Paul were staring at each other.

Kim answered, "Yes, maybe he was dumping them on the highway because he ran out of houses? Here is the list: four vagrants, six cars, nine bodies." She waited for his reaction.

Roger said, "This is in addition to the thirteen bodies in the homes he actually owns, the one we found yesterday, and the six we already had?"

Kim answered, "Yes, and Roger? There is one woman *still alive* but not by much. Mom says Devon has been starving them when he's done, less work than dumping them. This woman only has about six more hours. Somehow she has to be saved…please." Roger could tell Kim was crying.

Roger asked, "Do you have an address for her? I will send someone there now. We'll figure out some way to explain knowing about her." Kim gave him the address, and he hung up.

"You did it again," Paul said as he pointed to the phone.

Roger said, "Ah damn!" Normally he wouldn't have bothered to call back, but Kim had been crying. "Kim? I am so sorry I just hung up. Are you okay? Yes, I will the first minute I get. Thanks, goodbye." He looked at Paul when he said goodbye. Roger looked at Ellen, "Is there a way to sort the foreclosure list out from the tax properties Devon owns?" Ellen was licking her paw; she looked at Roger and winked. Roger said, "Is there a way I can get the foreclosure list first?" Ellen winked again.

254

Roger was still looking at Ellen, "When I am ready for the list do I just say that I am going to check to see if it has come in yet?" Ellen winked again. Roger said, "Ellen, you are a life saver." She winked again and then vanished. Roger called Detective Ed Mars and told him about the woman who was still alive. Then he said, "Ed, this is a tip from a very reliable source, can you get paramedics there ASAP? I will explain later. Report only to me or Paul when you are done," and he hung up. Roger rested his hand on the phone and exhaled, "Devon will be the topic at conventions for quite a while."

Paul looked at his watch and held it up as a sign to Roger. Then he said, "I am only speaking for myself, but I could not have dealt with today without that heads up we got last night."

Roger nodded, "I was just thinking the same thing. Our guys will be here any minute. I have a history with Dan Thor that hasn't always been pretty. He's Senior Agent – Indy, but I think I can play this our way. Just trust me."

Paul stood up to leave the room, frowned, and said, "I know the name. First class prick."

Roger nodded, "Yup."

When they got to the second Conference room, the guys from St. Joseph, Michigan, were already there and writing their names on name tags placed on the table for them. Roger introduced himself and Paul, and pointed to the coffee on the table across the room. The blonde agent named Todd Nelson said, "We have been following this in the news and agency bulletins. I've actually been hoping we would be called in." The other two agents were nodding agreement with his statement. Roger thanked them for their attitude. He heard the Indy guys coming down the hall.

A rough looking, grim faced guy in a black suit, gun and badge protruding, walked into the room. With his booming voice he declared, "Let's get this circus under control, so I can get back to my mess."

"Dan," Roger said and shook his hand. The other four men had followed him, and they were making their name tags and getting coffee. When everyone was seated, Roger introduced Paul and started, "I have scheduled a briefing for one hour for now with the entire task force. You will get particulars of what we have then. Right now I am going to give you the narrative on how we got to where we are today." He proceeded to speak for half an hour with only a few interruptions from Dan.

At the end of his oration Roger looked at Dan, "Most of this task force has put in fourteen hour days, seven days a week for almost two months. Being that I believe we may be at the end soon, I would like some of them to get the day off today to refresh." Agent Thor didn't say anything. Roger continued, "I see two distinct sides of this case right now, the surveillance and capture of Devon and hopefully the rescue of the hostages, and the ongoing collection of evidence. We have over three dozen identified properties that need to be visited in a very short period of time."

Agent Dan Thor spoke, "Todd here is our hostage negotiator and may give us the edge if we take

Devon." Paul looked at Roger, no way do I want to pull from this now with Devon!

Roger looked at Dan and started rubbing his neck, "Well, that would certainly give Paul and me a break. Just getting away from the press, the Chief, the DA. Most of forensics has come back, right Paul? I mean we would have to do the foreclosure visits, but…." Roger was nodding his head as he spoke. Paul was about to come unglued. He was biting the inside of his cheek to keep from talking. He couldn't believe Roger was throwing the cream of the case to Thor and not even putting up a fight for it!

Then Agent Thor spoke again. "On the other hand, you have a rapport with the hostage already, and it is your people at the house. I don't know, what do you think Tom, could we knock out these foreclosures in a couple of days?"

Tom looked at Dan's face, and answered, "The five of us could do the houses, and have the St. Joe boys here take the place of the task guys that will be gone today."

Dan looked at Roger, "I know you are overwhelmed here, but I think *that* would be the best use of manpower. Can you make it a couple more days?"

Roger looked at Paul then he answered, "You know Dan, I am just happy to see you guys. I will defer to your judgment on this one." Roger stood and announced there was breakfast being served across the hall, and he would join them as soon as he checked his computer. He was expecting Ray to send him the list of foreclosed homes Devon was the asset manager for, and he would give it to Thor the minute it came in.

Everyone except Paul and Roger left the room to enjoy the food the deli was serving. Paul said, "Remind me not to play poker with you." They left for Roger's office. When they arrived in Roger's office, there was a message to call Detective Mars. Nothing on the computer. "I guess I am ready for the list of foreclosed homes." He no sooner said it than an e-mail from Ray appeared on his computer with a message, "Let me know when you get this." Roger opened the e-mail, hit print, and handed it to Paul. Paul looked at the list and shook his head. Roger called Ray who told him the tax property list was stuck or something. He would send it as soon as he figured out the problem.

Then Roger called Ed Mars, "What did you find Ed? Wait, can I put you on speaker? Paul is here."

Ed answered, "Sure."

Roger said, "Okay Ed we're ready"

Ed came on the line, "Well, I wasn't prepared for what we found. She's alive all right, but not by much. It looks to me like she has been starved. She is at Memorial Hospital right now. I stayed to give patrol instructions on securing the scene. She had been duct taped and tied with rope to a pole in the basement. Nasty scene, Agent Dance." Roger thanked him for getting there so quickly and told him to report to *him* before he did his paperwork. He also told him to have someone at the hospital call him the minute this woman was up to answering some questions.

258

Then Roger dialed Kim, "We have her! She is at the hospital now."

Kim answered, "Great." Roger hung up. Paul just dropped his head to one side. Roger shrugged.

In the 'room' the deli had arrived and everyone was filling their plates, introducing themselves, and talking about the case. Five or six agents were studying the white boards, shaking their heads. Paul noticed Jack by the door with a name tag on that said in big black letters, POI : Jack Simpson. He nudged Roger, "Check out Jack's name tag." Roger just rolled his eyes.

Agent Dan Thor was looking at the white boards. Roger walked over to him. Dan looked at him and asked, "How the Hell did you make the connection of this house to Devon?" He was pointing to the address where they had found Sandy.

Roger answered, "We had heard that Nettie Wilson had paid her legal fee to Devon with a deed to an old rental property. We contacted the now former secretary to Devon who had the address and told us that Sandy Devon was actually going there on Christmas Eve to decorate. Devon had told us she was in Jamaica. From there it was just connecting the dots to Ginger Hall's accident site....piece of cake. Here is the list you wanted on the foreclosure houses." Roger walked away with Dan's mouth still open.

Roger cleared the room of everyone but task force people, and the meeting was over in thirty minutes. He was back in his office when he got a text from Sal, "He's here/ Told Sandy to get ready / Moving her to a new house."

Roger called Paul, "He's at the house now! I thought he would wait until a news break…..Damn. Get eyes around that exit. We can't lose him this time! I'll meet you there where we parked yesterday. We may need two cars." With that he grabbed his jacket and ran to his car.

Agent Thor and the other Indy guys were looking out the window as Roger ran by. Thor said, "Poor Bastard, he sure got the short end of this stick." He chuckled as he took another bite of his donut.

Then Paul ran past the window. Agent Thor set his donut down on a napkin. "I think we better get out of here before we get sucked into whatever is going on."

* * *

Teresa was flying around screaming, "Situation here. I need help!" Patrolman John was in the basement, she knew, and Detective Sal was in the closet with her gun drawn.

Devon was screaming at Sandy, "Get out of that shower and move it. I don't have all day."

She screamed back, "I have soap in my hair, just one minute." He slammed his fist against the wall and unlocked the chain from the bed. Sal was scared he was going to see where the slat had been loosened, but he didn't. He looked around the room and for a second she thought he was going to open the closet door, he had walked that direction and then stopped. He walked out with the chain and the bag of food. Sal heard the back door slam shut and then nothing.

Sandy had gotten out of the shower and was putting clean clothes on. Sal peeked out of the closet, and mouthed to Sandy, "We will follow you." Sandy nodded, and she heard the door squeal open again.

He walked into the room and grabbed her arm, "Just put the rest of that shit on in the car!" She had just pulled the sweatshirt over her head covering her bra with the phone in it.

She turned around, "I'm not walking out of here with no pants on! Just give me a minute." She actually pushed him.

He laughed, "You are such a stupid bitch."

Teresa was outside freaking out. Devon had splashed gasoline all around the house and up the siding. He had used two gas cans and just thrown them into the tree line. Then he went back into the house. Teresa flew in behind him and saw he was trying to get Sandy out of the house. Teresa called Ellen…no answer. "Oh, no you don't!" She kept trying, no answer. Sal watched Sandy and Devon walk out of the house, and she heard the car motor start up. She crouched against the living room wall and yelled for John that it was all clear. Just then Devon stopped his car, got out, took a lighter to a ball of old rags, and threw it at the house!

It was an explosion! Fire everywhere! The house was fully engulfed in seconds. Sal was screaming for

John who had made his way up from the basement but couldn't see for the smoke. Sal was coughing and crawling along the floor trying to find John. Teresa was in the house with them but didn't know what to do. She started hitting every button she could find on her watch. Nothing was working. She couldn't hear Sal or John coughing anymore. All she could see were flames from floor to ceiling. Teresa screamed, "GRANNY!"

Linda, Mary, and I were just leaving the last foreclosure house when a huge whoosh noise swept us away. Teresa had hit a very bad button on her watch. We were thrown into the middle of the fire ball! Teresa was screaming. There were flames everywhere.

Mary grabbed Teresa's shoulders and screamed, "What happened? Did we go to hell?"

Linda was screaming and hugging me. Then a strange tunnel developed down the center of the house. The air was cool and clear in the tunnel, but the sides and ceiling of the tunnel were solid walls of flames. We saw Sal and John fly through the tunnel and burst through the front wall to the outside. Then we all felt something push us out of the wall too. We ended up in the grass next to the tree line. The house was totally engulfed in flames and black smoke rolled up to the clouds above.

Linda was coughing and asked, "What happened?" Ellen was sitting in the grass looking at us. Sal and John were lying across the driveway coughing.

Teresa looked at Ellen, "Are they okay?"

Ellen answered, "Yes."

Teresa looked at Ellen again, "I didn't know what to do! I hit every button on my watch!"

Ellen said, "Oh yes, we know that, and then you called Granny which was the *right* thing to do." Teresa sighed with relief. I was thinking that I didn't want to go through that "whoosh" thing again for a while. Really didn't help my hair either. That ball of flames really made me appreciate that our little group had probably been graded on a curve to get into heaven. That was my only explanation for me being there.

Ellen said, "You girls just sit here a while. I will be right back." Ellen called Kim and told her to call Roger and tell him what had happened. Kim called Roger and told him Devon had set the house on fire, Detective Sal and Patrolman John were okay, but the fire department didn't know. Roger reported the fire, called Paul, and put his siren on. He arrived at the house about three minutes after talking to Kim.

Ellen went back with the gals, "Well, the good news is Teresa saved Sal and John's lives. The bad news is we have lost Devon." Ellen looked at Teresa, "Did you see what kind of car he was driving?"

Teresa said, "Yeah, a cute little Volkswagen, white." Ellen called Kim back and told her to call Roger again.

Roger and Paul pulled in the driveway at almost the same time. A state trooper had just arrived and positioned himself at the end of the driveway to guide the fire trucks. An ambulance was pulling in, and men were jumping out before it even stopped.

The fire truck actually ran over us! We weren't paying attention. That was weird. Sal and John were insisting they were fine.

Sal was showing the EMT guys that she didn't even have any singed clothes. Roger got to Sal and John and listened as they explained what had happened with Devon. Paul asked, "Did you see what kind of car he was driving?"

Sal answered, "It was a small car. I think a Volkswagen Beetle, white."

Paul said he would call it in and Roger gave him a signal, "I'll get that." Paul knew that meant he had already done it. Okay. Sal called a fireman over to the back of the ambulance where they had just hooked John up to a respirator.

"Sir? Have you ever been in a fire where the middle just opened up like a tunnel? And the air was okay in the tunnel?"

The fireman shook his head and said to Roger, "When their oxygen levels get low, they hallucinate." He walked back to the fire.

John pulled his oxygen mask off, "That is exactly what happened, and we were pushed out! Right through the front wall!" His eyes opened big, his face black with soot. Sal was agreeing with him.

Roger told them they had to go to the hospital to be checked out, no discussion. As the ambulance left, Paul and Roger watched the firemen fight the blaze. The Fire Chief came over to talk to them, "We'll have this out shortly. The old place was just a tinder box waiting to happen, but there was an accelerant used. Probably gasoline. This is arson. Your

264

people are really lucky. I don't know how anyone came out of that."

Roger's phone rang, "Yeah." He listened a while. "Okay, keep me posted. I want eyes on his house-office, thanks." He looked at Paul, "We lost him. They must not have taken the highway to wherever they're going." This was not a good development.

Paul said, "If we can get an excuse to call him, maybe we can get a trace. After you set a time for the press release, what if we call Devon and say his client wants to talk to him?"

Roger answered, "Good idea. Let's head back and get this press release time out."

Ellen and the gals were sitting under a pine tree watching the last of the firemen spray smoking embers. Teresa frowned at Ellen, "You didn't answer me when I called."

Ellen said, "There wasn't anything I could do. You did the right thing by calling Granny. You don't need your watch for that. You just call Granny." She added with a smile. Then Ellen continued, "We do need to take a minute and talk about our watches right now." Teresa moaned. Uh Oh. Ellen looked at her, "Yeahhhh. Do you remember smacking the big red one here?"

We were all looking at our watches, Teresa said, "Yeah, I think so. What does that do?"

Ellen rolled her eyes, then she said, "Let's just say about fifteen million people in the world are going to have a dejavu experience sometime today. That button repeats time, around the world, changes weather sometimes. Actually sends some angels to assignments they have already done. Betty is probably not too happy about now. I will explain someday, but let's just call that a no-no button for now." Oops. Sooo glad that was Teresa and not me! Then all of a sudden I was having this indescribable urge to hit that button. I couldn't quit looking at it. It was like, "Don't think pink elephants." Eeee gads!

Ellen looked at me, "Please do not hit the red button. Think about food or something." I crammed my nose into my wrist, and ate too much....ugh... but it worked!

Linda said, "You said Teresa did the right thing to call Granny, right?"

"Yup" was Ellen's answer as she got up. Ellen looked at Teresa, "One of the things you did with the buttons on your watch was change all of the animal genders. When this assignment is over you will have to go and fix them all."

Teresa looked mad. Then she asked, "Can we do it as a group?"

HEY! The group didn't hit the stupid red button! Boy, you have to stay alert with this bunch. We were not at all happy with that suggestion.

Then Ellen said, "Just messin' with ya!" That Ellen laugh. "I am trying to decide what would be the best places for all of you to go for a while. Any ideas?"

Linda said, "There was one whole stack of unrecorded papers for St. Joseph County I couldn't get to because it was on that one lady's desk, and she was there. I could finish that up."

Mary piped up, "I could help her. Last time Betty had to break the toilet, I saw how she did it." Ellen

266

laughed. She looked at Teresa and me, "What should I do with you two? How about you fly around the mall and see if any of the cars belonging to our women are there. We are missing about seven cars. Might help us narrow down where he took Sandy." Ellen watched them leave, and then Granny popped up next to her. Ellen said, "They really are making remarkable progress." Granny left. Ellen said, "Whew!"

Roger was back at the center and assuring everyone that Sal and John were going to be okay when his phone rang. It was Detective Ed Mars. "Agent Dance? Our girl is conscious, but really weak. They are giving her IV's, but she said she could talk to you." Roger thanked him, and as soon as Paul got there he asked him if he wanted to come with him to do the hospital interview.

"You bet," Paul said. "I'll get our picture of Devon and a couple of other head shots to take with us."

Roger said, "Get Jack's picture in there too." Paul nodded. Roger called Chief Doyle to see if he thought two o'clock would be too late for the press release. It was 11:00 a.m. now. He thought that sounded fine. Roger went into the 'room' to see how the St. Joseph agents were doing.

As soon as he walked in, they all stood up, "How are your people?"

Roger explained they were fine, got out without a scratch, but they had lost Devon and his hostage. He told them about the plan to trace their call to him. He also told them about the tip they had, and the woman they were getting ready to see at Memorial Hospital.

The young Agent Nelson said, "Is this how it has been every day here? How in the world have you compiled your reports so well? I've got to tell you, I'm impressed." The other guys were nodding.

Roger said, "We have had a good team working on this all along."

One of the other agents said, "Yeah, I saw on TV where you called in the heavens." Then he said, "I hope you don't mind, but I told your POI he had better remove the name sticker before anyone in the press saw him. I told him they have cameras pointed at the building at all times."

Roger just smiled and said, "Jack is making quite a sacrifice for this investigation, but it does come with some challenges."

Roger's phone rang again. It was Agent Thor. "Yeah Dan….really?....Damn, bad luck. Well, I just spoke to our M.E. yesterday, and he is going nuts already. Do you have any pull with Grand Rapids? I know, you have pull everywhere. Well, I'm in the middle of something on our side of this case but keep me posted," and he snapped his phone shut. Roger looked at the St. Joseph agents who were listening and said, "Be grateful you are here. Dan just found a body at the first house he went to."

There was a collective, "Shit," and Roger left the room.

Paul joined Roger in the hall outside of Roger's office. Paul looked in, but there was no cat. Paul looked at Roger, "Do you think someday we will sit down over a couple of beers and remember when a black cat was our boss?" They started walking out from the building to go to the hospital.

Roger laughed, "If we ever get through this case. Dan just found number one. I can tell he is pissed he'll have to do the work up on it." They were in the parking lot going toward Roger's car.

Paul opened the passenger door and said, "Wait until about five o'clock tonight."

Paul asked at the reception desk at the hospital how to find the critical care unit and was given directions. As he and Roger rode the elevator to the third floor, Roger said, "Sal and John were pretty lucky. You ever heard of a tunnel before?"

Paul looked at him, "Nope."

"Why do you think he torched the place?"

Paul pushed his chin forward and answered, "He may be thinking we would get there eventually, and he had to have left DNA everywhere at that place."

Roger said, "Or he may be in his final stage of frenzy."

Paul looked at him, "Or that."

They walked down the hall to room 342 where Detective Ed Mars was waiting outside in the hall. Detective Mars pointed, "She's in there." Paul and Roger walked around the beige curtain and almost gasped. She was a skeleton. Her eyes looked so sunken. She motioned them over and even offered up a weak smile.

Roger cleared his throat and said, "We will not stay long. We want you to rest and get better. The officer in the hall will get information from you later.

Can you look at some pictures, and tell us if you see the man that kidnapped you?" Her eyes were tearing up, but she nodded yes. Paul pulled out an 8x10 paper that had six photos of men's faces. He handed it to her, and she pointed at Devon right away.

Roger asked, "Did this man also rape you?" She nodded yes. Roger thanked her, and stood up. She grabbed his sleeve. She was whispering, and Roger strained to hear. He thought she said but he's not the man who stopped feeding me. Roger said, "There was another man that knew you were in that house?" She nodded. Roger continued, "He was in charge of feeding you?" she nodded. Roger said, "Did he rape you too?" She shook her head.

Paul gave her the page again, "Is *that* man's picture here?"

Paul and Roger looked at each other, *what if she picks Jack?* She handed the picture back to Paul. She shook her head. They thanked her and asked Ed if he could stay for about another hour, get what information he could from her, and arrange a replacement. They wanted him back at the center. Roger asked at the nurse's station if Jenny Camp was there. One of the nurses said she was down the hall and should be back in a minute. Roger said "Thank you." Then he looked to Paul, "We have to keep this gal out of the news." Jenny Camp walked to the nurse's station and saw them.

Roger motioned for her to come over to where he and Paul were standing, and she did. "Jenny, I have a huge favor to ask of you."

Jenny said, "Of course, anything."

Roger explained, "The woman in room 342 is a victim of our murderer. Only she got lucky. I have to keep her out of the news. He can't find out she is alive, or two other hostages may get killed. Our investigation is at a critical point. Can you come up with some kind of cover story on her? Just for a couple of days? If you have a supervisor that will need to talk to me, that is fine, I gave you my card. Please let her know what we're doing." Jenny said she would do her best, even if it meant sleeping in the woman's room to protect her. Roger and Paul thanked her and left.

On the ride down the elevator they were silent. They got to the car, and Paul said, "We have two doers."

Roger said, "Yup. Let's stop at the PUB and have Larry fix a dozen or so burgers we can take to Dan's guys. They are going to need it. They won't have any time to leave." Paul agreed. When they got to the Pub, they gave Larry their 'to-go' order and had burgers themselves while they waited. They were not too sure the next time they would get a chance to eat. Roger called Dan and told him they would drop off food to his guys if he gave them the addresses of where they were. Roger wrote the addresses down.

Dan asked, "You heard we have found three now?"

"Three?" Roger tried to sound surprised, "I'm glad we are bringing you food. We should be there in about twenty." He hung up.

Paul said, "You didn't say goodbye." They both started laughing.

"Man," Roger was rubbing his neck again. "We have another guy, but *he* didn't kidnap her or rape her? He was supposed to keep her alive? What for? Why bother? Devon has a partner in this for a reason. Let's just hope he has been printed before, and we get lucky."

Paul said, "You mean hope Thor and the CSI get lucky."

Larry brought the burgers out and said, "An order this big usually means things are real good, or things are real bad."

Paul said, "Or, we really like your burgers!" Larry smiled as he rang up their bill.

It only took a few minutes to locate the Indy guys. Then they went to the third location to find Agent Dan Thor. Dan was in the front yard with EMT guys waving his arms, red faced, and shouting. Paul moaned, "Oh brother, he's all yours."

Thor saw Roger and Paul pull up. He came over to their car and yelled, "Nobody wants to drive to Grand Rapids." Roger asked him to give him a minute. He excused himself to get back into his car and make a call. He called the director. After about five minutes Roger joined them again.

He spoke to Dan, "I have been told to tell you, you should be receiving more cooperation shortly."

Dan said thanks, unwrapped a burger, and one of the EMT guys walked over, "Agent Thor?"

Dan glared at him, "Yeah?"

"I was told to give you this phone number and tell you we will drive to Egypt if that is what you need, sir. Transportation arrangements are being made for your needs on a standby basis. I am sorry, sir. I didn't mean to sound disrespectful."

Thor took the number and said, "Thanks." He looked at Roger and said, "You got some serious connections boy," and kept eating his burger. "These are *damn* good. I know you didn't have any way of knowing what we were walking into, but…" he was shaking his head. He frowned at Roger and said, "I look at this e-mail you get at 8:47 (He was waving the list Roger had given him), ten minutes after I convince you to give me these damn death houses! You got angels." Roger and Paul glanced at each other. Thor wadded up the burger wrapper, took another one and said, "You want to see what I have in here?" He started walking back up to the house.

Paul stayed outside with the EMT guys to get their impression of the scene, and so he could view the victim. When her face was uncovered, there was only the slightest hint she may have been beautiful. He made a note to get missing person's records from the entire surrounding area. Had these women been reported missing or not? Sandy said Devon used the phrase he was going 'shopping.'

Paul was trying to pull something from his memory, hadn't Claudia, Devon's secretary said he went to a lot of funerals? Roger had said the senior center gal made a reference to that also. Could he be 'shopping' at funerals for victims? If he had a conversation with them at a funeral, their guard would be down, and they would probably assume he was a good guy. Sick bastard.

Roger and Agent Thor were out of the house and standing near the front door. Paul saw Thor answer his phone and swing around to glare at Roger. He screamed into the phone, "Another one? What the..." He clicked his phone shut. He looked at Roger and said, "With your original six, yesterday's gal, and my four, we've got eleven women. Plus he is holding two? *These gals* have been dead a while. This isn't new for this guy. This crap didn't start in November. You want to place a bet where this ends up today?" He wasn't being flip. He was worried.

Roger said, "I wouldn't bet against you on this, Dan."

Paul walked over to where they were standing, and Agent Thor turned to him, "I understand you have a personal interest in our judge." The bluntness of the question took Paul by surprise.

Paul answered, "I used to. She is a great gal."

Thor asked, "What happened?" Paul knew that Thor had the right to ask, to make sure there wasn't any sinister relationship between Devon and him, or any revenge issues with Ashley.

Paul took a deep breath and answered, "I think it was more what didn't happen. I just didn't make enough time for her. We just stopped calling each other."

Thor said, "Casualty of employment."

Paul answered, "Yup."

Thor shrugged, "I have four ex- wives that could relate to that." He walked away.

In the car driving back to the center Paul said, "Do you believe that four women married him?"

* * *

Chief Doyle was waiting for Roger when he walked in the door of the center. "Thank God you are here! Any way we can move up the press release to like now? You've got to understand the heat I am getting from everywhere. You can't turn on the news, without them showing our guys taking a body out of a vacant house! My phones have jammed, twice! I won't even tell you what the mayor said!"

Roger said, "I'll go you one better and do a press conference. They can ask me questions." Roger knew he was taking a risk, but he had to get this case moving in his direction. Roger said, "Contact your media people, and tell them we will be out front in thirty minutes. It's cold out there, and that might help this stay short." Roger went into his office to call the director. He had promised to keep him up to date. Once the real story of the total crimes of Devon emerged, he knew this case would be reviewed for years as a case study, and he wanted the file pristine.

Paul had started sending FBI bulletins to surrounding jurisdictions requesting information on missing women as far back as August. He was amazed at the calls that started coming in instantly. Funerals would draw people from out of town and delay identifying victims, but not forever. Devon had to be close to leaving the country. Devon's partner might already be gone. Maybe that was why he stopped feeding the women? The heat was on, and Ashley was in the middle of it.

Jack knocked on the door of the office Paul was using. Paul said, "Hey, Jack! I bet you think we've forgotten all about you."

Jack smiled, "I should be so lucky. Can I sit a minute?" Paul said sure, and Jack plopped down with the weight of the world on his shoulders. "I have been practicing talking to Devon in the mirror in my bathroom."

Paul laughed, "How is that going?"

Jack looked serious, "I don't know. I'm worried I might screw this up."

Paul thought a moment and said, "When you were drinking heavily, did anyone ever accuse you of something and you thought there was a chance they were right, but you argued that it wasn't true?"

Jack smiled, "Probably weekly."

Paul said, "See? You are an actor, but I don't think you are the one that has to act today."

Jack was thoughtful. "I didn't do it for real. I didn't do it! And he is going to be acting like he is helping me, right?"

"Exactly, he is the one who has to *act* today, not you."

Jack said, "That makes it easier for me. I can do this!" He smiled and left the room. Paul was thinking, oh please Lord, and he watched Ellen follow Jack down the hall.

CHAPTER 22

S andy threw up in the car when Devon set the
house on fire. He turned on to some country
road and made her get out of the car while he
threw away the floor mat. He made her clean the
seat with hand wipes while he watched for traffic.
Even though it was only thirty degrees outside, he
had all of the windows down. He kept calling her a
bitch. She didn't care. All she could think about was
Sal and John dying in that fire because they were
helping her. She looked at Devon with the morning
light that was on his face. He didn't look right. He
had dark circles under his eyes, and he looked
more unkempt than usual. His facial expression
was an unnatural looking stare, intense. His eyes
kept darting around, and he wasn't blinking. She
wondered if he wasn't taking some kind of drugs.

She knew she had to pay attention to where they
were going in case she got a chance to call Agent
Dance. The phone was ice cold in her bra. Agent
Dance had told her to leave it off to conserve battery
life. Maybe she could just turn it on every now and

then for a minute. Devon stopped the car, reached into the back seat, and pulled a pillow case to the front. He glared at her, "Get your fat ass down on the floor board, and put this on your head! Now!" Sandy did as he said and was surprised how dark it was with the pillow case over her head. She had hoped she could see through it. They drove for a while making a lot of turns, and Sandy could tell from the noise they were back in traffic. They had to wait at a couple of lights, a couple of more turns, and he stopped the car.

He pulled the pillow case off her head, "I am going to come around and open your door. You are going to get out of this car and into this new car. I will have the door open. You will keep your eyes shut, and you will get back onto the floorboard. *Got it?*" Sandy nodded. He moved her to the other car, and while he was walking around to the driver's side she looked at everything she could outside. They were at the mall.

Teresa and I were checking on cars at the mall. Ellen had told us to look for certain plate numbers. It was only mid-day and the parking lot was already full. People were returning Christmas presents. Teresa said she wanted the JC Penny side of the mall because that was her favorite store, so I was flying around the Macy's side. Out of the corner of her eye Teresa saw a woman crawl from one car into another. She was at the far edge of the mall lot where employees parked, and there was a high berm protecting the cars from view from the highway. Teresa called me, "I've got something weird over here." She told me about the woman and how the man driving looked like Devon. In seconds Teresa and I were hovering over the car like helicopters.

I said, "What is he doing?"

Teresa flew down to the driver's window and said, "He's trying keys out. There is a woman sitting on the floorboard with some kind of sheet or something on her head! It is probably Sandy." Devon looked right at Teresa. She knew he couldn't see her but it scared her. "Shit! He's one ugly dude."

"What do we do now?"

Teresa said, "Let me think a minute. I want to be sure we don't manipulate. That fire kind of convinced me things could be a lot worse for us." I had to agree with that. I couldn't imagine what the classes were like in Hell. I was having issues in Heaven!

Devon started the car and put it into reverse. Teresa said, "If we do something that will make him mad, he might hurt Sandy. The FBI guys were hoping he would lead them to where the judge is. I say we just follow them."

"Good call." We flew about five feet over the car for about twenty minutes when Devon started fishing around in a paper bag pulling out garage door openers. He was looking for one in particular.

Teresa said, "We must be close. Find out what street we're on."

I flew back to the street sign, and as I turned around I heard a big WHOOSH sound. Oh not again! Sure enough, I was back in the mall parking lot. One second later Teresa was next to me.

"That was fun."

Teresa frowned at me and said, "I'll tell you later. Let's go back and find them." We found the street sign and searched for fifteen minutes. Finally, we sat under a tree on a split rail fence and called Ellen.

I heard Teresa explaining she was so worried about hitting a wrong button on her watch that she touched one to make sure it wasn't pulled out. Problem was that button was supposed to be pulled out, and she and I went back in time again. Ellen explained it wasn't the no-no button but a close cousin. She ended that it wasn't Teresa's fault. They needed to find a better system for us. Whew! Ellen was happy that at least we had a general area where Devon probably was, and we knew Sandy was still alive. Ellen told Teresa we should join up with Mary and Linda at the county clerk's office. Turns out the documents they were trying to get were going to be very important.

Ellen called Kim and asked her to call Roger with the update. Roger thanked Kim for the information and tried to decide how to best use it. He called the patrol assigned at the mall and told him to look specifically for the white Volkswagen. Then he called Paul to come in if he had a minute. "How fast can we get the tracer on Sandy's cell? That's what he's using, and his home phone?"

Paul answered, "One phone call. We did the red tape yesterday."

Roger told Paul about Kim's call and said, "I am going to change the order of things. I am going to call Devon now and tell him as a courtesy we are notifying him in advance of the press conference. Kim's mom and her friend had a location on him minutes ago with Sandy in the car….a trace right now might tell us a lot."

Paul said, "Go for it." He left the room to make his call. He was back in a minute, and Roger dialed Devon's office number. Roger was pretty sure he would get the answering machine, but Devon picked up, "Attorney Devon."

Roger's eyebrow rose, "Attorney Devon, this is Special Agent Dance, FBI. We met at your office a couple of days ago." Roger clicked his pen repeatedly.

"Yeah, I remember. What can I do for you?"

Roger said, "Actually, I'm doing something for you. I'm calling to give you a heads up. We've picked up Jack Simpson for the recent murders, and we are holding a press conference in about fifteen minutes." Roger laid his pen down, he was annoying himself.

Devon took his time answering, "Have you been questioning Jack?"

Roger smiled to himself, "Not yet. We are aware you are his attorney and need to be present for questioning. Would about 1:00 at police center be okay for you?"

Devon answered, "Police center? You don't have him at county?"

"Not yet. We don't plan to name him until he's actually arrested. Right now he is a Person of Interest. As I said, this is a courtesy call to you." Roger was clicking his pen again.

Devon replied, "Yeah, one o'clock is fine. Boy you federal boys do things differently." and he hung up.

Paul pushed his chin forward in a quick motion, "So?"

"He picked up on the first ring. On the office line. We know from Kim he had Sandy less than fifteen minutes ago. I bet anything they are at his house!"

Paul stood and shifted his weight back and forth, "I can have the search warrant in ten minutes. Do him while he's here."

"I would rather not go in with a warrant. Let me call the DA."

Agent Nelson from St. Joseph popped his head into the doorway, "Just thought you might want to know that Agent Thor is on body number six." Nelson made the announcement while waving a fistful of papers.

Roger tried to look surprised. "Oh Man," he said and looked at Paul.

The young agent said, "I am so glad we pulled this side of things. This is crazy!" He was shaking his head as he left the office.

Roger looked at Paul, "Our patrolman at the mall is going to call any minute with the plate number on that Volkswagen. Take it to the kid there (he was pointing at the new agent Nelson), and get him to run that against the missing persons info coming in. Let him think it was his idea."

Paul smiled, "Going to give the kid a boot up the ladder if you can?"

Roger smiled, "Yup, and Paul, could you call Joy and let her know about the press conference? I don't want her to hear this on TV. With what they are doing for us I want her to have a heads up. I'm going out there right now." Roger stood, put his jacket on, and Ellen appeared on his credenza. "I hope you are just here for moral support!" Ellen winked at him, stretched out, and circled for a nap. Roger stroked her fur and said, "I'm trying to do you proud girl." And he left.

The Chief, Paul, and one of the senior agents from St. Joseph were waiting at the main door for Roger. There was a media mob outside. Patrolmen were moving reporters back and placing a podium with a microphone in the middle. The local and national news trucks were blocking the entire parking lot. Reporters were trying to get statements from the patrol officers. Roger looked at Paul, "How's Jack?" Paul shrugged. Chief Doyle whispered to Roger that the agents checking houses were up to eight bodies. Roger thanked him and said, "Shall we meet the press?" He walked through the door. Immediately the crowd tried to push forward to surround him, but the patrolmen did a good job of showing that force would be used if necessary. When the crowd calmed somewhat, Roger approached the microphone.

"Good morning ladies and gentlemen. I am going to make a brief statement, and then I will answer what questions I can. I request you allow me to finish my statement before asking questions. I will try to return the courtesy by answering as many questions of yours as I can. Do we have a deal?" The crowd chuckled. Paul thought this is why he is the big boss; he can control almost any situation.

Roger resumed talking, no notes, just looking at the audience in front of him. "I am probably going to shock you first, and just get it over with. The man who has murdered six women in South Bend since October, probably started much sooner than that. Our agents are retrieving bodies from vacant homes that can be linked to our killer that go back months. These woman had been kidnapped, raped (we presume), and left to starve to death." The crowd was silent. "I have just been informed that counting the body of a young woman we found yesterday, at this moment our victim count is at fifteen." There was a gasp in the crowd.

Roger continued, "We are detaining, at this time, a Person of Interest that can be tied by direct evidence to the murders of some of our victims. As this is an ongoing investigation, and we are awaiting forensic results, we are not making an arrest at this moment. I can assure you the man being detained has been removed from the streets of South Bend." There was a cheer in the crowd, and one young reporter was wiping tears from her eyes.

Roger took her question first. She asked, "Can you release the name of the man you are holding?"

Roger answered, "No."

The young man behind her raised his hand, "Can you release the names of the new victims?" Roger said those names would be released as soon as families had been notified. Paul was noticing that news reporters were raising their hands and being polite. Another miracle.

Roger pointed to a woman in the back row that had her hand up, "Yes Ma'am?"

She identified herself and said, "Are you confident that there is only one person responsible for all of this?"

Roger thought for a moment, "We always keep the door open to thinking of multiple perpetrators, but our evidence so far does not indicate such." Roger held his hand up to speak, "I am hoping that within the next day or so, I can give you more detailed information. I am feeling good that this nightmare your community has endured is almost over."

A man in the back yelled, "How much help did you get from the Heavens?"

The crowd laughed, and Roger answered, "I suspect quite a bit more than we realize." With that he ended the conference.

When everyone got back in the building, Paul said he was going to talk to Jack, let him know he had called Joy, and tell him of his 1:00 with Devon. Paul finally found Jack in the Chief's office patching dry wall. Paul said, "Jack, what are you doing?"

Jack looked around and said, "Well, I got bored. I had one of the guys go get me some mud and a trowel. I thought I would patch some stuff around here. Is it okay?"

Paul laughed, "Your acting debut is at one o'clock. I think you better clean up, get a bite of lunch, and wait in your room back there 'til I come to get you."

Jack said, "Okay." Paul asked him how he was feeling. Jack answered, "I think I will do okay. Is my name still secret?"

Paul nodded and said, "So far. We are really trying hard to keep that secret for your sake."

Jack said, "I saw all of those news trucks. Some of them trucks had national news channels. Joy and I talked about that being the worse part, but we get that it might happen."

When Roger got back into the office, he asked Ellen if he could get the list of tax properties Devon owned. She winked, and his computer told him an e-mail from Ray was waiting. Roger printed it off and decided he would give it to Thor right away. They are already in the field. Just get it over with. He called Thor. "Dan," Roger started, "I just finished the press conference, and we have Devon coming here at 1:00 to talk to Jack. Ray in IT just sent me the nineteen properties Devon owns. Do you want me to send someone with the list?"

Thor was silent for a moment, "Man, I don't know. I guess it doesn't matter. Do you know that I have had EMT's from two States following my guys everywhere we go? Got one wagon with four bodies in it! It's a friggin' Death Parade! I'm up to nine!"

Roger didn't want to tell him that was all he was going to find on that list. "Well, it's up to you Dan. I am dying here too."

Thor answered, "Yeah, I heard about the fire. Send someone with the list, might as well get this nightmare over with." And he hung up.

Roger called for a patrolman to take the list to Agent Thor. He didn't want to risk sending an agent. Thor would keep him.

Paul knocked on the door, came in, and sat in the chair across from Roger. "I've been trying to decide if I should prep Jack for questions. I'm thinking, no. What's your gut?"

Roger took a minute, "I agree with you." Then he said, "I just sent the list of tax properties to Thor by way of a patrolman. I asked him if he wanted it. They are up to nine bodies. I really think he figures Devon wouldn't be so stupid as to keep them in properties he owns."

Paul said, "I would think that too. He was planning to take that money and run out of the country. Isn't that the list of nineteen properties and thirteen, you knows?"

Roger answered, "Yup." Roger noticed an e-mail from Stan at CSI. He opened it and hit print. It was phone records for Devon's cell for the last three months. He looked at Paul, "Do you want this, or should we give it to our newbie?"

Paul chuckled, "Newbies are good. I want to be sure I am available in half an hour." Roger looked at his watch. It was already 12:30. Shit.

Jack was pacing in the little room. He couldn't believe he was actually meeting with Devon. He couldn't eat any lunch...12:30....*Oh Lord.*

Agent Thor was just locking the front door of the last house on their list. Thank God it had been empty. He saw a patrol car pull up and a young officer ran up to him with the list of properties Devon owned, "Agent Thor?"

Dan looked at him, "Yeah."

The officer was clearly nervous, "I am supposed to give you this list." He reached out his hand with the list in it.

Dan grabbed it, caused a paper cut on the young man's hand, and said, "What the hell do I want with this?" loud enough that another agent walked over. The young patrolman had retrieved a handkerchief from his pocket and was wiping blood from the cut. Thor continued, "You make a practice of bleeding all over a crime scene?" The young patrolman was stunned at Thor's outburst.

Agent Cross came to his rescue, "Thank you officer, we'll take it from here." Cross frowned at Thor who was smiling.

Thor asked, "They make any with balls anymore?" He walked away. He hated this job. It was only 12:30. Shit.

Joy was in the middle of the lunch hour at the nursing home. She could swear people were looking at her funny. She knew it was impossible, nobody knew yet. She was scared for Jack. She looked at her watch. 12:30. Damn.

The decision had been made not to get a search warrant for Devon's house but to send in a team. If they got caught or found something, the DA was willing to work with them on it. Everyone agreed they could not afford to alert Devon. Roger had also made arrangements for GPS to be installed on whatever car Devon drove to the center.

Roger's phone rang. "Dance." It was the surveillance team. Devon had just left, and they were going in. Roger asked to be kept on the line. He could hear voices in the background yelling "clear". He waited. Then he heard, "They're going to the basement now." Then the voice on the line said, "Sorry boss, nobody here." Roger thanked them, told them not to leave any evidence they were there but to snoop around for a bit.

Roger called Paul, "Nobody there." Paul just hung up.

Devon arrived at the police center about ten minutes later. Paul walked him into the interrogation room and told him he would go get Jack. It took all of Paul's control, every fiber of his being just wanted to just shoot Devon, but he wanted to find Ashley. When Paul got to Jack's room, he asked him if he would consent to handcuffs and ankle bracelets. Jack said yes. After he was cuffed, he really looked like a criminal. Paul said, "You know Jack, you are going to do fine. Just try not to think about Devon being the bad guy. He's your lawyer. He's supposed to get you out of this mess. That's how I would play it."

Jack was nodding his head, "Yeah, he's supposed to get me out of this mess. I like that, 'cept I know he's the one that put me in it!" Paul opened the door of the interrogation room and had Jack sit next to Devon across from the observation window. Paul announced he would let Special Agent Dance know they were ready.

Roger was already in the observation room when Paul entered and closed the door. They turned on the microphone, so they could hear what was being said. Jack started, "Well, hello again." He actually smiled.

Devon looked at him, "They are probably listening to us. They're not supposed to, attorney client privilege and all that." Devon looked at the window with a sneer, he looked back at Jack, "So Jack, how did you get into this mess?" Devon had tilted his chair back and was checking his fingernails.

Jack looked like he would come unglued. Then took a deep breath and said, "I don't know! One minute I'm drinkin' a beer at my bar, and the next minute I look like this! (He held up his cuffed hands) The only thing I can think of is maybe I did some shit when I was drunk or something. I don't remember anything!"

Devon actually laughed. "Maybe you didn't do this stuff. What did they tell you when they arrested you?"

Jack took a minute, "They said they had direct evidence that placed me at a murder scene."

Devon rolled his head a little, "That's not good Jack. Not good at all. Which murder scene?"

Jack answered, "Hell, I don't know! All I know is that I know a bunch of these women that have popped up dead….Nettie, Darla, Karen. Doesn't look good. You gotta get me out of this!"

"You knew three of the women?" Devon was smiling again. Then he got a serious look on his face, "Do you think you could pass a lie detector test?"

Jack thought a minute and said, "How does, 'I don't remember' register on a lie detector?" Devon said he didn't know. Might be a 50/50 chance.

Jack remembered they wanted Devon's DNA. He reached over and poured two glasses of water and pushed one to Devon through his cuffs. Devon ignored it. Jack took a drink. Devon asked Jack, "Exactly when did the police pick you up?"

Jack answered, "Last night."

Devon looked angry, "They just called me this morning? Have they been asking you questions?" Devon glared at the observation window.

Jack raised his wrists, "They put all this metal on me, put me in a cell, and asked me if I had a lawyer. That's all I know until...now."

Roger figured it was a good time to go in the room. He decided to change his strategy a little. Ellen followed him. Jack noticed the cat and spent five minutes trying to get it to come to him. Devon watched annoyed as Jack talked 'baby talk' to the cat. Devon finally asked, "You guys keep animals here?"

Roger said, "Science says they help with blood pressure." Then Roger sat down at the far corner of the table. Roger said, "Attorney Devon, we have accumulated a great deal of circumstantial evidence, and some direct forensic evidence that your client is the man we have been looking for. The FBI is willing to discuss a plea agreement if Mr. Simpson here will provide names and locations of all of his victims."

Devon leaned back in his chair and let out a laugh, "What are you crazy? Just like that, huh? Hit us with your hardest ball up front. You want to talk plea agreement? No arrest, arraignment, grand jury? If you have so much, why haven't you arrested and named him?" Devon looked smug. They want this done. He had them.

Roger answered, "Oh, he will be arrested and charged. What's the hurry? We're still finding bodies. You know how this is played Attorney Devon. As long as Jack is a POI we have more latitude in our investigation. The more we find out, maybe the less likely we'll be to make a deal. This is today's offer."

Jack looked at both Roger and Devon and said, "Will somebody tell me what you guys are talking about? Use real words. Damn."

Devon looked at Roger, "Can I have a moment alone with my client?"

Roger stood to leave, "Of course." Right as Roger reached the door Ellen jumped right towards Devon's face. He swatted at her and pulled back a bloody hand.

Devon yelled, "Jesus! You lookin' to get sued here?" Roger apologized, grabbed Ellen from the table and left the room.

He handed her to Paul and said, "Swab that paw!" Ellen was holding the offending paw out like it was a treasure.

Roger went back into the observation room and listened. Devon started, "Jack. How much money do you have?"

Jack looked at him and said, "About three thousand dollars…and my truck."

Devon was shaking his head, "That buys about one court appearance. Do you have any idea how long a trial like this could take? Years! If they have your DNA at a crime scene, well…."

Jack said, "What are you saying? I should take the deal?"

Devon answered, "Not this deal. You told me you don't remember anything. How can you give them names and locations of bodies?"

Jack frowned at him, "How 'bout this? Maybe I don't remember because I didn't do it!" Jack leaned back in his chair with an appropriate amount of disgust on his face. "I don't want no deal! And you know what else?" (Roger held his breath) "It is your job to fix this! You are my lawyer!"

Devon looked at him and chuckled, "Not really, I am retiring after the first of the year. You are probably the last client I will see. If we don't figure this out soon, you are going to get stuck with some court appointed lawyer. Let's give this a day and see if I can't think up a better deal."

Jack was astonished. He looked at Devon and asked, "You mean you want me to plead guilty?"

Devon looked at him with ice in his eyes, "Can you prove you're not?" Then he smiled, got up, and left the room. Jack actually smacked his head down on the table. Roger met Devon in the hall. It looked like Roger was bringing him a wet cloth.

Devon said, "No thanks…to the cloth or the deal. Sweeten the pot. The guy's a drunk. He doesn't know what he did yesterday morning. Save yourself and the county some money and time. Just bring me a better deal, one that doesn't require this asshole to remember anything."

Roger was stunned and asked, "He'll plead?"

Devon was walking away, "Probably."

Roger just shook his head. Cold. Set the guy up and throw him under the bus without blinking an eye. Roger waited until Devon left the building and went into the interrogation room where Jack was waiting. Jack looked apprehensive, "How did I do?" Roger clapped his hands, and Paul came in clapping his hands. Before Jack knew it there were about ten people standing there clapping their hands. Jack was beaming.

Roger said, "Let's take off these cuffs."

Jack was saying, "Did you hear him? He wants me to plead *guilty*! I told him I didn't do it!"

Roger said, "I heard Jack. Not much of a lawyer is he?"

Jack just kept saying "I don't believe the nerve of that guy. This could have been real! You guys might have really thought I did this!" Then Jack said, "Don't get rid of that cat because of this. They know how to read people."

Roger laughed, "That cat got us our DNA sample."

Jack's eyes got real big, "Yes it did!" He left the office obviously looking for Ellen.

Paul came around the corner and said, "You better get in here." Roger went into his office. Devon was on the TV news, in the police center parking lot, giving an interview to the reporters.

Paul turned up the volume on the TV, "All I can tell you is that I will mount an aggressive defense for my client, Jack Simpson, regardless of how much forensic evidence the FBI claims to have."

Roger and Paul looked at each other. Roger slammed his fist on his desk, "Damn it. Damn it!" Paul was clenching his fists and said he would go tell Jack. They needed to get someone assigned to Joy for security. Roger stood at the window in his office glaring at Devon surrounded by reporters, microphones pushed to his face, smiling for the cameras. "If it's the last thing I do," Roger whispered.

Roger got a call from CSI. They had a fingerprint hit from the house where the woman at Memorial Hospital had been held prisoner. The hit came from the Financial Institutions Bureau. The FIB reported the print was that of Mr. William Patterson, Sr., Vice President of Commons National Bank and Trust. Trust Officers that were responsible for large sums of money were required by the Insurance Bonding Companies, the Banks Risk Management policies, and the FIB to have fingerprints on file with the Regulator.

Roger wrote down the information and went into the 'room'. He wasn't surprised by the chaos. People were huddled in small groups, dashed in and out of the doorways. Papers were being passed about, voices shouted. There was so much happening in such a short period of time that the stress was palatable. He asked the Senior Agent Phillips, from St. Joseph, if he could talk to him a minute, and then took him to the far side of the room.

Roger started, "Agent Phillips, I understand you have about as much seniority as I do with the Bureau?"

Agent Phillips answered, "Yes, I think I do. I tried to retire last year, and they wouldn't let me go. What's up?"

Roger smiled at him, "I just got confirmation of a print match from the house of our survivor who is in the hospital. Did you hear about her?"

Agent Phillips nodded, "I heard that if we hadn't found her today, she would have died. Starved."

Roger continued, "The print is that of a Sr. Trust Officer at Commons National Bank, who I believe we'll discover he's in charge of a fifteen million dollar trust for Devon's wife, Sandy. When she hits her thirty-fourth birthday on January 13th, she will inherit it all."

Agent Phillips raised an eyebrow and whistled. Roger continued, "I bet if someone takes a DMV pic lineup sheet to the hospital, we will get a positive identification that he is the second guy in this Devon mess. The one letting the women starve. Then of course we will serve warrants for arrest and seizure of documents immediately."

Agent Phillips was looking at him, "Are you telling me you are looking to give this career creampuff away?"

Roger smiled, "I was thinking about your boy Nelson, seems to be a kid on the rise. If you would like it yourself, it's almost all laid out."

Agent Phillips was stroking his chin, "I don't want even a piece of it! I'm bloody sick of all this shit. Good choice. Let's give it to the kid, but you do it. I have to keep working with the other one." He had nodded his head toward a desk in the corner where the other agent looked totally overwhelmed.

Agent Phillips was back at his spot at the table and heard Agent Nelson saying, "Yes Sir. Yes sir." Roger was smiling to himself. Fairly early in Roger's career an almost identical thing happened to him, and really boosted his status within the Agency. He was still smiling when Agent Nelson stood up, "I won't disappoint you sir."

Agent Phillips just smiled and said, "If Agent Dance gave you any details to follow up on he expects them ASAP!"

Agent Nelson said, "Yes sir!" as he spun around and started making calls.

Agent Todd Nelson poked his head into Roger's door as he was leaving for the hospital. Roger looked up as Nelson said, "I am going to the hospital now, sir. I have the six DMV photos one of which is William Patterson."

Roger looked at him, "Take two patrolmen with you. Call me from the hospital if she ID's this guy. I will have the arrest warrant and seizure papers ready for you to go immediately to the bank." Then Roger said, "Confirm…quietly that he is working today… his auto is in the lot…that you are at the right branch…I do not want him to have any warning that you are coming…okay? I do not want him afforded any courtesy. Cuffs and leg irons. He's earned this."

Roger's phone rang, "Dance"

It was Agent Thor, "I'm not screaming "uncle" yet, but I am thinking about it."

Roger prepared himself, "What's up Dan?"

"We started on those properties that Devon owns. Three visits…three bodies! This is one sick bastard. If this guy isn't gone yet, you can bet he's getting ready. This crap will be all over the news tonight. There won't be any getting out of this for him. Are any of the St. Joe guys available?" He sounded spent. Death can really take its toll.

Roger answered, "The St. Joe guys are down to two, one just left on an assignment. The Director did give me authority to call in three Chicago boys if you want them?"

Agent Thor said, "They can be here in a couple of hours! You're damn right I want them!" Roger asked if he needed any patrol to help and Thor said "Anybody! Not to mention I am killing off the CSI, and don't even talk about the M.E. The EMT guys said they have filled the halls of the morgue and put the last two in the break room."

Roger cringed, "I'll see what I can do about the Chicago Medical Examiner. Maybe we can send some of these bodies there and borrow their CSI."

Thor said, "Thanks. Just let me know," and hung up. Roger thought Thor was right. Devon and Patterson have no choice but to leave after tonight's news. They were out of time. So were Sandy and Ashley.

Roger placed a couple of calls and found out three agents from Chicago were actually just fin-ished with an assignment in Merrillville and should be able to be there within the hour. Roger also called the Chicago Medical Examiner, got permis-sion to bring no more than twenty bodies to them, and a CSI team would be dispatched immediately. Chief Doyle said he would pull available patrol to at least help with traffic issues and reporters, maybe get a couple more State boys. Roger called Thor back with the news.

Paul came in and said, "He has to have them somewhere near his house. I can't figure out how he is doing this; all the bodies, all the cars. He answered the phone way too fast when you called."

"I know."

Paul started pacing, "I just talked to the guys watching his house, and the Buick is right there outside his office door. We followed GPS, he went straight to this office from here."

Roger asked, "Are any of the houses he owns on that list within walking distance of his house?"

"None. I mapped them out earlier and they are scattered all over South Bend, but none by his place."

Just then Roger's phone rang, "Dance." It was Stan at the forensics lab, "We have your boy Devon's fingerprints matching prints found on the outside driver' s window of Karen Smith's car. I got the lawyer's prints from the court records. Also, lawyer prints on that little piece of duct tape you found by Ginger Hall's accident site."

Roger said, "Thanks," and hung up.

He repeated to Paul what Stan had said and they both agreed that it was nice to have direct evidence to Devon other than Sandy's testimony. The unspoken fear was that Sandy and Ashley Tait might not live to testify. Paul gave Roger an update of what the "Talking Heads" of the news were saying about Jack, comparing him to Bundy and others. "I wouldn't be surprised if a lynch mob doesn't show up at Joy's house. We have security there, but I am worried. We may need to bring her here too. The public wants blood!"

The officer watching Devon's house called Paul, "He's on the move! I'll follow him. Do you want more eyes on this if he goes into traffic?"

Paul answered, "No, the GPS is still working. We'll watch him from here and keep you posted." Roger entered a few keystrokes into his computer. Paul and he were watching Devon's car move toward the highway in real time.

Roger said, "You know its four o'clock and this shit hits the news at six if not sooner. Two hours. It's going to get harder to keep eyes on him, and he has to run. Maybe he's going to where he has Sandy and Ashley. Could we get so lucky?"

Paul shrugged and realized the cat was on his lap. He knew that meant Jack wasn't far behind. Jack was trying to make claim to Ellen, and she wasn't buying it. Sure enough Jack showed up in the doorway. He knocked on the open door even though they both were already looking at him. Paul spoke, "Hey, I have your little friend here if you are looking for her."

Jack frowned, "I don't think she likes me anymore. I tried to give her a bath." Roger and Paul looked at each other and cracked up. Ellen wasn't winking, and she did look a little wet around the ears. Jack continued, "It's not like a dog. They get mean!" He showed them the fresh scratches up and down both arms and on his neck. Paul was wiping his eyes thinking how bad that could have been. He looked at Ellen, and she winked. They had needed the tension relief of Jack's visit.

Roger stretched his neck and asked, "How you holding up Jack?"

Jack answered "Okay. I feel useless. I wish I was doing something. And I'm mad. I can't believe my own lawyer gave the press my name and everything. You know I have been thinking, he might have them women in some house by his office. You said he got to the office awful fast after your guys lost him, right in his own neighborhood!"

Roger realized that Jack had been doing a little eavesdropping of his own. He really didn't blame him. Roger answered, "We're thinking that too Jack. We just can't start barging in a lot of private homes, and we don't want to alert him. We'll figure this out." Roger smiled, trying to ease some of the tension.

Jack nodded his head and said, "Just sayin'." He left the room. Ellen did not follow him.

Paul asked Roger, "How are you staying so calm?"
"I'm not."

* * *

Linda, Mary, Teresa, and I were sitting in chairs near the ceiling at the county clerk's office. Linda said, "Right there! That lady has her elbow on the stack of files that I need." They were looking at a fairly chubby woman who was taking a snack break at her desk. Linda said, "She better not spill that pop on those files. Look over there! I had those all organized and now look. No wonder they are three months behind."

Teresa said, "Maybe we should feel sorry for them. This is a lot of work, and there are only two of them to do it."

The other office gal was trying to politely explain to a young man that everyone has to pay property taxes if they own a home. He was shouting, "Well, nobody ever told me. My grandma gave me this house free and clear, and now you want two thousand dollars. Suppose I just don't pay it?"

The lady said to him, "Then the County will seize it for nonpayment of taxes!"

He looked at her, "What does that mean?"

She was exasperated, "We will take the house and sell it to pay the taxes." He went nuts! She called for security and the chubby lady finally moved over by them when she heard the security officer arrive.

Teresa flew into action and exchanged a pile of files from the table with the pile the lady had used as an elbow rest. She took the 'elbow rest files' into a storage closet. Mary guarded the door, and Linda told Teresa and me what to look for as we sorted. We finally had four files that were property transfers to Devon that we hadn't seen on our previous trip. Teresa looked at Linda and asked, "Now what?" Linda said the last time the IT guy Ray, got the property addresses from the tax record legal description.

She didn't know if we could do it that way or not. I had the brilliant idea of checking where the bill had been sent before the transfer. We had the names of the people who deeded the properties. They paid the last bills.

Mary spoke through the crack in the door, "How do we find the billing records?"

Teresa was looking around the office, "How about these filing cabinets that say "Billing?" Smarty pants. Now the problem was how to open the filing cabinet and sort through files without being seen.

The cabinets were smack dab in between these two ladies. I had another idea. Teresa must have heard it because we were both studying the ceiling when Mary asked, "What are you guys thinking..." Just as I pulled the fire alarm switch. Wow was that loud!

Our little chubby lady could really move. It looked like she was going to run over anything or anyone that got in her way.

In three minutes we had the room to ourselves, but the noise was deafening. We were shouting at each other things like, "Hurry!" "Look in the bottom one!" "We need the M's" "Got one!" "Here's one!" We found three of the four, and the sirens stopped. We heard people in the hall starting to come back. Linda shouted, "We have to fax them to Roger yet! You have to stall them!"

Mary ran out of the room and spread herself across the hallway. People just walked through her. "That was weird," she said. Teresa ran down the hall knocking over the indoor potted trees. Dirt and broken pots were everywhere. It did cause people to stop and wonder what had happened long enough for our fax to go through. Teresa was better at controlling mass than the rest of us were. She reminded us to concentrate our 'will', and we had greater force than mass. Whatever.

We went outside of the courthouse, and I said, "That might be considered manipulation of mortal environment."

Teresa looked at me, "Uh oh."

Linda said she was going to let Ellen know we had finished at the clerk's office and find out what she wanted us to do next. We were all sitting in the back of some guy's pickup truck playing with a big German shepherd dog when Ellen told us to get to the Commons National Bank and stop William Patterson from leaving.

We all looked at each other, "Who the heck is William Patterson?"

Ellen explained that he was a "friend" of Devon's who had been bribed into helping Devon. His job was to kill the women. Devon would call him with an address, and he was supposed to get rid of them. Patterson decided to keep them alive long enough for him and Devon to get out of the country with Sandy's money. Now the women were being found, dead. Patterson had been watching the news. The cops were finding bodies all over the city. It was all over. He decided to "advance" himself a little of Sandy's money…three million. Patterson decided he would take her records and leave now. He was sure the FBI would find his prints, and he wasn't going to stick around.

Ellen told us the FBI was going to show up to arrest him, but probably not for another half hour or so. Teresa asked what we could do to stop him. We knew the real question was how far can we go? Ellen was thinking and then said, "I can't be with you. I am going to have to trust whatever you do could be explained by mortals, other than him. We don't care about him."

Teresa was rubbing her hands together, "NINJA ANGEL!" Ellen was in Roger's office shaking her head.

CHAPTER 23

Roger and Paul were still watching the GPS screen and saw Devon's car had stopped. They quickly searched the address and discovered it was a funeral home in town. Roger called and found out that the services for Ginger Hall were going to start in fifteen minutes. Roger almost choked when he said, "He's at Ginger Hall's funeral."

Paul shouted, "No way! Jesus! Is there no bottom to this guy?"

Roger noticed the fax message on his computer and printed it. The fax was from Kim, right, it said, "There are four more properties. Here are four legal descriptions, but we only found three street addresses to match." Paul dashed from the room.

Roger called Ray in IT, "I have one legal description that I need a street address for. Can you get it for me?" Ray said he would call him back. Paul had seen the list and already left to get a map.

Roger felt it was entirely possible Devon was planning on leaving the country, tonight. Surely once he saw the news of today's discoveries of bodies in the houses he owned, he would know the jig was up. That meant Sandy and Ashley would not live to see tomorrow, if they weren't already dead. Roger knew that Paul was having the same thought. They were out of time.

Paul returned with the map. All three street addresses were within walking distance of Devon's office. Paul declared, "We should go now...while he's at the funeral." Roger knew Paul was making an emotional decision, and this had to be done right.

"Let's give Ray a minute to get us that fourth address and I want to make sure Nelson can handle this Patterson guy. That is going down right now too."

"She could be ..."

Roger looked at him, "Paul, he just talked to Jack. If he is comfortable enough to go to a funeral, he isn't feeling pressured by us at the moment. I just want all of the information. We have men ready. She could be in the one address we don't have. Fifteen minutes, okay?"

Jack had been listening in the hall. I told them. Right in this neighborhood. Well they might have to wait but I don't. He went to his little room, grabbed his truck keys, and walked quickly out of the building.

Roger's phone rang. It was Agent Nelson, "Special Agent Dance? She has positively identified William Patterson as the man that stopped feeding her." Roger told him the warrant and seizure notice would be ready by the time he arrived at the bank. Roger told Nelson that he would send the paperwork with a patrol unit. Not to wait. He asked Agent

Nelson if he had verified Patterson was there. Agent Nelson said he had spoken with Patterson's secretary about coming in without an appointment. He had pretended he was an investor and was only in town for a couple of hours. She assured him she was looking at Patterson as they spoke.

Roger said, "Good, and Agent Nelson? You do not need to be polite." Roger then called the DA for the arrest warrant and the seizure papers. He specified he wanted listed any documents and records in the bank that referenced Sandy Nelson Devon, including any un-posted transactions, for all standard accounts and all trust accounts. He was learning from this deed thing.

* * *

It took a while for the gals to find Patterson's office. He had a big corner suite, and he was bent over loading a bunch of files from his desk drawer into a box. He also had a stack of what was titled Account Transfer Receipts, and he had obviously been signing Sandy Devon's name to them. He had made a few computer entries and neatly put the transfer slips into an envelope and into his pocket. His secretary had walked into his office and said, "Oh. Were you planning on leaving? I just told a gentleman you were here. He's on his way over."

William Patterson looked at her and said, "I have an appointment I am late for already, so if you could just reschedule for me, I would appreciate it."

"He said he was only in town for a couple of hours."

Patterson glared at her, "His poor planning is not my problem. Now, if you will *excuse* me, I have a few things to finish before I leave." She walked out of the office and shut his door.

This was one big guy. We were trying to think how we could stop him once he tried to leave his office. Teresa said, "Maybe we can just drop that file cabinet on him."

We all looked at her and Mary said, "I think killing him is going to set us back in class a little."

"We could throw things at him." I thought that was a good idea until Linda pointed to the large picture window to the waiting area, clear view of the secretary's desk. "How does she not see that?" He started to stand up and put his overcoat on. Teresa tied one sleeve into a knot. He wrestled with it, and then his phone rang. His secretary was bent around looking at him.

He sighed, sat in his chair, and picked up the phone, "Patterson." He listened for a minute and said, "Why don't you just do whatever you want Fred? No, I'm not mad. I don't care."

Then he got up again and reached down to pick up the box. He had a money wire on his screen, and I hit the print button. His printer started, he stopped, and looked at it. When it finished printing, he folded it, put it in his pocket, and started walking away from his desk again. I hit print again. He slammed the box onto his desk, closed down his computer, ripped the paper out that had just printed and put it in his pocket. He opened his cell phone. Dialed and waited, "Hey, you sick son of a bitch, I'm leaving now. There is an extra jet at the airport if you need it, and I called to let our 'friends' know we need plan B. You better move your ass boy!" Patterson snapped his phone shut, looked around the office, and started walking to the door.

I yelled, "Out of ideas here!" Mary knocked a bunch of files off the corner of his desk. He just looked back and left them. Shit.

Teresa yelled, "Grab his legs." We all dived to the floor, and he walked right through us.

He was next to the secretary's desk when Linda screamed, "Trees!" There were four indoor potted trees in the waiting area. We each grabbed one and threw them at him.

He dropped his box and was brushing dirt from his suit when they heard, "William Patterson? FBI. You are under arrest for murder." Patterson had tried to turn, but Agent Nelson had him on the floor with his knee in his back. He was handcuffing him. Then he had the leg irons put on him and stood him up. Agent Nelson handed the seizure warrant to the secretary and said, "Please call whatever staff can assist you in collecting the documents on this list. Our agent will remain with you. There will be no computer entries or other persons allowed in this area until we are through." She looked like she was going to faint. Then he read Patterson his rights, loudly, and proceeded to walk him through the front lobby and out of the building.

Teresa called Ellen, "Hi, we…"

Ellen interrupted her, "Yeah I know. What's with you and *trees*? Now I need you guys to go follow Jack. He is going to get into trouble real soon. Big trouble. Head towards Devon's office. You should find him somewhere in Devon's neighborhood. I have to stay with Roger and Paul a few more minutes." Ellen looked up and said a small prayer.

* * *

Paul jumped up from his chair, "Devon's moving again! Bastard must have just wanted a look." Paul's raised voice startled Roger. Roger made a motion with his hands for Paul to calm down.

Roger called Ray again, "I am sorry, but I am out of time. You got that address for me? I'll wait on the line."

Paul was pacing, looking at the screen, "He's heading back towards his office." Roger started writing and then hung up. He turned the map around and the last address looked like it actually was just behind Devon's back yard. Paul said, "That looks like the house where we parked and watched his house the first time."

Roger said, "He could park in any one of these garages, do whatever, walk home and our guys might not even see him."

Paul was looking at the screen. He was nearly out of his mind, "He's half way home!"

Roger handed Paul the list of addresses, then said, "I have one quick call."

Roger called Agent Nelson for an update and told him to bring Patterson to the police center, not county and put him in the interrogation room. Not to un-cuff him. Then he added, "I think your senior and you can handle any statement he may make. You can be sure he is going to lawyer up." Roger called the DA for search warrants on the four addresses for Devon and asked that they be delivered to him by patrol as soon as they were ready.

The DA barked, "Are we at the end of this thing?"

Roger answered, "One way or another, it ends now."

That was all Paul had to hear. He ran into the 'room' with printed copies of the addresses. Paul held the copies over his head as he announced, "Time to take Devon down. These four addresses, we are rolling now! Go silent. He has two live hostages. We need to surprise him. Park and walk." Chairs scraped the floor and the twelve agents in the room began checking their weapons. The metal clacking sounds of their weapons were deafening. One by one they rushed through the door and ran towards their vehicles. Chief Doyle pressed his body to the wall in the hallway to keep from getting run over. He would let these guys finish this up. They had earned it.

* * *

Jack had parked his truck behind a Smoke Shop and walked two blocks to the neighborhood directly behind Devon's office. He was hiding by a large pine tree trying to decide which house to start with. There were a few that looked empty, but he could see tire tracks going into the garages in the light snow. He decided to try to look like a utility meter reader, except he didn't have a notebook, so he peeled a big piece of bark from a fallen log. It actually was about the right size, and he walked up to the first house. He stood by the meter, pretended to read it, and walked across the patio. He was going to peek in, but he saw a lady feeding a baby in a high chair. He tipped his hat to her and just kept walking to the next house.

When he got to the next house, he pretended to be reading that meter and walked across that patio. He was ready to tip his hat, but the house looked empty. There was a sliding patio door which anyone in construction could pick. They usually have to break in to go to work. He slid the door open slowly and peeked in. He couldn't hear anything, and he didn't see any furniture.

The house was dirty, and he was immediately hit with a terrible smell. Not good. His instincts were telling him to turn around and run. He was not the hero type, but he knew he had to find Sandy and Ashley. He slowly made his way down the hall with his jacket pulled up over his nose. He slowly pushed open a door and peeked in a back bedroom. He saw a woman tied to a chair with duct tape and rope. She was dead. The chair had tipped over and her body fluids had soaked the carpet around her. He figured she had probably been gone for a while. Jack gagged as he ran towards the patio door to get out. He throat was making some kind of noise he couldn't control. When he got outside, he threw up against the air conditioner. He actually thought he was going to faint.

Teresa spotted him outside of the house and pointed to him. Mary said, "Great. What are we supposed to do with him anyway?"

Linda said, "I think we are just supposed to follow him and make sure he doesn't get into trouble."

Teresa said, "That's all?" I was thinking this little adventure had potential for hurting our class score.

Jack went to the next house, same story. There was another dead woman. Once outside again he leaned against the back wall and took deep breaths. It struck him that he was seeing these women like this before their families even knew they were dead. He had a steady stream of tears he couldn't control running down his cheeks. How do the cops do it?

He decided to go to the house that backed up to Devon's back yard next. There wasn't a patio like the others because it was an open basement in the back. He slid down the embankment on the light snow, looked around, and started unlocking the patio door. He slowly slid it open and heard strange noises around the corner of the wall. Maybe this house wasn't vacant.

He tiptoed to the end of the wall, peeked around the corner, and saw two women, alive! They were bound to chairs with duct tape and had big long chains locked around their ankles. Jack was suddenly struck with paralyzing fear. This was the real deal! He was in the Monster's Den! Both women were looking at him with panic in their eyes. There was no turning back now. He ran over to them and was introducing himself, "I'm a good guy. I'm going to save you. Can I take this tape off your mouth?" He was talking to Sandy. She nodded her head.

When he removed the tape, she said, "Please undo my hands! I have a phone in my bra!" Women are so weird, Jack thought. Why would you keep a phone in your bra?

We were just outside of the house Jack was in and saw Devon leave through his back door. He started walking through the light snow heading directly for the house. What would be the word that describes panic times ten? That would be the word to describe the moment. I was wildly trying to find something to use as a weapon. We have not been prepared properly! There was a squirrel chattering at me. I grabbed it from its branch and threw it at Devon. The squirrel wildly slashed at Devon's face as it tried to get a hold of something solid, then it jumped to a nearby branch and resumed chattering at me. Sorry.

Mary frowned at me, "What's wrong with you? A squirrel?"

Linda saw a small branch that she pulled back so it slapped his face. He was annoyed but kept on walking. "What do we do now?" Devon was within twenty feet of the patio door.

Mary screamed, "Stick a branch between his legs and make him trip!" That worked, but he got back up and kept walking. We kept sticking branches between his legs.

Jack got a small pen knife out of his pocket and was sawing on the tape. He noticed that both women were taped just like the ones in the other houses. He looked at Sandy after he got her hands free and said, "I am going to undo your friend now." He walked over to Ashley and carefully removed the tape from her mouth.

Ashley wailed, "You have to get us out of here! He's coming back!"

Jack was saying, "I know, I know. I almost got this cut." Ashley's hands were free. He noticed their bodies were taped around the basement support poles, and he started cutting the tape on them.

Sandy said, "This stupid phone isn't working!" Jack couldn't imagine who she was trying to call that was more important than what they were doing. Women!

Jack tossed her his, "Try this one." He had Ashley free, but her ankle was still locked to a very long chain. Jack looked at her and said, "I need to get her undone from that pole." Ashley was nodding, and Jack went back to cutting the tapes on Sandy's pole. Sandy couldn't get Jack's phone to work either.

They all heard the patio door slide open, and then Devon was standing in front of them. "What the Hell are you doing here?"

Devon pulled his fist back to hit Jack. We had just flown into the room and were trying to find something to hit Devon with. I remembered the old man in the basement of one of the foreclosure homes, and how easy it was to conjure up items by just wishing it. I put a frying pan in Jacks hand. As if he wasn't stunned enough, Jack looked at the pan, pulled his arm back, and hit Devon on the side of the head. Devon stumbled backward a couple of steps, and then shouted at Jack, "You're dead!" He lunged at Jack and put his hands around Jack's throat. Jack was trying to pull Devon's hands away, but he just wasn't strong enough. Devon was laughing. Jack's face was getting red, and his knees were starting to buckle. All four of us were beating on Devon, he just couldn't feel it. Sandy and Ashley were screaming for Devon to stop!

Ellen appeared and said, "Get Back! I'm going in!" We saw her enter Jack's body. Jack's face got a determined look, and he brought his arms straight up and broke Devon's grip on his neck. Then he hit Devon three times in the face and one to the gut. With each blow Devon stumbled backwards. Devon doubled over and went down to the floor. Jack jumped on him, grabbed Devon's arms, pulled them behind his back, and started taping his hands with duct tape. *That just happened to be next to the wall.* Then Jack taped Devon's ankles, and did some kind of hog tie type thing with the tape. Devon looked like an ugly rocking horse. Jack just sat on the floor and exhaled. Ellen was out.

Devon was screaming profanities, so Jack wrapped a piece of tape around his mouth and all the way around his head. Devon was done. We all collapsed on the floor. Ellen took a bow and said she was going to get Roger and Paul. Then she looked at me, "A squirrel?" Uh oh. Sandy and Ashley had stood up during the fight. Sandy was punching the air and screaming the whole time like she was actually helping....about as much help as we had been. Now they were clapping and hugging Jack. He was out of breath, but he managed to say, "You know the FBI is planning on checking out this neighborhood soon, so I guess we should just wait."

Ashley had started crying. Jack put his arm around her shoulder, "It's okay now. You're okay now. What do you need? What can I do?"

Ashley was shaking her head, and then she wiped the tears from her cheeks and smiled, "My hero, Jack. You have done plenty, unless you can figure out a way I can shower?" She pointed to the bathroom behind them, "It's been three days, and I got sick last night." Ashley looked miserable.

Jack said, "How far will this chain go if we go this way?" he was dragging the heavy chain across the furnace duct which gave her another ten feet.

Ashley yelled from the bathroom, "I'm in. But..."

Jack said, "Oh…hey, take my clothes. I just put these on an hour ago." Ashley and Sandy started laughing,

Jack had kicked off his boots, dropped his pants and taken his shirt off. "Here, take your shower and put these on." Ashley gave him a big hug and went into the shower. Jack put his boots back on, and pulled Ashley's chair over by Sandy so he could talk to her. He was wearing his briefs, his socks, and his boots. In minutes he and Sandy could see steam rolling from under the door.

Sandy looked spent, "You know he just took me this morning from that house, and he set the house on fire! My friends were in there."

Jack looked at her, "Sal and John? They're fine. I saw Sal before I left the police center. They got out!" Sandy was so happy she couldn't quit giggling. Every now and then she looked over to Devon who was glaring at them. She turned her chair, so she didn't have to see his face.

"How could I have married him?" she whispered.

Jack looked at her and said, "I think we all get fooled every now and then. You can just start over. I am just starting a new life myself." He proceeded to tell Sandy about what he used to be like, four days ago. How he had volunteered to be a Person Of Interest, so they could trick Devon, and how he was trying to better himself. "This stuff takes time."

They heard the water shut off in the bathroom and a scuffle around the corner by the sliding door. Roger, Paul and two other agents burst into the room with their guns drawn. Roger looked at Devon on the floor, and then at Jack, "Ashley's not here?" Paul went pale.

Jack answered, "She's in the shower," and pointed to the bathroom.

Paul ran over to the door, "Ashley?"

Her voice screamed, "Paul?" The bathroom door burst open, and Ashley threw herself into Paul's arms. She was sobbing uncontrollably.

Paul held her close until she seemed to calm down and said, "Jack's clothes sure look better on you." Everyone started laughing.

Roger had three patrolmen secure Devon and carry him outside to the caged patrol car. He called for an ambulance for Sandy and Ashley. One of the troopers removed the locks on their ankle chains. Roger looked at Jack and said, "I've got to tell you Jack, I'm impressed. He is as strong as a pit bull."

Jack said, "I don't know what happened. I don't know how I did it. He had me, I was goin' down. Then all of a sudden I was kickin' ass!" Sandy and Ashley told them how brave Jack had been.

Roger interrupted, "That doesn't excuse that he interfered with a federal investigation."

Jack said, "Yeah, there is that. Just a detail, right?"

Roger couldn't resist, he pointed at Ashley, "Ask a federal judge." Jack went pale and his jaw dropped. Roger winked at Ashley, and she played along by frowning at Jack.

Then she laughed, "How can you tease a man standing in his undershorts in a 40 degree basement?"

Jack said, "Yeah, what she said."

Then Jack got serious, he whispered to Roger, "You got a whole neighborhood of dead people out there. Well, two that I know of." Roger sent a trooper out to retrieve his wool overcoat from the back seat of his car. They had already found the other women, and there were three.

The ambulance attendants were there, and Paul said he would ride with the girls to the hospital and have a trooper follow him. Roger asked Jack if he needed to go to the hospital and he said he just wanted Joy, and some clothes. Roger handed him the phone and said, "Tell her to meet us at the police center, fix herself up pretty and bring you nice clothes. You both are going to be all over the TV news tonight."

Jack grabbed the phone and kept talking to Joy even as Roger was guiding him back up the slippery slope of the yard to the cars. They got to the car, and Roger told Jack he needed his phone back. After about four, "I love you too, honey's," he finally got it.

Ellen told us to go back to the police center. Linda said, "Ellen said we're done."

Mary gasped, "How did she mean that? Done how?"

Teresa said, "I think we did well on this. There was a lot going on!" I didn't say anything, I had been counting issues all along, and I think we were about a C+. It's not like they can grade us on a curve. We are the only 'group'! Also, I'm not sure, but I bet squirrel tossing is not an allowable sport in Heaven.

Ellen didn't say what she wanted us to do at the police center, so we decided to check out parts of the building we hadn't seen before. We ended up in the non-violent section of the holding cells. There were only a few of the cells occupied so we took turns going in and out of the empty ones. It was pretty cool. We decided to go out to the parking lot and see what the reporters were up to. Teresa kept standing in front of the cameras and making faces. I did too, until Mary mentioned that we weren't *sure* that we wouldn't show up on film. We had never thought about that. Guess we wait to see the six o'clock news.

One reporter's truck had the radio on and none of us had heard any new songs lately, so we sat in his truck and listened to the radio. We were bored, like four kids. We went out into the field by the station and made a bunch of snow angels, which turned into a snow ball fight 'til we realized someone might see the balls flying around. Poor Ellen, I think we are hopeless.

* * *

CHAPTER 24

Roger finally was able to get his phone from Jack, call Chief Doyle and the DA, and tell them he wanted a news conference scheduled for 6:00. That gave them one hour. He wanted Jack and Joy on the evening news. Roger filled them in on the developments of the arrest of Devon and the rescue of Sandy and Ashley. He could hear the relief in their voices. He also filled in the Chief on Patterson, as much as he could. Roger and Jack were still in Roger's car. Roger hung up his phone and looked at Jack, "You are a real hero today. I am going to make sure the world knows that tonight, but you also could have really screwed this up and cost those two women their lives. I want you to think about that. I want you to promise me you will never involve yourself in something unless someone you trust asks you to." He looked Jack in the eyes and said firmly, "I mean this Jack."

"I promise. Man, do I promise." Jack laid his head against the headrest and cried.

When Joy got to the station, she looked really nice. She took one look at Jack and said, "Where are your clothes?" He was talking to a group of officers in the main hall in Roger's wool coat, his underwear, socks, and boots. Everyone around them just started laughing.

Paul had returned from the hospital where Sandy and Ashley were being checked by medical staff. He had asked them to call him when they were ready to come home. He went looking for Roger and found him talking to Agent Nelson about the Patterson arrest. Agent Thor and his team had returned to the center for the press conference. Thor and his guys looked like they had spent the day in Hell, and in many ways they had. Paul thought, I bet Thor is right up on the podium before it's over.

The guys from Indy were bringing the task force up to date on the body count...nine at the foreclosure homes, and so far eleven on the tax property list. Everyone was shaking their head in disbelief. They knew this case, and Devon, was going to make FBI history. Unfortunately, this probably wasn't the last case like this they would get. As soon as Paul was seen in the room, everyone wanted an update on the rescue. Even though Paul felt absolutely spent, he took the time to recount all of the events for them. They had worked hard on this case too.

Roger was congratulating Agent Nelson and Senior Agent Phillips when Paul joined them. Agent Nelson looked at Paul, "We got a full confession." Paul glanced at Roger.

Roger rubbed the back of his neck and said, "Why didn't he lawyer up? This doesn't make sense."

Roger gestured he was going to his office and asked Paul if he had a minute. They went into the office, shut the door, and both of them dropped their heads on the desk. After about two minutes, Paul raised his head and said, "Oh my God."

Roger lifted his head, "I think it's over, for the most part. Thor's got some work to do." They both started laughing. It would be months before the tension from this case would really be gone, but tonight was a start. Ellen appeared on Roger's lap. Roger looked at her and said "Please, don't tell me I have a problem." Ellen shut her eyes. Roger said, "Good." Ellen put her paw on the phone. Roger looked at Paul, "Do you believe this?" Then he looked at Ellen, "You want me to call someone?" Ellen winked. Roger asked, "Kim?" Ellen winked. Roger dialed Kim, and Ellen went over to lie on Paul's lap.

Kim answered, "Hello?"

Roger said, "It's me. We got him."

Kim said, "I know! Mom has called *twice*. She is so excited. Are you okay?"

Roger answered, "Yes."

Kim said, "I know you are probably beat, and I'm not sure this is even appropriate. Tonight is the memorial for my mom and her friends down at the bar they used to lunch at. More of a wake I guess. I know they will be there. I wouldn't mind you seeing that I have a 'normal' side too. They have good burgers if you haven't eaten."

Roger didn't even have to think about it, "Kim, that sounds great. I would like to see your normal side, but I have a couple of hours here yet." Kim gave him directions and hung up.

Paul looked at him, "You are going on a date? Tonight?"

Roger laughed, "Not really, a wake for Kim's mom and her friends at their bar."

Paul said, "I'll be staying at Ashley's tonight. She's still pretty spooked. This was a bad one."

Roger added, "Jack said Sandy is going to move into Nettie's place until she figures out what she wants to do."

Paul shook his head. "Strange world." Paul pushed his chin out in a quick motion, "What is the story on Patterson? I'm with you. Something doesn't pass the smell test."

Roger said, "I'm going to give you the short version. He and Devon met because Patterson was going down for child molesting. Devon negotiated a way for him to buy his way out of it. They became scum buddies. When Devon married Sandy and found out her Trust money was at Commons National, he told Patterson he could have a couple of million if he got Sandy to sign papers transferring all her money to him on her birthday. Once Devon started collecting so many women, he literally didn't have *time* to kill them all. Patterson agreed to get rid of them for Devon, but later decided to keep them alive by feeding them. I don't think he has the stomach for killing. Get this, Patterson's reason for not feeding them anymore was that there were too many. He claims Devon took too many. That wasn't the deal. He had work and social commitments. There just wasn't enough time."

"Doesn't explain why he confessed."

Roger tapped his pen on his desk, "He isn't stupid, and I bet he has a ton of money hidden. He has a plan."

The press conference was unbelievable! There wasn't a dry eye in the crowd. Roger had walked them through the horrors of Devon, the unselfish decision Jack had made to become the POI, and Jack's heroic, albeit unauthorized, rescue of the two live hostages. Jack was signing autographs for the reporters while holding Ellen. One of the reporters asked him about the cat, and he answered, "This is Ellen. She doesn't really belong to me, but she brings us good luck. And she doesn't like baths!" Ellen had raised a paw for the pictures. (The photo had been picked up by AP Wire Service and caused Ellen a small reprimand. Another story.)

Paul had left for the hospital to pick up Sandy and Ashley, and Roger was reviewing the directions Kim had given him. The Tavern, Niles, Michigan, just over the state line she had said. He found the street on his map, grabbed his coat, looked for Ellen, but she was gone.

Roger found the bar and there was a bright neon orange sign on the door that said "Shallow End Gals –Memorial Wake." He went in and saw Kim sitting at the bar with a bunch of people around her. She saw him come in and said, "Roger, I saved you a seat." The little crowd moved away, so he could sit. He gave Kim a little kiss on the cheek. She was so beautiful. She looked like she was actually glowing when she smiled, "You did it." Kim smiled.

"WE did it," Roger said.

Roger looked around. It was a medium size bar, clean, and the people there looked to be from all walks of life. It was a long "U" shaped bar, with a walkthrough space so the staff could get to the kitchen and back side of the bar, with booths lining the other walls. Roger asked, "The sign says; Shallow End Gals?"

Kim nodded and said, "See how this part of the bar only has six stools and the other side has maybe twelve?"

Roger laughed, "So they call this the Shallow End."

"Right, this was Mom, Mary, Linda and Teresa's favorite place to sit at lunch time. The staff would put napkins out, so no one else would sit here." Kim pointed to the bartender wearing a Statue of Liberty Costume. "That is Carol. She likes to dress up. Then she pointed to another waitress, "That is Lou, she owns the place. Then there's Jocelyn, Sadie, Sandy, and Marianne. They have all been here forever."

Kim looked at Roger. He was smiling. Then he said, "Were all these people friends of your mom?"

Kim looked around, "I don't think so. I knew most of the people Mom knew. They had a lot of mutual friends. I think a lot of these people knew Linda, Mary, and Teresa more than Mom. Mom didn't get out much over the last ten years or so. She was what we called 'Transportation Challenged'."

Roger laughed, "Wonder how that works now?"

Kim laughed, "I hear there are issues."

Roger realized how difficult Kim's position was. He looked at her, "How long will things be like … this?"

Kim said, "I don't know, but I feel lucky. She hasn't been totally taken from me." Roger thought her eyes looked like pools of Caribbean water. He felt like he could see her soul, and her pain.

He looked around the bar again, "Are they here?"

Kim cleared her throat, "Not yet."

Ellen had told them to take some personal time and enjoy the wake, but to behave. Hmmm, that is pretty limiting. In mortal life I could only think of two people I really didn't like. I had daydreamed that if I ever had the chance I would get even with them, nothing mean. Just a little payback. Now was my chance, and it didn't seem worth it. Life is funny. After- life is funny. I decided to super clean house for Kim before I went to the wake, and play with the cats. That was me then, and I guess that is me now. I put some more cat food out for the strays, made sure Kim's door was locked, and went down the street to the bar.

Mary had decided to visit the Coldwell Banker Real Estate Office where she had worked. She had some good friends there that in life would pester her too. Ray, the main culprit, was at his desk getting ready to go to the wake. Nicky McFarlan, another realtor friend of Mary's, yelled from the kitchen, "Ray! Did you know there is a cake in here with your name on it?" She was taking a finger full of frosting.

Ray came into the room, "Don't do that! It says 'Ray", not just anybody."

Nicky shook her head and said, "You are such a shit! Are you planning on eating the whole cake yourself?" She watched as he retrieved a large knife from the drawer and slammed it shut with his butt.

"I most certainly am." He took a big swipe of frosting with his finger and made a long moaning sound. "Oh this is good!" Then he took the knife and tried to cut it, frowning, he scraped the frosting to one side and saw it was metal. "This is spooky," he said to Nicky. "Only Mary would do this to me."

Nicky was laughing, and Ray came over and jokingly was choking her. Nicky laughed, "Stop —stop. I didn't do this, honest!" Ray sort of backed away from the cake.

Henry, another agent in the office, yelled, "Jesus! That doesn't sound very professional out there."

Ray said, "I don't know if I'm going to the wake or not."

Nicky said, "See? I told you to quit choking Mary four times a day! Karma!" Ray went back to his desk to finish up the BPO for Equinox World Services.

He had been working on it for over two hours, and it was almost done, "I hate this website!" Then, "<u>AAAGH!</u>" All his data was gone. "What happened?" Ray was furious. Mary had pushed the delete button.

Nicky grabbed her jacket and leaned over Ray's computer, "Karma." Mary felt that was a job well done and laughed all the way to the bar.

Linda went home to visit family. Bob was asleep in his chair with the TV going. She could see he had been reading the newspaper. She went to the kitchen and cooked some fried chicken, made some lasagna, and put them in the refrigerator. She didn't know what Bob would think when he found them, but she knew he would know they were from her. If that's breaking the rules, then so be it. While the food was cooking, she cleaned the house a little and did some crafting. She made each family member a little scrap book in the two hours she was there. She put them right on the dining room table to be found. She knew they would be treasured. Then she left for the bar.

Teresa decided she could not pass up the opportunity to mess with her sister Sheila. Sheila took great pleasure and pride in playing tricks on her 'older sister' at any opportunity. Teresa decided that Sheila's doll collection, which filled an entire room of Sheila's house, would be a perfect way to 'spook' little sis.

Teresa flew around Sheila's house placing the dolls in unexpected places, like peeking out of air vents so you could only see the eyes, sitting on a shoe rack, holding a yogurt in the fridge. She even tucked one in Sheila's bed. Her favorite was the ugly doll she hung from a hook on the back of the bathroom door so that when Sheila looked in the bathroom mirror the doll was staring at her. Teresa put some hair gel in the dolls hair to make it look even more crazed, and used Sheila's eyeliner to 'enhance' the doll's creepy look. That ought to get her, Teresa giggled. Then she left for the bar.

* * *

Roger and Kim were talking to people who came over to offer their condolences. Roger was impressed with the number of people with funny memories. Kim had said to him more than once after someone left, "I'll tell you someday. There's a lot more to that story."

Carol came over to Roger, "Okay. How do I know you?" Kim pointed up to the TV where a repeat of the press conference was playing with Roger speaking. Carol went crazy. "You're that dude! WHOA! F-B-I-!" Half of the people at the bar stopped talking, and Carol screamed as she pointed to the TV, "This is the FBI dude that caught the killers." Everyone cheered, clapped, and whistled.

Kim looked at Roger who looked embarrassed. She said, "Oops, so much for a quiet little night in Niles, Michigan."

Carol got his autograph, along with about twenty other people, and then Carol came back over. "Dude! You have about fifty free drinks here. I'm puttin' them in the register 'cause I know you're not drinkin' tonight." She winked at Roger. Then she looked to Kim, "You go girl!" and walked away.

Kim winked at Roger, "Pretty much what it's like here." They both laughed. Kim gently elbowed Roger, "They're here now." She held her glass up. Half of the bar did the same thing not knowing what they were toasting, but what the heck. Then she said, "So is Ellen." Roger looked at the floor and down the aisle. Kim laughed, "When she is around mortals she is a cat. If she isn't going to show herself..." and Kim whispered to him. Roger's eyes got real big. Kim said. "The real one is alive. This was a comfort thing. Do you really expect any of this to make sense?" Roger was shaking his head. He had eaten, and they had been there about two hours. Kim knew the party would go 'til closing, she said to Roger, "I think I am ready to leave. It has been a long day."

Roger got up also, "I'll get you home."

They said their goodbyes to the people around them, and once they were outside Kim said, "I walked here. It's only two blocks. I think I'll just walk home. Thank you for coming tonight. I enjoyed being with you, and I know you must be tired." She gave Roger a little kiss on the cheek. Roger thought he saw her eyes starting to glisten with tears.

Roger held on to her hand and said, "I'll walk with you."

Kim looked at him, "I don't know that I'm the best company."

Roger said, "We don't even have to talk." They didn't. The whole two blocks they just walked. It was a nice crisp evening. Roger felt good with Kim. When they got to Kim's front porch, there was a black cat eating the food she had set out. Kim looked at Roger, and they started laughing. They knew it wasn't Ellen. She didn't eat cat food. Roger walked back to the bar, got in his car, and put the window down, so he could hear the sounds of laughter and feel the night breeze. He was very glad he had come to the wake.

****

CHAPTER 25

***One year later, the first day of the
Prosecution's Case in
The United States of America
VS James Devon***
AFTER-PARTY: South Bend PUB

Roger had received an invitation to attend an after-party at the PUB, on the eve of the prosecution's first day of trial. It was a celebration of Devon finally getting justice. Everyone from the case would have to be in the area for testimony a while once the trial started. In the invitation had been a hand written letter from Joy. Highlights of the last year were, Sandy found out her trust was actually worth more than one hundred million. She had given the City of South Bend five hundred thousand dollars to reimburse for police costs in catching her ex-husband. The FBI is prohibited from accepting personal donations, but allowed their employee's participation in the huge college fund Sandy established for the children of law enforcement personnel.

Sandy had also purchased Nettie's house from Joy and Jack for much more than it was worth, so they would feel financially comfortable. She also bought the PUB, gave it to Jack, and is providing five years free professional advice from business and financial people she uses. She gave a million dollars to the Humane Society *and* built them a huge new facility. The list went on and on....

Jack was still not drinking and was taking college classes in business. Roger shook his head through the whole letter, but especially that part. Joy had quit her job and was the cook at the PUB. Sandy helped cook and waitress when needed. Her money really meant nothing to her other than allowing her to do what she really wanted in life. Sandy and patrolman 'Basement John' were engaged.

Roger pulled into the parking lot and could see that a large addition had been added to the building. There were also new parking lot lighting and signage. He walked in and saw Paul and Ashley at the end of the bar. Roger gave Ashley a kiss on the cheek, and Paul a gentle slap on the back. "Hey Paul, how you been?"

Paul nodded, "Okay, how about you?"

Roger nodded looking at the TV news, "You know, I don't want to jinx this, but my gut has been churning all day thinking about this trial starting."

Paul looked at him, "Wow! I was afraid to say anything. I don't feel right either."

Larry came over and shook Roger's hand. "I never saw you again after you guys solved this thing... good job."

Roger said, "Thank you."

Paul piped up, "Larry is the new manager of the PUB."

Larry interrupted, "Huge salary." They were all laughing. He handed them menus and pointed to the wall behind him that said, "TIPS NOT ALLOWED" Then Larry explained, "The wait staff is on good salaries and benefits too." He was pointing at the menu, "If you notice there are only prices for the booze...look here," and he pointed to a big line that said **P**ay **U**nless **B**roke...**PUB**. Leave what money you feel the food was worth or what you can afford when your waitress clears your table."

Roger asked, "How is that working out?"

Larry smiled, "You know it's funny. We have people who never can pay for their food. Sometimes they come around and volunteer to do some work. People who make up for it next time they are here. Most people overpay because they think it's cool. Business manager says he's never had a new restaurant this profitable...so I guess for us, it works!"

Just then Jack came out of the kitchen and yelled, "Roger! Paul!" He came around the bar and hugged them both, "Man what a year, huh?" Jack couldn't smile any bigger.

Roger said, "Did I hear you are going all college on us?"

Jack was nodding his head "Yup, Yup. You know the kids now days are so smart."

Jack said, "I'll have Joy and Sandy come out and say "hi" when they catch up, they're cookin'."

Paul looked shocked. He knew Sandy was extremely wealthy now, "Sandy cooks here?"

Jack said, "Yeah, she likes it. Not every day. She goes to the Mission a lot too."

Then he said, "This a cop bar, did you know that? Got a funny story. Not long after we opened up, about an hour before closing, this kid in a hoodie comes in. I'm bartending, and he says, 'This a stick up,' with his finger in his pocket, you know. And I said, just like the movie, 'This is a cop bar.' And everyone in here pulls a gun on him. 'Bout shit his pants. I asked him if he needed money for drugs or food. He says food. So I showed him I don't charge anyway. Freaked him out. He's my dishwasher. Hey Jimmy, come here."

A young man, clean cut, came out of the kitchen, "You better not be tellin' that story again. I've got work to do!" Jack waved him away. Paul and Roger laughed so hard they were wiping tears.

Roger noticed Kim come in. He got up, gave her his stool, a kiss, and introduced her to Ashley. Paul noticed Roger had his hand on her shoulder quite a while. Yup, he thought that might go that way. Ashley asked Kim, "How do you know Roger?"

Kim looked at Roger, smiled, and then said, "A long time ago we shared a cat."

****

United States of America VS James Devon: <u>*Day 2*</u>
Prosecutors Case: First Witness

The prosecutor glared at the defendant's table, the defendant in particular. The witness on the stand tried to keep from laughing...this was better than he expected. The judge pounded his gavel and the prosecutor asked for a hearing in the judge's chambers. The judge cleared the courtroom and brought in extra security to watch Devon.

"Just what the *hell* do you think you are doing out there?" the judge shouted once they were all in chambers.

The defense attorney was clearly shaken. "Sir, I had no idea Patterson was going to say that! I don't know what is going on. He's a prosecution witness."

The judge looked at the prosecutor, "Has there been any opportunity for Devon to pull something? What are we doing here?" William Patterson, witness for the prosecution, had just stated in open court that the man at the defense table was not James Devon. The prosecutor was ready to slug someone.

The judge fell back in his seat and stated he was going to declare a two day recess, so the fingerprints and DNA of Devon could be double checked, again. "While you are at it double check that asshole Patterson too! I'm going to find out what the hell is going on, and there will be hell to pay!" The judge told them to leave his chambers, and he would be in the courtroom shortly.

Roger was driving to the courthouse. He was scheduled to testify mid-morning. His phone rang, "Agent Dance....What? I'm five minutes away." He checked his phone list and dialed Paul.

Paul picked up on the first ring, "It's all over the news."

Roger asked, "How soon can you be at the courthouse?"

"I'm about ten minutes away." Roger declared he would be with Devon.

Roger parked in the underground garage and entered the courthouse through the secured stairwell. The national news vehicles had dominated the exterior of the courthouse grounds even before this surprise declaration of William Patterson. Now it was a full blown circus. Roger made his way through the halls by holding his badge up and saying FBI whenever someone official looked like they wanted to question him. He was practically running.

Roger made it to the holding room and pushed his way in. The man sitting at the table in a black suit looked up and grinned at him. There was no recognition in his eyes or Roger's. It wasn't James Devon. A good look alike, but it wasn't James Devon. Roger sat across from him and demanded the room be cleared of everyone but one guard, the defense attorney, and whoever this man was. For a moment it felt as if the room was spinning. Roger took a deep breath and asked, "How long has he been gone?"

Paul was waiting outside of the holding room. He couldn't believe it was just last night they were all celebrating Devon's trial beginning. Roger came out to the hall and motioned to Paul. They walked over to a small area that had a window looking down on the parking lot. The chaos below was surreal and growing. Roger spoke first, "If you don't mind, I need you to line up at least two agents to help us. I need you to interview this defense attorney, the guards, any prison staff who would have had contact with Devon, and get the surveillance tapes from February 15th to now." The silence between them was deafening.

Paul didn't even try to hide his shock, "That isn't Devon? He's been gone since February?"

Roger choked, "Yeah, probably both of them, Patterson too. This attorney said he was called in to represent Devon in February and first met him February fifteenth. The man in there, Daniel Warren, was the man this attorney met with. Devon was already gone. And Paul, I am going to negotiate a transfer of this piece of shit to here, at the Indy Office, for interrogation. I will set us up there. I would like it if you could be with the transport."

Paul answered, "No problem. Are you okay?" Roger was feeling sick to his stomach, said no, and excused himself to run into a nearby restroom. Paul worried that either one of them could have a stroke from this damn case.

Roger was back after a few minutes and apologized. He looked a little pale but said he was fine. Then he said, "I just can't bring myself to think about what they have been doing for the last eight months. How many ....?" He couldn't finish. Paul told him he would start with the interviews and for Roger to concentrate on working out something with the DA for getting custody of the prisoner.

Roger was worried about Paul and asked, "Have you talked to Ashley?"

Paul rubbed his chin and said, "Oh God no.... I haven't." Paul had heard that Ashley wasn't the same after her experience with Devon last year. He had tried to stay close but Ashley had seemed to shut down. He had seen her last night at the 'After Party' but she hadn't stayed very long, and she did seem distant.

"You can be sure she knows. I'd give her a little time. Then let her know we are on it. Damn this sucks!"

Roger walked away. He went looking for the DA and the prosecutor. He found them in the courtroom chambers where they were huddled over a stack of files and talking in low tones very animatedly. Roger didn't have to introduce himself. They had established a very close working relationship during the case to catch Devon and Patterson.

The DA invited him to join them and said, "This is just some kind of trick to delay the trial! You were the lead agent on this…"

Roger interrupted him, "That is not James Devon in the holding room." The prosecutor and the DA looked stunned. Even with the courtroom accusation, they didn't for one minute believe that James Devon was not the man in the defendant's chair. He had been in federal custody since his arrest in December of last year.

"How the hell can that be?" The prosecutor was standing now, his neck beet red.

Roger gave him a moment and said, "Obviously there are a lot of questions to be answered. But the man in the holding cell is Daniel J. Warren, not James Devon. He has a proposed deal for you." Roger handed the offer to the DA. The DA took the paper and read it. He was grasping it so tightly that Roger thought it might tear.

"This is crazy!"

Roger told them what the defense attorney had said and finished by saying that it appeared this had been the plan all along. That 'somehow' Devon was able to get Daniel Warren, the man posing as Devon, to disguise himself as an attorney, switch out clothes with him in the law library at the prison, and Devon just walked out of the jail in February. He has had eight months to cover his tracks.

Roger finished with, "I have never met with William Patterson, but I would bet money he's gone too. Even though he has been in a different prison, they are all basically the same. Especially when the defendant is representing himself at trial, they are afforded special privileges to protect their rights. These guys are rich, and smart, and probably had this all worked out before their arrests. I have a feeling that the law firm that contacted this attorney is in on it, if there is such a firm." Roger continued, "Obviously this is an open case again. I am going to need full access to prison staff and records now. We won't know the particulars of what has happened until later. Right now, I'm telling you, Devon is gone."

The DA and the prosecutor just looked at each other. The media nightmare waiting outside would be a picnic compared to the governor's office. Roger pressed forward, "I need you to do that deal, now. I need every piece of information I can get from this guy, *and* whoever is pretending to be Patterson." The prosecutor excused himself to go puke. This case was the largest case of its type in memory and maybe in United States history. To admit the killer had escaped, and they didn't even know until trial, was unbelievable.

The DA sat looking at Roger. Neither could speak for a while. They both were remembering the horrible nightmare caused by Devon and Patterson: thirty- one dead women, two hostages, one starvation survivor. The largest federal fraud case in Indiana history at Commons National Bank. The manpower, months of accumulating mountains of evidence for the jury, the jury selection, and finally...finally the trial. The second day of the prosecutor's case, first day for witnesses, and this? It had been a full year of preparation under national media scrutiny. The DA's office had prepared a text book case. The staff had sacrificed beyond what anyone could have expected. The driving force of their dedication had been the knowledge that they were bringing evil to justice.

The worst part, Devon had been free for eight months. He had to be caught, again.

* * *

Hundreds of miles away Devon was laughing. This was worth the two months he had spent in jail. He placed a call to William, "You watchin' the news?"

****

Jack Simpson and Joy Covington stood at their bar with customers watching. They grabbed each other as they listened to the news and broke out wailing. Sandy had been in the kitchen and came out to see what was wrong. She listened to the TV for a minute and grabbed Joy to keep from fainting.

****

Judge Ashley Tait had been presiding on the bench in another trial when she was handed a note by her bailiff. She called for a recess and was now in her chambers crying. The monster that had kidnapped and raped her, was free.

****

Chief Edgar Doyle, South Bend Police, had his head in his hands as he sat at his desk. Outside his office, time had stopped. Everyone was huddled around the television in the conference room. His phone was ringing. His arm felt like concrete as he reached to answer it. It was a reporter wanting a statement.

****

The warden from the prison was told by his assistant to turn on CNN. He couldn't believe what he was hearing. Surely this was some kind of trick? Nobody escapes from his prison.

****

Kim had been on break at the casino. She was watching the news. She wondered if her mom knew what was happening. She couldn't believe this evil man was free. Oh my God... Roger!

****

The prosecutor was back across the street at the Justice Building. His staff was silent, standing like soldiers, waiting to hear that this was some sort of trial trick, that surely Devon wasn't free?

****

CHAPTER 26

We were all in the stupid NINJA angel class (my nickname). Teresa was the only one that could get the stupid mannequins to move right. It looked like some kind of *stupid* drunken aerobics' class. Linda and Mary were trying to dance. I had given up and was sitting on the floor. I know we need to learn how to move mortal mass if we were ever going to pass this class, but I still think our little 'group' could function with just one NINJA, Teresa. I got back up to give it another shot. It would have been easier if the mannequins didn't all have this look of shock on their overly painted faces. Only Teresa's had hair. I got into the mannequin okay, I just couldn't get the hips to move. It looked like I was marching. Ellen had said that real mortals would be harder because we would be fighting their "will." Oh goody- goody.

Teresa yelled for us to watch her. She was doing some kind of Michael Jackson "Thriller" dance move, so we got behind her and tried to copy what she was doing. Being in front of the wall of mirrors helped *some*, but I don't see this ever being a hit video.

Ellen showed up and turned off our music. "Hey gals, I need you to come over here."

She sat on a bleacher that appeared from nowhere and looked pretty serious. After we had all gathered around (we were still in our mannequins) she said, "I have really bad news…"

Okay, here it is. I was expecting this. We had done so awful in this class they were going to kick us out of Heaven after all. I felt bad now because it was probably my fault. I was having an attitude problem with this whole Ninja thing.

Ellen continued, after giving me a look. "James Devon escaped from prison eight months ago. So did William Patterson."

What? We couldn't believe it!

"Does Roger know?" Teresa asked.

Ellen answered, "Yes, they all found out today at trial. It's all over the news." Ellen continued, "Yes, before you ask, we did know this was the plan, but there are more important things we do than to monitor mortals. However, it *does* mean that our assignment really isn't completed." Ellen exhaled and shrugged her shoulders.

Mary asked, "I know we have been taking classes for almost a year, and we are a lot better at some things. But this NINJA stuff…"

Ellen said, "I know. This assignment was a tough one for me too because we really didn't think it would result in so many challenges that you weren't ready for. Still aren't ready for!"

I asked Ellen, "Will we be able to help Roger and Paul find out where these guys are and catch them?"

Ellen nodded emphatically, "Absolutely! In fact, they need you now more than ever! We need to implant new filters for you in case Betty and I can't get to you quickly enough. These men are evil. You all still retain a great deal of your mortal minds. The risk is certainly present that you will be in harm's way or put a mortal in harm's way unintentionally."

Linda asked if we would still be using Kim to communicate with Roger and Paul. I was holding my breath. I hadn't seen Kim while we had been in classes.

Ellen said, "Of course!" Once again, she reminded us that all we could really do was discover information 'our way' and guide Roger to the mortal discoveries quicker than he would have found them on his own. We could not manipulate mortal environments. Boy they were really big on that. Still.

Then Ellen looked at us all and said, "Let's figure out these mannequins right now. I am going to teach you a few 'tricks.' After about an hour of testing Ellen's patience, I am pretty sure I read her mind. (We might be a bad influence.) We had all figured out how to make the mannequins move, somewhat naturally. Looking in the mirrors we did the 'Hokey Pokey.' Ellen had our grand finale be our version of the Can Can. Not ready for Broadway, but not bad. I tried belly dancing after that and nearly broke my mannequin. At least she had the appropriate facial expression on. Utter shock.

Ellen said we had no time to spare, and while usually only authorized as a 'special' assignment, we were going to practice moving real mortals.

Teresa asked, "Why would we ever want to move a mortal?"

Ellen answered, "Remember when Devon was choking Jack?"

We all answered, "Oh yah!"

Ellen continued, "Also, you may need to save a mortal by moving them out of harm's way." Then she looked at me, "Vicki, you are thinking that this is a form of manipulation of mortal environment, aren't you?"

"Well yeahhhhh," I said. "I suppose it is all in whose definition you go by?"

Ellen frowned, "We go by mine." Of course. "You remember stories of women who lifted cars off someone trapped? Or people who survived being under ice for hours? Or, people being thrown to safety from an accident?"

This was me, "Speaking of that, why didn't someone throw us to safety from our crash?" It seemed to be a valid question. Since we were dead.

Ellen had a serious look on her face. "No one was near to help. There are actually only a few of us that can manipulate mortals." I was shocked.

Mary said, "You mean we are getting 'special' training?"

Ellen answered, "Oh Yes, very special training, for very special angels. We had no idea allowing you to retain as much of your mortal mind as we have, would

352

have resulted in your spiritual minds performing as they have been. This is very advantageous!"

Something is very wrong in heaven if the way we think is advantageous.

Ellen stood up, "Okay, this is what we are going to do. There is a biker bar in Nevada that is hosting a big four day blast. Some of these are pretty bad boys. Get used to the interior mortal signals, lots of drunks to choose from. You are going to do whatever it takes to stop them from driving a motor vehicle. I am just going to watch. Remember, you can mess with *them*, but not their environment."

I cleared my throat. My voice cracked when I squeaked, "Wait." *This was not sounding good.* "I need an example here."

Ellen chuckled, "Maybe in your attempt to subdue one, his mortal anger starts a fight. You can't let them involve machinery or weapons, no knives, guns, you know. They can't get hurt in any way."

"Can I have another example?" This was still me, not real happy with that example at all. "Don't you think it is quite a leap to go from a mannequin to a drunken biker?" I was starting to speed talk now. "Can't we start with animals and work our way up… or babies…teach them to walk. Old people! That would be good. They wouldn't even remember! You know, easy stuff?"

Ellen said, "Nope, we don't have time. These drunken bikers are babies compared to what you are going to face with Devon and Patterson. This is the easy stuff."

Linda asked, "I have to go inside a drunken biker?"

Ellen answered, "Yup."

Teresa said, "I get the first one!"

Mary looked at me, and I started cracking up. The look on her face. Mary inside a drunken biker was going to be 'interesting.' (There's that word again.)

* * *

Nevada was nice this time of year, not too hot, September, pretty pink sunset on the horizon....

There were five large barn type buildings and a long tent structure. There were rows and rows of motorcycles, trucks, and strange cars. Really hairy people all tattooed, spinning their vehicles in the dirt, other people cheering them on. There were people lying in the parking lot. Alive. I checked as I flew over. Women wearing very little clothing, more than one band playing, and at least a dozen bar areas. Little groups huddled in secret transac-tions.....ah shit.....and various other activities.

Ellen pointed to a big sign that said 'Parking.' "I will be watching from on top of the sign. When you enter into someone take a moment to listen to their thoughts. Make sure they are drunk. No sense messing with the good guys. Besides, if you lose your balance they will think it was their fault."

I saw a real scrawny guy trying to start his motorcycle. He could barely hold it upright, and he was having trouble with his kick start. I can do this. I entered through his ear...ugh. He rubbed his ear and all I could hear in his head was, "Come on you damn piece of shit...start!" Yup, I had me a certified drunk here. I leaned real hard to the left and he completely fell off the bike. Two guys, who had been talking nearby, came over to help him up. I had him kick one of them. Mistake! The big dude pulled a gun on me! Shit! Before I knew it, Ellen was in there with me. (Getting crowded.)

She looked at me, "What made you do that?"

"I don't know. Must have been my mortal." Good an excuse as anything. Ellen had the guy get down and pray for forgiveness, said he was drunk and didn't mean it, said he would polish the other guy's chrome on his bike.

When we left him, I am sure he was wondering how he ended up polishing that guy's bike. Ellen called a quick meeting. Teresa was mad. She had picked out her first guy, and now he was driving away.

Ellen started, "Look for weapons! You are not playing with mannequins anymore! Vicki, that guy's gun was in his hand! He had been shooting beer bottles. Now you guys try again and be careful."

Teresa said, "Geeesh, Vicki."

Mary said, "I'm going to stay close to Linda." *Whatever.* I told Teresa we should pick two guys together and experiment between us. That way we knew who we were.

Teresa thought for a minute and said, "It really worries me that makes sense." We found two guys talking to each other as they stumbled out to the parking lot. Looked like they were heading for their trucks.

I looked at Teresa, "I think they are going to drive!" We swooped in.

Mine had a distinct case of beer breath, and he was thinking he needed to pee. I was just about to tell Teresa we needed different guys when both these guys stopped and started peeing in the dirt. I sent Teresa a message, "Now what?"

Teresa messaged back, "This is really different isn't it? I'm going to try to write my name." When Teresa's guy got done, he was so startled to see that he had written 'Teresa' in the dirt, he told his buddy to go on without him. He was going to nap in his truck. One for the good guys.

Mary and Linda had decided to do the same thing Teresa and I had done. Pick two guys together. Their guys were definitely drunk, and the bartender had just told them to go sleep it off for a couple of hours. They were determined to drive to town, so they were perfect...*and no guns.*

Mary had some trouble deciding how to go in. It didn't look good anywhere. All of a sudden her guy threw his head back laughing, and she dove in. He started gagging and said he just ate a bug. That started another round of back slapping, and Mary almost fell out again. Linda was already in her guy and reading his thoughts, "Oh, you've got to be kidding me!"

Linda sent a thought to Mary. "My guy thinks your guy is cute!"

Mary didn't answer right away. "My guy isn't thinking at all. He is *really* drunk. Now what?"

Linda asked Mary, "They are almost at their trucks! How do we stop them?"

Mary said, "All I know how to do is dance."

Linda was thinking, "Okay, let's start dancing and see if they don't just get tired."

Ellen was sitting on top of the parking sign shaking her head. To the delight of the crowd, the two brawny bikers started to waltz together. Not too bad, she thought. Then they started bitch slapping each other. (The only way we knew how to fight.) Guess one of them got frisky. Finally the crowd separated them and made them sit down which eventually led to them falling asleep. Someone covered them under one blanket. Hmmmmm.

Teresa and I sat on a huge rock and watched Linda and Mary dancing with two new guys. We needed a short break. I looked at Teresa and said, "You know I am pretty proud of how you are doing in this class! You really rock!"

Teresa looked at me and said, "I think I need to get a lot better, fast." Her facial expression said she knew something I didn't.

"And you think that *why?*" I really didn't want to hear her answer.

"Ellen asked me if I had any issues with alligators....or Voodoo."

I was right. I didn't want to hear that.

357

From Book Two

* * *

Jeremiah Dumaine was seventy-four years old, a fourth generation swamp man with a tuft of long gray hair, and one blind eye. He had seen a lot in his years of living in the haunting bayous. His cypress clad home had been his grandfather's, and he had helped his own father carve the belly of this boat. These were dark waters tonight...silent...as if life itself was holding its breath. He stood, his bent frame nudging through the thick muggy air, and slowly glided his craft to Mambo's den on the other side of Honey Island.

His eyes moved to the half dead woman in the corner of his boat. Almost didn't see her curled on that cypress root in the swamp. Lucky a gator didn't find her. Mambo would know what to do. He stooped as the draping moss tickled across his shoulder, and he listened for the whispers of the marsh. The occasional soft splash of his paddle and the subtle ripples on the water were the only hints he was there. His skin twitched with fear tonight. This was the second woman he had found in the swamp.

Jeremiah secured his boat to a large cypress root at the edge of the swamp near Mambo's den. The dirt path into the marshland was well worn from many visitors. Tiny animal skulls and colorful clumps of feathers tied with thin leather straps adorned the low branches of shrub trees. Where the path met the green iridescent crust that cloaked the black water edge, the swamp gasses bubbled and occasionally released tiny spurts of blue flame.

Scientists had explained the phenomenon as decomposing organic material mixing with the stagnant swamp waters, creating methane that would ignite and create a 'pop' like sound. That didn't explain the concentrated pockets of activity. In spite of the efforts of numerous research teams, this mystery of the swamp remained impossible to duplicate in a lab. The scientists were left with unproven theories.

Nights like tonight, the blue haze from the gasses made the wings of flying insects appear florescent and the huge webs of the Cypress spiders glow blue. Jeremiah didn't care what the scientists thought. He knew that in all his years in the swamp, the most flames were at Mambo's. The eerie blue glow surrounding her hut could be seen for miles at night. Any fool could see the spirits lived here.

Jeremiah came to Mambo last month when he had found the first woman in the swamp. Mambo had taken her in and brought her back to health. Instead of leaving, the woman had stayed to help the aging Mambo in her daily chores. Mambo had named her Heeshia, meaning 'chosen one.'

The path to reach Mambo was narrow and overgrown. If you didn't know where her hut was, you would never see it. There was a large clump of giant knurled Cypress trees where her hut had been built in the center. Decades ago moss and wetland shrubs had enveloped the entire structure except for a small chimney opening in the roof. The Cypress clad door was covered in moss, and piles of offerings were scattered at the threshold.

Believers brought staples and gifts for the gods in exchange for potions and amulets. They wanted Mambo's blessings and protection, and believed in her abilities to summon the Saints. Mambo was the recognized Voodoo Queen of the faithful.

Jeremiah helped the woman he had just found out of his boat, and he wondered what Mambo would say. He didn't know what else to do.

Heeshia met him at the door and helped him walk the woman over to a cot in the corner of the large main room. Mambo was sitting on the floor in front of a small open fire pit throwing pinches of powder into the flames and chanting softly. The powder would briefly ignite and shoot colorful flashes of light that danced around the walls, casting moving shadows from unseen sources. Her large dark eyes followed them across the room and she slowly stood. "Heeshia, bring our guests food." Mambo sat on the edge of the cot and put the woman's hands inside her own, "You are protected here."

The young woman burst into tears and Mambo stroked her hair. "You have seen evil and survived. We will build from that." Mambo slowly walked back to her place in the center of the room and lowered her crippled body to the floor. She had her arms held up over her head and was chanting loudly. Then she closed her eyes and began swaying to a softer chant. She slowly lowered her arms, crossed herself and began a slow rocking motion. She looked so frail. No one really knew how old she was. She had always been an old woman, even when Jeremiah was a boy.

Jeremiah went outside and cut firewood for Mambo's stack. He filled a water bucket from the rain cistern and carried supplies he had purchased for his home, to Mambo's little porch. Heeshia stepped outside to speak to him. Her long black hair was pulled tightly back from her face and she was wearing clothes that probably had once belonged to a man. Her boots were worn and she had made a belt of rope. Even in the middle of the swamp she was a *striking* beauty.

"I need to leave here. Mambo will need to help the new one. Did you find her, like you found me?" Jeremiah nodded. Heeshia said, "Evil men are bringing women to this swamp to die. I am strong enough now to stop them. Can you take me to the city tomorrow?"

Jeremiah looked at her frail body and wondered how she could stop the evil that had come to his swamp. He started to speak, then saw something in her lavender blue eyes that was very powerful, almost hypnotic. He was instantly reminded of a story his grandfather had told him. A band of Polish warriors came to Haiti on the orders of Napoleon, but soon changed affections and helped the Haitian people win their revolution against the French Army.

A few decedents of these folk legends could still be found in rare blue-eyed Haitians. Almost exclusively women, Voodoo lore professed them to have special warrior skills. They were believed to be cherished by the Saints, messengers of Erzulie Dantor, sometimes called 'Black Madonna'. A female warrior spirit, and fierce protector of women and children. Jeremiah was quite certain Heeshia was a blue-eyed Haitian. Mambo called her the chosen one. Jeremiah would not question the wisdom of the spirits.

He nodded respect to Heeshia, and slowly walked back to where his boat was tied to the shore. He pushed his long paddle against the tall swamp grasses and quietly steered his craft into the open black water towards home. Heeshia stood at the swamps edge and watched his boat slowly glide away. He could see her form fading in the blue haze, yet he could still see those eyes.

Jeremiah had a plan. He had a large stash of mink furs and alligator skins he would take to the city tonight to get money for Heeshia, and buy supplies for Mambo. He would also purchase ammunition for his guns. Jeremiah didn't like guns, but evil had come to his swamp.

A single frigid breeze whipped around his shoulders and vanished. Jeremiah shuddered as the icy sensation tickled down his spine. He looked around for some source of the sudden chill. It was unseasonal, unexplained. The moon peeked from behind the dark clouds and offered a brief display of diamonds sparkling on the black water. Sounds of the wildlife rose from the marsh like an orchestra warming for a performance. The long grasses rustled and began to dance near the shore from invisible trespassers. The swamp was coming alive again.

* * *

Book One: Alcohol Was Not Involved
Book Two: Extreme Heat Warning
Book Three: Silent Crickets
The Shallow End Gals
Linda McGregor
Teresa Duncan
Mary Hale
Vicki Graybosch
Kimberly Troutman

33928062R00219

Made in the USA
Middletown, DE
01 August 2016